"*Ambush* is electric—the [...] and characters you swear are real. With a deadly mystery, past trauma, and future hope, *Ambush* is just one more proof of Coble at the top of her game."

—Tosca Lee, *New York Times* bestselling author

"Coble's *Ambush* takes off at a roaring speed with razor-sharp writing. Expect the suspense to put claw marks on the pages as you hold on for the thrilling ride. This is an up-all-night must-read!"

—Jessica R. Patch, bestselling author of the critically acclaimed Strange Crimes Unit series

"Engaging characters, irresistible intrigue, and a slow-burning romance make *Fragile Designs* a captivating read."

—Mary Burton, *New York Times* bestselling author

"Excitement, evil antagonists, action, and romance are a few of the items that stand out in *Break of Day* by Colleen Coble . . . The world-building is excellent."

—*Mystery & Suspense Magazine*

"A law enforcement ranger investigates a cold case and searches for her kidnapped sister in this exciting series launch from Coble (*A Stranger's Game*) . . . Coble expertly balances mounting tension from the murder investigation with the romantic tension between Annie and Jon. This fresh, addictive mystery delivers thrills, compassion, and hope."

—*Publishers Weekly* on *Edge of Dusk*

"Colleen Coble's superpower is transporting her readers into beautiful settings in vivid detail. *Two Reasons to Run* is no exception. Add to that the suspense that keeps you wanting to know more and characters that pull at your heart. These are the ingredients of a fun read!"

—Terri Blackstock, bestselling author of
If I Run, *If I'm Found*, and *If I Live*

"This is a romantic suspense novel that will be a surprise when the last page reveals all of the secrets."

—*Parkersburg News and
Sentinel* on *One Little Lie*

"There are just enough threads left dangling at the end of this well-crafted romantic suspense to leave fans hungrily awaiting the next installment."

—*Publishers Weekly* on *One Little Lie*

"Colleen Coble once again proves she is at the pinnacle of Christian romantic suspense. Filled with characters you'll come to love, faith lost and found, and scenes that will have you holding your breath, Jane Hardy's story deftly follows the complex and tangled web that can be woven by one little lie."

—Lisa Wingate, #1 *New York Times* bestselling
author of *Before We Were Yours*, on *One Little Lie*

"Colleen Coble always raises the notch on romantic suspense, and *One Little Lie* is my favorite yet! The story took me on a wild and wonderful ride."

—DiAnn Mills, bestselling author

"Coble's latest, *One Little Lie*, is a powerful read . . . one of her absolute best. I stayed up way too late finishing this book because

I literally couldn't go to sleep without knowing what happened. This is a must read! Highly recommend!"

—Robin Caroll, bestselling author
of the Darkwater Inn series

"I always look forward to Colleen Coble's new releases. *One Little Lie* is One Phenomenal Read. I don't know how she does it, but she just keeps getting better. Be sure to have plenty of time to flip the pages in this one because you won't want to put it down. I devoured it! Thank you, Colleen, for more hours of edge-of-the-seat entertainment. I'm already looking forward to the next one!"

—Lynette Eason, award-winning and bestselling author of the Blue Justice series

"In *One Little Lie* the repercussions of one lie skid through the town of Pelican Harbor, creating ripples of chaos and suspense. Who will survive the questions? *One Little Lie* is the latest page-turner from Colleen Coble. Set on the Gulf Coast of Alabama, Jane Hardy is the new police chief who is fighting to clear her father. Reid Dixon has secrets of his own as he follows Jane around town for a documentary. Together they must face their secrets and decide when a secret becomes a lie. And when does it become too much to forgive?"

—Cara Putman, bestselling and
award-winning author

"Coble wows with this suspense-filled inspirational . . . With startling twists and endearing characters, Coble's engrossing story explores the tragedy, betrayal, and redemption of faithful people all searching to reclaim their sense of identity."

—*Publishers Weekly* on *Strands of Truth*

"Just when I think Colleen Coble's stories can't get any better, she proves me wrong. In *Strands of Truth*, I couldn't turn the pages fast enough. The characterization of Ridge and Harper and their relationship pulled me immediately into the story. Fast-paced, with so many unexpected twists and turns, I read this book in one sitting. Coble has pushed the bar higher than I'd imagined. This book is one not to be missed. Highly recommend!"

—Robin Caroll, bestselling author
of the Darkwater Inn series

"Free-dive into a romantic suspense that will leave you breathless and craving for more."

—DiAnn Mills, bestselling
author, on *Strands of Truth*

"Colleen Coble's latest book, *Strands of Truth*, grips you on page one with a heart-pounding opening and doesn't let go until the last satisfying word. I love her skill in pulling the reader in with believable, likable characters, interesting locations, and a mystery just waiting to be untangled. Highly recommended."

—Carrie Stuart Parks, bestselling and
award-winning author of *Relative Silence*

"It's in her blood! Colleen Coble once again shows her suspense prowess with a thriller as intricate and beautiful as a strand of DNA. *Strands of Truth* dives into an unusual profession involving mollusks and shell beds that weaves a unique, silky thread throughout the story. So fascinating I couldn't stop reading!"

—Ronie Kendig, bestselling author
of the Tox Files series

"Once again, Colleen Coble delivers an intriguing, suspenseful tale in *Strands of Truth*. The mystery and tension mount toward an explosive and satisfying finish. Well done."

—Creston Mapes, bestselling author

"*Secrets at Cedar Cabin* is filled with twists and turns that will keep readers turning the pages as they plunge into the horrific world of sex trafficking where they come face-to-face with evil. Colleen Coble delivers a fast-paced story with a strong, lovable ensemble cast and a sweet, heaping helping of romance."

—Kelly Irvin, author of *Tell Her No Lies*

"Coble . . . weaves a suspense-filled romance set during the Revolutionary War. Coble's fine historical novel introduces a strong heroine—both in faith and character—that will appeal deeply to readers."

—*Publishers Weekly* on *Freedom's Light*

"This follow-up to *The View from Rainshadow Bay* features delightful characters and an evocative, atmospheric setting. Ideal for fans of romantic suspense and authors Dani Pettrey, Dee Henderson, and Brandilyn Collins."

—*Library Journal* on *The House at Saltwater Point*

"Set on Washington State's Olympic Peninsula, this first volume of Coble's new suspense series is a tensely plotted and harrowing tale of murder, corporate greed, and family secrets. Devotees of Dani Pettrey, Brenda Novak, and Allison Brennan will find a new favorite here."

—*Library Journal* on *The View from Rainshadow Bay*

AMBUSH

ALSO BY COLLEEN COBLE

AMBUSH

A Sanctuary Novel

COLLEEN COBLE

THOMAS NELSON
Since 1798

Library of Congress Cataloging-in-Publication Data

Names: Coble, Colleen, author.
Title: Ambush / Colleen Coble.
Description: Nashville, Tennessee: Thomas Nelson, 2025. | Series: Sanctuary novels; 1 | Summary: "She'll do anything to uncover the truth of her parents' murder—even work alongside the man who once broke her heart"—Provided by publisher.
Identifiers: LCCN 2024022199 (print) | LCCN 2024022200 (ebook) | ISBN 9780840714220 (paperback) | ISBN 9780840714350 (library binding) | ISBN 9780840714251 (epub) | ISBN 9780840714336
Subjects: LCGFT: Christian fiction. | Novels.
Classification: LCC PS3553.O2285 A83 2025 (print) | LCC PS3553.O2285 (ebook) | DDC 813/.54—dc23/eng/20240520
LC record available at https://lccn.loc.gov/2024022199
LC ebook record available at https://lccn.loc.gov/2024022200

Printed in the United States of America

25 26 27 28 29 LBC 5 4 3 2 1

For my grandsons Elijah and Silas whose love of the Out of Africa Wildlife Park provided the nugget for this story. Love you both!

CHAPTER 1

WHAT HAD POSSESSED HER to agree to this crazy idea? Once Paradise Alden left Barnwell behind, turned east on 98, and entered the confines of Nova Cambridge, Alabama, she braked her green Kia Soul and, for the first time in fifteen years, took in the moss-draped trees lining the narrow streets.

Home.

She hadn't thought she would ever return to this place again. Once upon a time, she'd thought this corner of Baldwin County held everything her heart could desire—until that hopeful place inside had exploded into a thousand pieces.

Was she ready for this?

She passed Tupelo Grove University, west of Foley, where her mother had worked a lifetime ago. Beyond the city limits she left the memories behind for now and ran down her window to inhale the intoxicating scent of Weeks Bay. In early January the humidity lacked the fierce heat that would come in the summer, but the air held enough moisture to remind her.

The sound of a siren chased away her memories, and she instinctively let up on the accelerator. The speedometer hovered eight miles an hour above the speed limit. The bubble-gum light atop the tan car behind her flashed, and she pulled to the side of the street. Her window was still down, so she pasted on a smile and angled it at the officer who strolled to her door.

His surly expression vanished. "Howdy, miss. You have any idea how fast you were going?"

His deltoid and trapezius muscles bulged under his short-sleeved shirt, and the rest of his body had the disproportionate appearance of someone who took steroids. The breeze ruffled his thinning brown hair, and his green eyes appraised her like a slab of steak.

"I forgot to turn on my cruise, and I'm afraid I was speeding, Officer."

He tapped his badge. "Deputy Creed Greene." He leered as he leaned on the top of the door. "Passing through? How about catching some coffee with me and I'll give you the lowdown on our nice town."

What a lech. She'd met his type plenty of times over the years. County deputies in this area would be stationed at the Bon Secour substation, and some felt they could do whatever they wanted. A quick peek down the empty street let her know she was on her own. "I'm starting work at The Sanctuary Wildlife Preserve. I'm the new vet, Paradise Alden." Her gaze dropped to his left hand. "And it appears you're married, Deputy. I doubt your wife would appreciate your having a coffee date with me."

His leer vanished, and he straightened before he whipped out his pad. "Driver's license."

She reached into her bag and pulled out her wallet, then passed over her license without comment. He walked to the back of her car and glanced at her plate, then got in his car.

Paradise tapped her fingers on top of the steering wheel as she waited for her ticket. The tin-pot dictator behind her was likely to stretch out the time as long as possible. The unfortunate truth was he was the law, and she wouldn't have much recourse for a complaint.

Twenty minutes later, he returned and handed her the copy of the ticket. "Slow down, Ms. Alden. I'll be watching you." He held on to his side of the ticket longer than necessary before he finally released it.

The ominous glare he gave her tightened her chest. Great. She'd made a formidable enemy on her first day back in the area. "I'll be careful." She stuffed the ticket in her bag, then waited until he went back to his car before pulling back onto the road to finish her journey.

Her pulse accelerated as she turned at the sign to The Sanctuary. The drive to the cluster of buildings next to the big parking lot wound through cypress trees interspersed with pawpaw, catalpa, and black gum. The undulating fields had vegetation and grasses for the African herds roaming that area, and she caught glimpses of water as well. The serene appearance soothed her fears. Maybe it would be okay. She glanced down at the angry red scars on her left arm and shuddered at the realization of what awaited her.

She parked in the lot and grabbed her bag. She glanced up into the giant oak tree reaching moss-draped limbs out over the roof of her car. No big cats up there. She shut her door and turned toward the people.

Time to face Blake Lawson, the man who had destroyed her life.

Her employment email instructed her to proceed past the ticket booth and the gift shop to a small building tucked under another oak tree and its accompanying moss. The low-slung building appeared to have had a new coat of green paint, and through the window she spotted Blake and his mother, Jenna Anderson.

While Paradise stood unobserved, she let her gaze roam over Blake. In the past fifteen years, he'd grown bulkier muscles and a couple of inches, but she would have recognized him anywhere. That shock of dark brown hair that stood out from his head like a plume had been tamed only with a short cut.

She'd heard he used to be a combat paramedic before the death of his stepfather, Hank Anderson, the town vet she'd worked for as a teenager. After the accident, Blake had managed to get discharged from the Marines to come help his mother at the wildlife refuge. Jenna had two small sons now too, and from what Jenna had told her, his little brothers had also played a part in the decision.

Paradise hadn't talked to Blake directly, and she suspected he wouldn't be any happier to see her than she was to see him.

She clocked the moment he noticed her by the stiffening of his shoulders and the way his smile fell away from his tanned face. Those blue eyes raked over her, and his mouth flattened as she stepped through the door into the open space that held two desks, a dilapidated sofa, and a small table and chairs for lunch breaks.

The muscle in Blake's jaw flexed. "Paradise?"

He'd had no idea she was coming? "Hello, Blake." She tore her gaze from him to greet Jenna. "You didn't tell him?"

Jenna shook her head. "Um, Blake, Paradise has agreed to help us out for the next year."

She couldn't gauge his thoughts, but before he could reply, a piercing scream came from outside. Was it a big cat attack? Paradise froze with her blood roaring in her ears. Sympathetic pain shot from her left shoulder down to her wrist at the sound. The confidence she'd mustered to take this job drained away and her knees went weak.

Blake slapped a stun gun into her hand as he ran past. "Come with me!"

She tried to obey the command, but her legs barely supported her as she went in the same direction. What if a jaguar was out of its enclosure? This time it might rip her arm right off instead of leaving her with weakness and a bad scar. Her mouth bone-dry, she wobbled as she ran after him toward the barn.

A horse trailer was behind a pickup, and an old, swayback horse stood off to one side. Several people circled the elderly animal, and they stared with horrified expressions into the trailer.

Blake approached the group and spoke to a man standing by the back bumper of the truck. "What's going on?"

The man gestured toward the trailer. "Call the police station, Blake. There's a body in there."

What body? Then Paradise spotted a mass of blonde hair. Not a mane, not fur. Hair. A woman's hair. And she was clearly deceased. "Call the police."

———

The forensic team swarmed the scene, collecting evidence into bags. Blake luckily stood upwind of the stench of manure in the paddock, but he hadn't had the good fortune to avoid examining the body. Deputy Greene leaned against the fence with his thumbs hooked in the loops of his belt, and Blake approached the officer. "Got an ID yet? She was on her stomach and I didn't see her face."

Greene nodded, and his gaze sharpened on Blake. "I'm not at liberty to say. You touched the body?"

The accusation in Greene's voice stiffened Blake's spine. "I was a combat paramedic in the Marines. I checked for a pulse, but she was already dead. Looked like someone used a knife on her." He'd seen several slashes on her arm.

Greene frowned. "The medical examiner will determine cause of death. Where did the horse come from?"

Creed had moved to town during Blake's senior year, and he'd been a bully back then too. They'd had a fight in the hall once when Creed slammed a friend's head into the wall. Becoming a law enforcement officer had only made his power trip worse. And now, apparently, he was also a detective in the sheriff's department.

Blake wanted to be as uncooperative as the deputy, but he restrained the impulse. "Dillard Ranch." The ranch abutted the preserve a half mile to the east, and the Dillards had been generous with their dying livestock ever since Mom and Blake's stepfather bought the wildlife refuge.

He spotted his mother under a towering magnolia tree and headed that way. His steps slowed when he saw Paradise standing with her. Seeing his first love again after fifteen years had been a bolt out of the blue. Why had Mom asked her to come, and even more importantly, why hadn't anyone told him? He wasn't sure what kind of pressure Mom had exerted to get Paradise to agree either.

He pasted a neutral expression on his face and joined the women. "Did anyone mention the woman's identity?" It wasn't hard to keep his attention on his mother, who stood wringing her hands and biting her lip. The trauma of this situation would leave its mark on his tenderhearted mom.

His mother's eyes were red, and she nodded. "It was Danielle Mason."

His eyes widened. "The animal rights activist?"

He should have recognized the frizzy blonde hair. The woman had been a major nuisance for the past two months. It was hard to get past the protesters and into the park on some mornings. When he'd offered to show the Mason woman around and prove how well the animals were doing, she refused. She'd made up her mind with no evidence.

"You realize the police will suspect us," his mother said. "It's no secret how the protests have adversely affected the park's profits."

His gut twisted. This kind of publicity could only make things worse. "No wonder Creed was so accusatory. He practically blamed me for tampering with evidence."

In his peripheral vision he caught a movement from Paradise, and he let his full attention swing toward her. Ignoring her wasn't going to improve anything. The sun touched her curly light brown hair and enhanced its red and gold lights. Standing about five-seven, she was a little taller than she had been at fifteen, but the last fifteen years had only increased her beauty.

Her amber eyes still wore a wary expression though. Maybe any kid who'd been through the foster-care system would wear the same armor. Getting past that steel plate she wore back then had been a rare honor, and he'd blown it.

"You haven't changed much, Paradise."

"Neither have you," she said in a subdued voice.

He wanted to ask her what brought her back, but now wasn't the time. One thing was certain—it wasn't a job. Some kind of big enticement had gotten her past her vow never to step foot here again.

Blake tore his gaze away and glanced around for his little brothers. "Where are the boys?" They were five and seven, and he wouldn't be surprised if they were poking around in the chaos.

"I saw them a minute ago." His mother turned to peer around.

He spotted the youngest first. Five-year-old Isaac was in the fork of a tree branch, and his brother, Levi, sat under him in the shade with a book. The older boy was an avid reader already. The two looked a lot alike, but Levi had dark brown hair like Mom and Blake while Isaac's was blond like Hank's.

"Hey, boys, let's go get some lunch. You hungry?"

Isaac jumped down from the tree. "I am." He approached Paradise and stared at her. "Are you a girl lion? Can I touch your hair?"

She darted a glance at Blake, and her lips curved in that enchanting smile he remembered so well. "Did you coach him?"

Blake splayed out his hands. "Innocent of the charges."

She had that mane of hair that exploded in the Alabama humidity, and her eyes were a golden amber color that reinforced the similarity to the big cat. It was so striking, even a little kid like Isaac noticed. Blake used to call her Simba, a nickname she'd hated when he first met her. Until it became a pet name. Even if it had been used for a male lion in a Disney movie, it suited her.

She squatted in front of his youngest brother. "You can touch it."

Isaac grinned and thrust both hands into her wild, curly hair. "It's so pretty. I wish I had hair like yours."

"Trust me, you don't."

He studied her. "I peeked in your car, and you have a teddy bear in the back seat. He looks old."

"He is. My parents gave him to me, and he goes with me everywhere."

"But you're a grown-up."

Her cheeks reddened, but she didn't ignore his little brother. "Even grown-ups have favorite things from when they were little."

She'd always liked kids and had often taken care of younger foster kids in the home. Yet here she was, still unmarried and childless. At least Blake assumed so since she'd shown up alone.

Paradise stood and glanced at the office. "If you tell me where to find my lodging, I'll get unpacked."

"I'll take you over and help carry in your luggage." A few minutes alone might help dissipate the tension between them.

Or maybe intensify it.

CHAPTER 2

WHEN PARADISE HAD LIVED in Alabama, this Sanctuary property had been a respite from the turmoil after her parents died. Since she'd worked for Hank Anderson, the vet in Nova Cambridge, the former owners sometimes let her help feed the handful of roadside zoo animals they'd collected and clean up the excrement. But this place had been her happy place, even more so than the vet's office. She'd felt needed by the wild animals. Now she would be responsible for caring for the wildlife she glimpsed as she followed in her car behind Blake's truck. There were a lot more of them now than back in her day.

She got out, he grabbed her large roller bag, and they walked toward a row of shotgun cottages. She shot a side-eyed glance Blake's way. Seeing him again had been a punch to her gut. She'd always heard you never got over your first love, but she'd minimized that notion in her head until the moment her heart stuttered in her chest at the sight of his face—until she remembered his betrayal.

Blake had been her world for the six years she'd spent as his next-door neighbor. Maybe it had been a mistake to come here, but she wasn't sure of her path forward or how to get over her fear of big cats. Jenna's offer had been a lifeline she'd clutched with both hands. The possibility of getting to the bottom of her nightmares made the offer irresistible.

Blake stopped in front of a cute cottage barely bigger than a garage and set down her suitcase to unlock the door. "It's not big, but Mom had it renovated last year. It's got all new furnishings and a fresh coat of paint." He handed her the key, then folded his arms across his chest and stared at her. "Why'd you come back, Paradise? I thought once you'd shaken the dust of Nova Cambridge off your feet, you'd never step foot in Baldwin County again."

She searched his face for some reaction at seeing her again, but Blake had always been good at masking his feelings when he wanted to. She wasn't sure she was ready to reveal her nightmares and what had driven her back to face them.

His attention moved from her face to the scars on her left arm, and his eyes widened. "You get that in an attack?"

She instinctively covered them with her right hand. "A black panther mauling. Jaguar. Someone accidentally left a door open while I was working in his habitat." Reiterating the incident always stole her breath and left her shaking. She didn't want Blake to realize how traumatized she'd been. "I was on leave and afraid I could never work with the big cats I loved so much again. Your mom's offer felt like it was meant to be." She dropped her hand away from her scars.

Blake stared at her arm. "Ouch. It's still painful?"

"It is. And I don't have full strength back in it yet. I'm working on getting that back with exercises the physical therapist gave me."

He gave a quick nod. "Think you can do the job here?"

"I wouldn't have accepted it if I wasn't sure of that. I can take care of myself."

"You don't have to take on the whole world, Paradise. I'd hoped you would have learned that in the past fifteen years." His gaze dropped to her hand. "Not married?"

"Never could trust a man."

He flinched when her barb struck him. His betrayal had cost her everything—her home, her peace of mind, her ability to trust.

When he opened his mouth, she knew she couldn't listen to one more platitude or excuse. Not today when the past was hitting her so hard. "I'd like to unpack. I'll report for work at seven. Piggly Wiggly still in the same place?"

"Yeah, not much has changed in Nova Cambridge since you left. A few new stores opened when old ones closed. A few more paved roads, another gas station." He pushed open the door to the cottage and stepped out of the way. "For what it's worth, Paradise, if I had the chance to do things all over again, I would have talked to you first."

Small comfort now. His remark didn't deserve a response. Nothing could change what had happened to her life. She was the one who had to live with the consequences. Were any girls in her meager circle of friends still around? She wasn't about to ask Blake, so she picked up her suitcase and stepped inside the cottage. He'd already turned to walk away when she closed the door, which helped ease the tension from her shoulders.

The interior was surprisingly airy and felt spacious. The open studio layout held a full-size bed on one side and a minuscule kitchen with a love seat and armchair on the opposite side. The cottage smelled like new furniture. Paradise found a walk-in closet near the bed with plenty of space to hold the meager belongings she'd brought. It took fifteen minutes to stow everything, and then she decided to run to the Piggly Wiggly to stock the kitchen with food.

As she drove away, she spotted Jenna still talking with Creed. The deputy stared at her car as it passed before saying something to Jenna, who stiffened. Paradise could only imagine his comment. Her thoughts sank deeper into the past as she drove the familiar back road across the bridge to Nova Cambridge, four miles from the preserve. It had been her home for her first fifteen years.

Before she could stop herself, she turned onto Oak Street to drive past the house she'd called home for the happiest years of her life. She parked across the street and stared. The last time Paradise had been here, it had a forlorn, abandoned appearance. Someone had brought the plantation style into the present decade and spruced it up. The shutters and trim were painted black instead of the brown they had been when her family lived there, and the roof was metal now. They'd painted the tan vertical siding white, and it contrasted with the black trim in an appealing way.

Did the people who owned the home now know what had happened inside? The murders had been all over the news twenty years ago, and the place had sat empty for several years.

As she watched, the door flew open and two children spilled into the yard. The little girl appeared to be around ten, and she ran to the tree swing with her long blonde braids flying. Paradise watched her with a growing lump in her throat. If only she could turn back the clock to before she'd awakened that night. Maybe she could have saved her parents.

───────

The boys' bedroom had all the toys put away, and Blake sat on the edge of the bottom bunk. "One more story," Isaac begged.

His big brown eyes were impossible for Blake to resist, and he pulled out *Green Eggs and Ham* for the umpteenth time. Seven-year-old Levi hung over the top bunk to see the pictures while Blake read the familiar story. He was barely two pages in when Isaac's eyes fluttered shut and his breathing grew even. Levi exhaled and moved away from the edge, then closed his eyes one page from the end. Blake put the book away and tiptoed to the door, where he shut off the light before he slipped out.

His mother had gotten a visit from the sergeant in charge of the Bon Secour substation, and Blake strained to hear Roderick McShea's rumbling voice in the living room. He was still there, so Blake picked up the pace to join them. The murder had the potential to further harm the refuge, and they were already tee-tering on the edge of solvency.

His mom's blue eyes were anxious above the tremulous smile of relief she directed his way. "There you are, Blake. Sergeant McShea was asking about the altercations we've had with Danielle Mason."

McShea was in his fifties and had managed to maintain the athletic build left over from his star quarterback days in high school. He was a hometown boy who'd gone to school with Blake's mother. He hadn't married until he was in his thirties, and his three kids were just now going off to various colleges.

He swiped his light brown hair off his forehead and stood to shake Blake's hand. "Sorry to bother you both so late, but it's been a hectic day. I wanted to hear the story directly from you both."

Blake settled beside his mother on the sofa while the sergeant dropped back into the armchair. "You have cause of death?"

"That will take a day or two for the medical examiner to de-termine. I will say she appears to have been stabbed. It wasn't an accident."

"I saw knife wounds on her arm."

"Ah yes. Detective Greene was upset you'd disturbed the body."

"I wasn't sure she was dead and was assessing whether I could help." Blake had known Rod all his life and didn't have to remind him of his past medical career.

"Of course." Rod's hazel eyes narrowed. "Your mom has told me what she remembers of the demonstrations outside the entrance to the preserve. Did you have any conversations with Ms. Mason?"

Blake controlled his dismay. Someone must have mentioned the two altercations. "Ms. Mason organized a group to blockade the entrance. About thirty protesters all held signs reading *Free the Animals* or *Death to the Keepers*. They banged on cars as they tried to enter, and screamed obscenities. I arrived at the scene and asked her to move back and allow entry to the park visitors. She refused and charged toward me. She barreled into me with her shoulder, then yelled that I'd hit her. She called your office, but luckily we had cameras at the entrance that showed I was telling the truth. She was very angry about it, and the next day her behavior was even worse."

"I reviewed that video this afternoon. Tell me about the next day too."

Unease moved through Blake's stomach. If the sergeant was reviewing the video, he must be worried one of them had killed the woman. "She set fire to the fence line. That night's video showed her pouring gasoline along the fence line and then lighting it. I confronted her about it the next morning, and she slapped me in the face."

"What did you do?"

Blake's face heated. "I took a step toward her, but I didn't hit her."

"You wanted to?"

"For a second. It was a hard slap that surprised me. I think she wanted me to strike her, and when I didn't, she got even angrier. I'd been carrying a bucket of raw meat for the bears, and I'd set it down to handle the situation at the gate. She grabbed it and threw the blood and meat in my face."

He couldn't remember ever being as mad as he had been that day. By God's grace he'd managed to hold on to his temper. The woman had been nearly apoplectic with rage, and all he'd done was turn around and go back through the gate. "I locked the gate behind me and wouldn't let her in until I called your office to report her assault."

"She wasn't arrested."

"No. I should have pressed charges, but I didn't want the negative publicity. Her group had caused enough problems without adding to them."

"I see. Did she have a vendetta against you personally?"

"It might have developed after the two altercations. I haven't been able to figure out why she targeted The Sanctuary. We rescue animals and give them acres and acres to roam. We love them and care for them. I tried to talk to her when she first showed up, but she'd made up her mind about us before she ever came with her followers. Her blog followers sent nasty messages too, and I had to shut down our social media accounts."

Rod's gaze fell away, and Blake read the heightening suspicion on his face. "I would never hurt her or anyone else." Hollow words. Every criminal probably protested his innocence.

McShea rose and adjusted his belt. "Thanks for the information. I'll be in touch if I think of anything else."

Blake ushered him out and locked the door behind him before he rejoined his mother. She sat with her face in her hands. She lifted her head and stared at him with tear-filled eyes. "He thinks we killed her."

"I know." Blake sank back onto the sofa. "We'll weather the gossip though, just like we always do."

She bit her lip and nodded. "And I'm sorry I blindsided you with Paradise. I tried to tell you several times but couldn't find the right words."

"Why would you hire her, Mom? She hates me now. It's going to be a source of conflict, and we don't need more stress."

"She's had a rough time, Blake. I heard about it through a woman who worked at her zoo. I was desperate for help here, cheap help, and she needed a place to heal. At least we could provide that."

Blake wasn't sure anything could heal Paradise Alden but God, and she thought God hated her. It was going to be a long year.

CHAPTER 3

AT SEVEN O'CLOCK THE next morning, Paradise had her hand on the lock to open the gate into the medical compound when a big cat screamed. Her heart pounded, and she wiped sweaty palms on her jeans as she forced her fingers to insert the key. The black leopard was in the other field, and she was safe.

She'd read the history of the rescued cats, and some of the stories of the living conditions were heart-wrenching. Still, when she was faced with the sight and smell of the big cats, her mouth went dry and she felt faint. This fear had to be eradicated if she held out any hope of living her normal life.

"Paradise."

She turned at the sound of Blake's voice and saw him striding across the grass toward her. He wore a safari shirt and camp shorts with boots, and she glanced at her watch. His first expedition wasn't due to start until nine, so she might have to put up with him awhile. She pinned a neutral expression in place and waited.

His gaze flickered over her and settled for a long moment on the scars on her left arm. "Doing okay?"

His fake concern didn't faze her. "Fine. The cottage is darling, and the bed was very comfy." She knew that wasn't his real question, but she wouldn't discuss her fear or her injuries with him. He'd lost all rights to any confidences long ago.

His jaw tightened. "That's good to hear." He paused and stared at the ground. "You're going to hear some stuff about the woman who was killed, Danielle Mason. She has been organizing protests against the refuge with some crazy claims we're mistreating the animals."

Paradise knew enough about him and his mother to know they'd take their care of the animals very seriously. "I'm sure that's been difficult."

"Very." He hesitated. "I think McShea suspects I might have had something to do with the murder. Danielle and I had two very public altercations. The going is likely to get very rough here, and if you want to bail rather than be involved, we would understand."

"You trying to get rid of me already?"

Amusement lit his face. "You know me better than that. If I didn't want you here, I'd tell you outright."

True enough. Maybe she should be open with him too, but the truth didn't come easily. Not yet. She wanted time to assess if she was here on a crazy idea that wouldn't pan out.

When she didn't answer right away, he pocketed his hands. "Well, I'd better get going. I have a large group in two hours, and I have paperwork to do first."

When he turned to go, she collected her thoughts and put her hand on his arm. "I never thought for a second that you would hurt anyone, Blake. Things have been a little—difficult."

He stared at the scars on her shoulder and down her upper arm. He reached out as if he wanted to touch them, then dropped his hand back to his side. "I can only imagine how bad it's been. It took a lot of courage to accept this job. I never thought you'd come back."

She released his arm. "I'll try to stay out of your way. This refuge felt like the right place to heal."

There was so much she wanted to say, but the words stayed locked behind her teeth. He had no idea how much courage it had taken for her to come here and face him again. But her only answers were here in this place, where shadows from the past still reached out to shape her life.

He smiled down at her, and this time she stepped back from the full strength of that warmth. She'd nearly forgotten how easily he related to people. Her guard had to stay up around him, and she was only here for the truth. Once she got her courage back, she could move on with her life. Getting involved with Blake—or anyone else for that matter—wasn't on her radar.

"I'll let you get back to work." She gestured to the enclosure. "I'm about to examine a fennec fox. Your mom thought she'd sprained one of her legs."

He nodded and walked away in long strides toward a safari truck parked at the equipment building. Paradise stepped into the medical building on leaden feet. She'd been off work for the past four months, and she was relieved not to have to take care of a big cat. Not yet anyway. A fennec fox should be easy enough.

The clinic was housed in a metal building with painted concrete floors. It held the smell of various animals being treated here, and she caught a whiff of big cat. Her throat tightened and she hurried past the room where the animal had been.

A perky brunette in her early twenties turned to greet her with a bright smile. "Hi, I'm Lacey Armstrong, your vet tech. I'm so glad you're here." She gestured at the cage. "This is Rosy.

She's favoring her right paw, and I think it's sprained. She's very domesticated and friendly. I don't think you'll have any trouble with her."

"Fennec foxes have fragile bones and are prone to sprains. Hopefully, that's all it is." Paradise glanced around the space. "Do we have an X-ray machine?"

Lacey nodded. "And an ultrasound machine. A vet's office in Mobile donated an old CT machine as well. We're pretty well set up even though we operate on a very tight budget."

Paradise opened the cage. "Hello there, Rosy. How are you doing?" The tiny fox stared at her with a mournful expression. "Not so well?" She reached slowly into the cage and the little creature let her gently touch her head. Rosy let out a protesting squeak when Paradise touched the injured paw. "Let's get this x-rayed."

"I'll do that for you." Lacey scooped Rosy out of the cage with gentle care and whisked her away to another room.

While she was gone, Paradise peeked in all the drawers and cabinets and found the exam room well equipped. Working here would be a pleasure as long as she didn't have to treat a big cat. At least not until she was ready to face that task.

Lacey returned and settled Rosy back in the cage. "All done. You can see the X-rays on the computer."

Fennec foxes preferred not to be touched, though they tolerated being handled, so Paradise let the little fox lay quietly until she saw the X-rays. "It's not broken, so that's good. I'll wrap it."

"We have a hospital area where injured animals are kept overnight, but there's no one to man it right now," Lacey said. "I live in town. Would you be able to check on her after hours? No other animals are in the hospital."

"Not a problem." In fact, she just might take Rosy home to keep her company.

Blake was never one to bury his head in the sand, and the current circumstances were severe enough that he had to act. After the first expedition, he sat on the fence by the wolf enclosure and pulled out his phone to call his cousin Hezekiah Webster. Hez was an attorney in the area and gave The Sanctuary ten free hours of legal advice a month. They hadn't had to use him that often, but the past few weeks had been challenging, and Blake might already be pushing that limit.

Hez answered on the first ring. "Hey, Blake, how's it going?" His cousin's deep voice held the calm strength of a man used to commanding center stage in a courtroom.

"Not so great, Hez." Blake launched into the discovery of the body. "I think I'm going to be their top suspect. And with good reason. She and I had a couple of altercations." He reminded Hez what had happened even though he'd consulted with his cousin when it all went down. "On the surface it would appear I had motive."

"This doesn't sound good. Let me see what I can find out about the case," Hez said. "For now, I'd suggest detailing your whereabouts the day before and the morning of the murder. Do they have a time of death?"

"The autopsy isn't back yet." Blake thought back to his schedule so far this week. "I think I've got a solid alibi. I've been staying at Mom's to help with the boys, and she and I watched a movie until late the night before. Isaac slept with me in my apartment that night too. Security cameras scattered around Mom's cottage should show I never left the upstairs apartment."

"That will help. Don't answer any questions without me present, and don't offer any information on your own. If you've got a detective gunning for you, things can get twisted."

"Will do. Thanks for the hand-holding. Maybe we'll get lucky and they'll figure out who really did this."

"Once they find the scene of the crime, they should uncover more information. Do you know if they've searched the ranch where the meat originated?"

"They aren't telling me much."

"No, I suppose they aren't. How's Aunt Jenna holding up?"

"She's worried. We were already trying to make it on a shoe-string, and now we have this to worry about." Blake slid off the fence and kicked at a weed with his boot. The action didn't do anything for his frustration level. "And if this isn't bad enough, Mom hired a new vet."

"That should be helpful."

"It's *who* she hired. Paradise Alden." A long pause followed, and Blake knew his cousin was trying to place the name. "My first girlfriend."

"The girl next door who was in foster care? The one you . . . ?"

"Exactly," Blake said grimly. "And Mom didn't even warn me. When Paradise walked through the door, I thought maybe I was hallucinating. I haven't seen her in fifteen years."

"And how'd she seem?"

"As beautiful as ever. And as prickly. She'll be as easy to work with as a porcupine. She assumed Mom had told me about hiring her and was none too pleased to be dumped into a surprise situation. The funny thing is—I'm not sure why she's here. She's got horrific scars on her arm and seems jittery around the animals. She was mauled by a black panther—a jaguar."

"That would make anyone skittish. Hmm, strange she'd come back after all this time."

Blake was done talking about Paradise. The bigger problem still loomed. "Let me know what you find out from the sheriff's office."

"I'll be in touch. Try not to worry."

"Easier said than done, but I'll give it a shot." Blake signed off and put his phone away.

His favorite red wolf, a female named Daisy, pressed against the fence and yipped a greeting. The preserve had acquired her after hearing of her need for a home. She'd lived most of her life in a crate, and when they'd brought her to the park, she'd run around the acres allotted to the wolves for hours as if she had to stretch her legs and never stop. Red wolves were critically endangered. Daisy had given birth to four pups, bringing the pack of red wolves to a total of twenty-one.

Daisy wagged her entire rear end and yipped at him. Her pups rolled and tumbled together, and their fat bellies made Blake chuckle. He rubbed their warm bellies, then loved on Daisy a few minutes.

He left the wolf enclosure and walked to where the black bears slept in the shade, then moved on to the big cats and on through the African bush area, where zebras roamed with antelope and wildebeest. He was especially fond of the capybaras and river otters. The aviary exploded with sound when he paused and spoke to the parrots. They all tried to talk to him at once.

By the time he'd made the rounds to the easily seen enclosures, it was nearly time for the next safari. He'd been here with his mom and the boys for six months, and he couldn't imagine living any other place now. Or doing anything else—not even paramedic work. These animals had helped him as much as he'd helped them. Mom thought he'd given up his career, when the reality was he'd been relieved for an excuse to try to forget that final week when he'd been responsible for the death of his best friend. If only forgetting was possible.

The current situations developing threatened this place he loved so much. And it wasn't just for himself that he wanted it to succeed—it was for his mom and little brothers. And it was for these animals he cared about so deeply. If The Sanctuary failed, where would they go? He had to do everything he could to save this special place.

CHAPTER 4

PARADISE PRESSED HER FINGERTIPS to her eyes, burning from lack of sleep. Every time she'd closed her eyes last night, she'd seen the body in the horse trailer. Some kind of distraction would help. She settled at her minuscule desk in the clinic and opened her MacBook. She called up the list of online articles she'd saved in a Scrivener file and began to read through them again. The first one was the article blaring a brief note about the murders:

> Nova Cambridge Couple Murdered. A neighbor reported a disturbance at the home of Granger and Becky Alden just after midnight on February 2. Law enforcement found the bodies of the couple in the home. A child was reportedly unharmed. Police are investigating.

Then she called up the next article announcing the sale of the Steerforth property to Hank and Jenna Anderson. The initial paragraphs mentioned the vision they had for founding a sanctuary for abused animals. Paradise knew some of Jenna's early story. She'd married Blake's dad at seventeen, right out of high school, and had given birth at eighteen. Her first husband had died in a Marine helicopter accident when Blake was a year old, and she'd raised her son alone.

When Blake enlisted in the Marines, she'd finally remarried. She would have been forty-two or so when Levi was born. Hank had been a wonderful man who'd inspired Paradise to become a vet herself. Paradise found the article a fascinating addition to what she knew about the family, but it was the final paragraph that had brought her here:

> The 120-acre preserve had been in the Steerforth family since the late 1800s. The property initially served as a working farm and ranch until the Steerforths added a roadside zoo. The property went up for auction after the owner, Mr. Steerforth, died in an auto accident. Hank and Jenna Anderson purchased the property and moved their animals to the ranch, then opened The Sanctuary Wildlife Preserve to the public.

Paradise stared at the words until the screen blurred. While there was no guarantee the answers to the murder of her parents were here, she had to come and find out for sure. And she had to find her way back to the career she loved. Her future depended on her success here.

"Knock-knock," a female voice said from behind her.

She turned to see Jenna smiling at her from the doorway. Though Blake's mother was nearly fifty, she didn't look a day over thirty-five with her stylish chin-length bob and boho-chic sense of style. Blake had gotten his thick dark hair and blue eyes from his mom, and they could have passed for siblings.

Jenna stepped into the office. "Settling in all right?" She dropped into a wooden chair near the desk.

"It's been a quiet morning." Paradise told her about the fennec fox. "I'm going to take a cart around the place and see what all we have to work with."

"Take Blake's expedition this afternoon. It's a behind-the-scenes excursion, and you'll see everything we've got."

Paradise would rather do it on her own, but she gave a jerky nod. Working with Blake came with the job. "I like what I've seen so far. The animals are well cared for and seem happy."

"We do our best."

Now might be a good time to dig out some truth. "How'd you decide to buy the property? I remember this place when I lived in town. The Steerforths let me help out sometimes when I wasn't working for Hank, but they only had a few animals. A couple of lions, a tiger, a zebra, and an ostrich named Katie. I think there was a bear too."

"You worked for Hank, so you already know of his love for animals."

Paradise nodded. "His passion was contagious, and when I left here, I knew I wanted to be a vet too." She didn't pry with more questions. When Paradise had lived here, Hank had been married to someone else. Paradise didn't know the details of his first wife's death.

"Too many people want an exotic pet without taking into consideration the needs of the animal. Those animals are often kept in tiny cages or enclosures and have poor quality of life. They're abused and abandoned. The animals the Steerforths took in here were in terrible shape, and the wife, Mary, was mauled by a tiger. The animal had to be put down, and the husband abandoned the farm, just walked away and left them. Then a week later he died in that auto accident."

Paradise winced. "That had to have been hard to watch."

"It was terrible. Hank went over twice a day to feed the animals, and we ended up buying the farm along with the animals three years ago. Blake went into partnership with us too, but he didn't participate except monetarily at first. When Hank died, Blake was discharged from the Marines and came to help out. I don't know what I would have done without him. He handles the boys like a pro and jumps in everywhere I need him. I won't sugarcoat it though—things have been tight, even with our generous donors."

"I know you kept some of the employees from the farm. Are you trying to keep too many of them employed?"

Jenna shrugged. "We can't run it alone, and at least they were familiar with the animals. I probably could let go of a couple, but I hate to do that. They love the animals."

"It's a little weird being back here after so many years. I drove past my old house yesterday. Someone has fixed it up."

Jenna nodded. "One of our employees bought the place. Evan Hopkins. You might remember him."

Paradise managed to hide her shock. Evan had been a seventeen-year-old neighbor when her parents were murdered, and she considered him her top suspect. After school the week before, she'd walked in on him in their house. His excuse about being too drunk to know he was in the wrong house had convinced her father, but all these years later, she thought it much too flimsy to be true.

To hear he'd purchased her home was a punch to the gut. Was

it to cover up evidence that might have existed somewhere? It seemed unlikely after all these years, but she wasn't sure she believed it was a coincidence he'd been the one to buy it.

"I'd be interested in seeing the inside sometime if he would let me."

"I'm sure he would. Evan is a hard worker and a great guy."

"Where does he work on the preserve?"

"He's a big cat keeper."

Paradise licked dry lips. She'd avoided the big cats, but she wouldn't be able to put it off much longer. Not if she hoped to accomplish her goals.

Blake glanced at his watch. It was the last encounter of the day, and half the seats were empty like usual. Most people liked the morning excursions so they could escape the Alabama heat and humidity, though in the winter the afternoon usually filled too. A young couple who seemed more interested in each other than learning about the animals sat on the bench seat that stretched across the back of the vehicle.

At the sound of quick footsteps, he turned an automatic smile toward the sound, but it died on his lips when he saw Paradise mount the stairs. "Uh, you need me?"

She shook her head. "Your mom suggested the encounter would be a good way to get familiar with the animals and the park." She slid into the long seat on the right side of the bus. "I'll sit here so I can face you and hear you easily."

And unfortunately, he'd see her out of the corner of his eye the entire time. Even with all that had happened between them, her guarded amber eyes drew him right in.

He flipped on his mic and turned around. "Good afternoon, you're about to embark on an inside tour of The Sanctuary. You'll see river otters, chimps, bears, the African delta, and lions lazing in the sun."

Paradise flinched at the mention of the lions. Was she truly up to this job? He hated to see her fear, but she would have to get over it. The big cats often required vet care.

He drove to the first stop, the grizzly bear refuge, and shut off the engine. He grabbed a bucket of raw meat morsels and opened the truck door. "You can get out if you want or watch from the windows." The vehicle was open air with a canvas roof, and the couple in the rear would be able to watch from their seats. The couple stayed put and didn't look up from their ardent conversation in the back.

Paradise followed him out of the truck and approached the fence with him. He rattled the fence and called for Serena, his favorite grizzly. She'd come to them when authorities closed down a roadside zoo. Even half-starved she'd been socialized and friendly. Since arriving here, she'd roamed the acreage with obvious delight. As usual she lumbered toward them, and he poked food through the fence for her and the three cubs who followed her.

Paradise examined her condition with a steady gaze. "She's beautiful, not even thin from the winter."

"She was a chub when she entered her cave. She gave birth last month and brought her babies out to show them off. She's a good mama."

They watched the cubs tumble together in the grass for a few moments. "It's a wonderful thing you're doing here, Blake," Paradise said softly. "I see the hand of love and kindness everywhere."

"We care about the animals. It's Mom's lifework."

"And yours?"

"It is now. I used to wonder why she cared so much. Now I know."

"What about your paramedic career? Are you sorry to leave it behind?"

Did she really care? "I came to help Mom and my brothers, but I soon loved it as much as they do. The animals all have different personalities, and every day I'm eager to interact with them. And I don't have to worry about getting shot." *Or losing a friend.* "I can't imagine doing anything else now."

A sharp, short report rang out, and his combat reflexes took over. He jerked Paradise down with him as he ducked. A bullet zinged by his head and hit the lock on the gate. "Get down, everyone!" The people who had disembarked hit the dirt, and several heads inside the truck ducked down below the windowless openings.

"This way." He scrambled on the ground with Paradise to just behind a small viewing shack where they squeezed into the space between the back wall and the fence. The four other people scrabbled after him too, and he checked to make sure no one was hurt.

"You okay?" he asked Paradise.

"Fine." She was pale but composed. "You tempted fate with that comment about not getting shot at any longer. More activists?"

"Looks that way."

Several more shots zinged off the metal lock at the gate. He thought the gunshots were from a 9-millimeter. Was the shooter trying to break the padlock and let out the bears? He popped his head out and saw the barrel of a pistol poking through the back window of the safari truck. The seemingly innocuous couple were the ones responsible for the attack.

He pulled out his phone and shot a text to his mom. *Active shooter.*

"You can't trust anyone," he said. "I thought that couple was more interested in making out than learning about the animals. It was all a front."

No more shots rang out, and he saw the couple running away down the path into the thick brush. Blake rose and held out his hand to help Paradise up. She ignored his help and scrambled to her feet. "Are the bears okay?"

He jogged over to the gate, now hanging open, but there was no sign of Serena and her cubs. "I don't see any blood. They probably took off at the first shot."

"Who would risk hurting the animals like that?" She brushed the dirt off her jeans. "The bears could have been hit by a ricocheting bullet. We need to check on them. Can we find them?"

"I'm sure Serena led her cubs to safety."

"You don't know that they weren't hit."

True enough. Normally, Serena had never shown a sign of aggression and loved attention from the workers, but her protective instincts could change that. "I'll get the tranquilizer gun."

Paradise had been around wild animals long enough to know it wouldn't do much to stop a charging grizzly. Serena could be on them before the sedative could work. All he could do was pray the friendly grizzly knew they were trying to help.

He walked to the truck and retrieved the tranquilizer gun, then reluctantly picked up a rifle as well. Paradise grimaced when he returned with the deadly weapon.

"I don't think I'll have to use it." He pointed to the bucket. "Let's take some food with us. That might distract her if she's hungry."

She grabbed the pail of food by the handle. "What if we try to call her over again like you just did? It might reassure her."

He nodded. "Be ready though. I'll need tools to fix the gate, and she might try charging through it."

Paradise banged the metal pail against the fence. No movement or sound occurred for several minutes. She did it again and called out Serena's name. Blake heard a snuffle, then the bears wandered into view.

"I don't see any blood on them," Paradise said.

A truck engine roared toward them before it stopped and two officers got out. The cavalry had arrived.

CHAPTER 5

PARADISE SAT IN THE conference room with Blake, Jenna, and Detective Greene, who was the last person she'd hoped to see after the shooting incident. She should have expected him to be the one to show up. Though the situation had been terrifying at the time, she hoped the incident would convince the detective that none of them had anything to do with the murder of Ms. Mason.

The room held the aroma of strong coffee mingled with the freshly baked sweet rolls Jenna had brought in. Paradise's stomach growled, and she realized she'd missed lunch. She rose and poured a cup of coffee while Greene grilled Blake. At least he was leaving her alone.

Greene clicked his pen off and on again before putting the tip to the green notebook in his hand. "You claim to have never seen the couple before."

Blake's eyes flickered at the way Greene emphasized *claim.* "As far as I know they weren't with the initial protests, though I could have missed them. The first group of protesters included probably thirty or so people. This couple today sat in the back of the vehicle and seemed more concerned with making out than with seeing the animals."

When Greene's lip curled as he wrote, Paradise decided she'd better jump in even though she hated to attract the man's attention. "I can corroborate that. When I boarded the vehicle, they were wrapped around each other and didn't interact with Blake through the tour. They didn't get off the truck either and didn't even seem to notice we'd stopped."

"Did you say anything to them directly about getting off the vehicle?" he asked.

"No. It's common for people to stay in the truck and observe the animals through the open windows. Some people are afraid or simply don't want to get out. Like I said, they seemed uninterested in the animals. I wondered why they even came." Blake ran his hand through his thick dark brown hair and it stood on end. "When the first bullet pinged on metal, I grabbed Paradise and hit the ground. I yelled for the few people who got out to take cover too. You can talk to them to corroborate our story."

"You recognized the sound as gunfire?"

"I've been in war zones, Deputy, so I immediately recognized it. I'm pretty sure it was a 9-millimeter."

"Did you feel threatened, like the shooter was aiming for you?"

"They never shot at us directly—only at the lock on the gate. But ricocheting bullets can kill just as easily as intentional ones, so I knew better than to ignore the danger."

"Did either of you try to confront the shooter?"

"Like I said, I knew better. When the shots ceased, I saw them running away."

When Greene's questioning gaze turned her way, Paradise steeled herself. "I kept my head down when Blake checked to see what was going on. I didn't see anything until he told me it was okay to crawl out from behind the lean-to. Our priorities then were making sure the visitors hadn't been injured and none of the bears were shot."

"Seems odd the shooter aimed at the gate knowing he might strike one of the bears. That doesn't show much concern over the animals."

"I thought the same," she said. "I was shocked to find the bears uninjured. It was very reckless of them."

"How did they get a pistol into the park?"

"We don't have a metal detector or anything like that," Jenna said. "They easily could have brought it in with a backpack or a purse."

Greene turned his attention back to Blake. "You're familiar with guns. Did you recognize the type of pistol?"

Blake shook his head. "I was too far away to see it well. I only saw the barrel, though when security arrived, I searched the bus for casings. I found none. I suspect the shooter's partner picked them up as he or she shot the weapon. A search around should turn up the ricocheting bullets though."

"He or she? So you aren't really sure if the man or the woman operated the weapon?"

Blake shook his head again. "As I said, I only saw the barrel sticking out the window."

Greene clicked off his pen. "That's it for now. I'd like you both to try to provide details for police sketches to see if we can track them down. Saturday afternoon work for you? I can arrange for a forensic artist to come here. That's typically best since the memory is often jogged by being where the incident occurred."

"We're shorthanded here," Jenna said. "The last excursion will be over at four. Blake would be free after that."

"I'll arrange for the artist to be here at four thirty." Greene rose and glanced at Paradise. "I'd like a word with Ms. Alden privately. Walk me out, please."

Paradise's gut tightened, but she stood and followed him out of the room. He said nothing until they reached his SUV.

He opened his door and gave her a coaxing smile. "I feel like we got off on the wrong foot. Dislike is radiating off you like a furnace, and I'd like to make amends for our first meeting. I'm sorry if I was out of line." He held out his hand. "Friends?"

Seriously? The guy clearly thought he was irresistible to women. Paradise ignored his extended hand. "It's all forgiven, Deputy Greene."

His smile wobbled a bit before he pinned it back in place. "That's good. Maybe our next meeting won't be so awkward. I'd hate for this to get back to the sergeant, you know? You sure we're square?"

"I handle my own battles," she said evenly. "You don't have to worry about me running to your boss."

Relief lit his green eyes. "Glad to hear it." His big hand came down on her shoulder, and he gave a slight squeeze.

She moved away immediately, and his hand dropped off. "I don't like to be touched."

"I'll keep that in mind."

His flat tone told her he hadn't taken the rejection any better than he'd dealt with her refusal to go out with him. She watched him get into his SUV and drive off. He was still going to be a problem.

—◡—

Paradise shut the door to her cottage behind her and sank onto the chair in the tiny living space. Rosy, the little fennec fox, trotted over to greet her. "Hey, Rosy." The fox settled by her feet, and she wished the small animal liked being handled. Having Rosy on her lap right now might give her a little comfort.

Her eyes burned, and she swallowed the lump in her throat. Was there some sort of sign over her head inviting men to hit on her or something? She'd had to deal with this kind of thing all her life, starting when she was in foster care. It had led to an unshakable distrust in men.

She gritted her teeth and rose to stomp to the bathroom mirror. Her eyes were luminous with moisture, and even her cheeks were pale. Where was that come-hither sign and how did she erase it? She pulled back her unmanageable mane of hair. The wind had left it even more untamed than usual, and she saw nothing that would draw anyone. Did men sense weakness in her somehow? All predators saw that in their prey, but she'd worked hard to project a strong, confident manner.

She splashed cold water on her face and wiped it with the towel before she sighed. Though she wasn't hungry, she should eat something. Rosy should be fed too. She went into the kitchen and fed the fox before she opened the fridge, staring at the contents. Nothing appealed to her, so she turned toward the coffeepot.

Someone tapped at her door, and she tensed. Surely Greene wasn't back. She turned that way and spotted Blake's dark hair through the window. The stab of relief quickened her steps to the door.

Blake's face held concern. "You okay? I saw the way you stomped off after Greene talked to you. What did he want?"

She stepped out of the way to allow him to enter. "He wanted to apologize for our first meeting. In reality, he was afraid his bad behavior would get back to the sergeant."

"Scumbag." He stopped by Rosy. "How's she doing?"

"Better. I should be able to take the wrap off in a day or two."

"You just let her roam here?"

"She's litter trained. Besides, she's good company. Want coffee? I was about to make some." She didn't want to be alone after that encounter, but her spine stiffened at the realization she was giving him the wrong signals. "Sorry, that was out of line. Let's maintain some professional distance."

He shut the door behind him and crossed his arms over his chest. "Let's get this out in the open, Paradise. I'm not the enemy here. I never was. Can we at least talk about what happened back then?"

"What good would it do?" she fired back.

He stepped past her and settled on the chair she'd just vacated, leaving the love seat for her. "I'm not leaving until we clear the air. Neither of us can work in this tension. You know it as well as I do."

She wanted to throw him out, but he was much too large for her to handle. And maybe he was right. They'd never talked about what he'd done—there'd been no chance after CPS moved in.

She crossed the small space and dropped onto the love seat. Her hands shook, so she clenched them together in her lap and said nothing. If he wanted to talk, he could start the conversation.

"What do you think I should have done?" He watched her intently. "Waited until Mr. Adams raped you? My options were limited."

She flinched at his bald statement. "I trusted you. You had to have known when you talked to the caseworker that they'd remove me."

"I didn't know they'd take you so far away! And I couldn't stand by and watch what was happening. No one could."

"I had it under control. I told him if he tried to enter my room again, I'd tell his wife. You should have trusted me to take care of myself. I don't need anyone's help. He wasn't the first man to try something. Nor was he the last."

He scratched his dark hair and it sprang back into its upright position. "No one is that strong, Paradise. When I was in Afghanistan, I was the one there giving aid. But even I needed help—a team. Allowing no one into your inner circle is a tough way to live. We all need other people. And God."

His voice gentled, and she knew his mention of God wasn't an accident. It had been a conflict during their teen romance too. She couldn't trust a God who would take her parents in one fell swoop and leave her dependent on strangers. Her views hadn't changed in all these years either. What kind of God did that? She didn't want anything to do with a being like that.

When she didn't reply, Blake leaned forward. "What would you have done if it had been me? I loved you. You know I did. I hoped your caseworker would listen to me. Mom would have taken you. I told the caseworker we would."

Paradise's eyes filled when he said he loved her. Past tense. And of course it was because it had all been so long ago for him. To her, his betrayal was still fresh. "You should have known better, Blake. We lived next door. Adams could have easily continued to have contact with me if I merely moved to the next house over."

Realization reflected on his face. "I never thought about that. You still didn't answer my question. What if you saw that same thing happening? Would you have ignored it and turned a blind eye?"

"I told you in confidence! Why do guys think they have to fix everything? Sometimes women need a shoulder to cry on. We don't expect you to rush in and make things worse. Talking it out can show the way to fix things. And I knew what to do. I had it in hand, but you ruined everything."

She saved the real blow for last because it would be the knockout. "Did you ever think that where I would be sent next would be worse, Blake? It *was* worse. They were a nice family but blind when it came to their son. They didn't believe me when I told them about him, and h-he raped me." She choked back her pain.

Blake's expression turned grim, and he reached for her. She shook off his touch and ran to the door to hold it open for him. "Please go."

"Paradise," he whispered.

"Don't say anything, Blake. Just go." She didn't look at him, and after a hesitation, he left. She shut the door and went to make coffee.

CHAPTER 6

THE MEMORY OF PARADISE'S revelation haunted Blake all the way back to the house. The noisy tussling of the boys on the living room floor was only a minor distraction from his self-recrimination. Why hadn't he considered the consequences of what he'd done? But he was just a kid himself, and he'd had no power in the circumstances. Once Paradise was in the foster-care machine, they were all helpless.

The aroma of frying catfish wafted from the kitchen, and his mother called his name. He went that direction and found her flipping the fish he'd caught last month and had frozen. Her face was red from the heat.

He grabbed a knife out of the block. "I'll do the salad. Smells like corn casserole in the oven too."

"You have a great nose. Is Paradise okay? That was a scary thing to happen on her first day of work. I hope it doesn't send her packing."

"She's doing okay with it. I'm not sure why she came. I mean, how easy can it be to return here when she hates me? I blew it, Mom. She landed in a worse place when she left here." He told her what Paradise had said. He'd failed the girl he loved just like he'd failed Kent. Would he ever be able to forgive himself for the wrongs he'd done?

His mother's eyes clouded. "I carry that blame too. We reported it together. We'll do what we can to help her now. God can heal those hurting places."

"It's made her hate God even more." He'd prayed for her occasionally over the years and had never really forgotten her.

"Then we just pray harder. He's the only one who can help her."

Blake nodded and opened the drawer with the cutting boards. They were a jumble inside. "The boys been playing in here?"

His mom glanced over to see what he was talking about, and she shook her head. "Not to my knowledge."

Given the weirdness of everything that was going on, Blake opened the junk drawer. His mother always kept it organized in a tray. The tray was in backward and nothing was in its usual place. He exchanged a long glance with her. "I'm going to check the office."

He strode past the boys, who had quit wrestling and were playing with Legos. The door to the office stood open, and he frowned. They usually kept it closed. His pulse quickened. When he flipped on the light, everything appeared in order. He pulled open the middle drawer and found papers askew, pens and pencils rolled to the other side. The alphabetized files in the side drawers were out of place.

From the doorway his mother's anxious eyes locked with his. "Someone's searched the house?"

"No doubt about it."

"But why? What could they have been searching for?"

"Your guess is as good as mine. Much as I hate to, I'd better report it."

She wrinkled her nose. "We'd better see if there's anything missing first."

"Good idea. I'll check the safe while you go through your bedroom. Make sure your jewelry is all there."

"On it. Oh, and dinner is ready," she called on her way to the bedroom.

He grunted and moved to the safe in his closet. The door stood open, and he curled his hands into fists. The loss of their backup funds would be huge, but when he stooped to peer inside, he let out a relieved exhale. The stacks of hundred-dollar bills were still inside.

So why open the safe and not take the money? Who had been in the house and why? He checked the papers inside too. Their passports and birth certificates were there. None of this made any sense.

His mother reappeared. "Everything is there. Did they take the money?"

"Nope, not a dollar. The safe was open, but everything seems to still be there."

"What on earth?"

He shrugged. "I'm going to report it anyway, but I doubt they'll even send out a deputy. We don't know who was here or why. Knowing Greene, he's likely to say the kids were into things."

"They wouldn't know how to get into the safe." She stared at the space in the closet. "How did the intruder manage to break into it?"

"The key was in it. I'm guessing they searched the kitchen and found the key, then checked the office before searching the closets."

"They had something specific they were searching for."

"I think so." He followed her out of the office and scooped up a brother in each arm. The boys squealed and slung an arm around him as he carried them into the kitchen.

He loved his life here, but his thoughts went to the little cottage on the other side of the complex. Could Paradise's return to town have anything to do with the events here? She had mentioned going to get food. Maybe they should invite her over for dinner. He deposited his brothers in their chairs at the table and glanced at the heaping plate of fish.

"You've cooked enough for an army," he told his mother.

"Well, I wasn't sure if we'd have company."

The glint in her eye told him she'd read his mind. "I doubt she'd come over."

"It can't hurt to ask. She's alone in a strange place, and she used to love fish."

He wasn't sure how much Paradise had changed over the past fifteen years, but he wanted to find out. "You text her. Maybe she won't take it as out of line coming from you. I'll call McShea."

"Coward." A smile tugged his mom's lips, but she reached for her phone on the counter and tapped out a message.

What on earth was she doing? Paradise walked along the brick pathway past the fields between her cottage and the main house. When Jenna's text came through, Paradise's stomach had rumbled with a reminder of how hungry it was and she'd agreed without thinking about the fact Blake would be there.

The truth was, she was lonely. She'd been okay with that for years, but being back here where things had once been so lively and fun had reminded her of what friendship and camaraderie felt like. Oh, she'd had a couple of good friends here, but their letters had ceased when she moved away. Then she had no one she'd opened up to and told about her previous life.

Jenna and Blake *knew* what she'd gone through. They had front-row seats to the fast demolition of the family she'd once had and the life she'd struggled to remake. They'd been part of the explosion that brought all of it down again.

Was the third time a charm and she'd find a place to call home permanently? She wasn't that lucky.

The main house was not familiar to Paradise. She'd only ever been to the business end of the place in its previous incarnation as the Steerforth Ranch with a roadside zoo. It was a cute shotgun-style house, yellow with white trim and an inviting porch. Painted gray stairs led to the red door on the east side of the porch. There were additional quarters over a garage that made the entire structure appear a bit lopsided but in an interesting, welcoming way. She liked it the minute she laid eyes on it. She suspected Blake had the quarters over the garage.

The door opened before she had a chance to knock on the red door, and Blake stepped out of the way. "Glad you could join us. Mom made catfish and there's way too much for us to eat."

Was he making excuses for Jenna's text? She lifted a brow and stepped inside. "It was kind of your mom to invite me."

He shut the door and leaned against it. "Everything okay at your cottage? Nothing out of place?"

She examined his tense expression. "That's an odd question. I haven't found anything out of place."

"Our place has been searched. Not sure what they were after, but I don't see anything missing."

She held her hand to her throat. "Did you call McShea?"

"I got routed to Greene. He wasn't much interested since nothing was taken."

"What's going on here, Blake?"

He took her arm, and she jerked it away. They would never be friends, and he needed to remember that.

He dropped his hand back to his side. "Sorry. I'm worried, Paradise. Did Mom mention we don't think Hank's death was an accident?"

She absently rubbed her arm where his touch had seared her skin. "No, she didn't talk about anything personal. She told me about the opening here and asked if I was interested. How did he die?"

"He fell out of the hayloft in the barn and broke his neck."

"That sounds accidental."

He nodded. "And I would agree if strange things hadn't been happening before that. This isn't our first break-in, and someone tried to run him off the road the week before his death."

"Could it have been the activists?"

"That's what we think. My cousin Hez is an attorney, and he poked around some, but without any real help from the police, he hasn't turned up any evidence. At least Mom got Hank's life insurance, which helped. It will give us a few months' breathing room to keep things going." He grimaced. "If we can get the activists out of our way long enough to draw people in here to see what we're offering. I'm going to try to catch McShea out of the office at lunch tomorrow."

Her heart stirred at the quandary his family was in. She'd taken a low salary because she had to come back here, and this job didn't ask much of her. Her affection for his mom had played a role in that decision too, but she hadn't realized the situation was so dire.

"So you think maybe someone tossed Hank over the edge of the loft?"

"Or broke his neck and staged it to make it seem like an accident." He ran his hand through his hair. "Shy of a confession from some unknown person, I don't know how we prove it though. We all have to be on guard here. Every one of us."

"Did anyone else want to buy this place before Hank and your mom purchased it?"

"Sure. It's 120 acres of prime land. Lots of hay grown here, good pastures for horses and cattle. Several farmers wanted it as well as a developer."

"I'm surprised the developer didn't buy it."

"It got snarled in red tape, and Hank managed to swoop in and snag it. Once the funding for the developer came through, they sent a guy to offer to buy it for much more than Mom paid, but we said no, of course. It's perfect for our needs."

He reached behind him and pushed open the screen door. The aroma of catfish and cornbread wafted out, and her mouth watered. She followed him through the small living room into the tiny kitchen with its round table for five. The boys smiled shyly in her direction.

"There you are." Jenna carried a platter of catfish to the table. "You're just in time."

Paradise took a seat beside the older boy. "Can I do anything to help?"

"I've got it. It's nothing fancy, but it's filling."

Had she made a mistake tonight? She hadn't thought about how she'd be looking across the dinner table at Blake, but it was too late to back out now.

CHAPTER 7

COUNTRY MUSIC BLARED FROM speakers placed around the patio areas that wrapped around the Tiki Hut, just outside Pelican Harbor, and the aromas of burgers and fries blew toward Blake on the breeze. The building had once been a shotgun house, but additions over the years had changed its shape.

Blake spotted McShea at a corner table with a sweet tea and a gigantic burger in front of him. McShea lifted a brow when he saw Blake. Blake hoped he'd listen better than his brainless deputy. He stopped beside the table. "Hey, Rod, mind if I join you?"

Rod set down his glass of sweet tea. "'Course not. Have a seat." He motioned for the server. "I'll even buy your lunch. I was going to stop by your place when I left here and see how you were doing. That shooter yesterday probably scared your mama half to death."

Blake pulled out a chair and settled across from the sergeant. "Yeah, it scared everyone. A server in our snack bar quit." He ordered a burger and sweet tea when the server arrived, then leaned toward McShea. "Any leads?"

"Wish I could say yes, buddy, but we're at a loss just yet. We found some spent 9-millimeter bullets, but they were pretty much destroyed from hitting metal. No casings, so you were right about that. Forensics took some prints, but you know better than me how many visitors touched things around there while watching the bears. Wish you had some outdoor cameras in places other than the entrance and the housing areas."

Blake made a mental note to grab a few. He wouldn't tell his mom he bought them from his savings. She worried too much about him. "Strange things out our way, Rod. Hank's death, then the body in the horse trailer. Now we've got that shooting and the break-in last night at our house."

About to take a bite from his burger, Rod closed his mouth and set down his sandwich. "Break-in?"

"Didn't Creed tell you? Someone rifled through our things. They didn't take anything, but every drawer in the place was searched—even the kitchen. Whoever it was didn't take Mom's jewelry or our laptops. They found the key to the safe and opened it too. The documents were moved around, but they didn't take the cash we had in there."

"Any idea what they were searching for?"

Blake shook his head. "I know you don't believe it, but I think Hank was murdered."

"Buddy, we've talked about this before. There's no evidence of that. None. No forensics, no sign of a struggle. Why are you so sure it was murder?"

"Hank was the most careful man I ever knew. For him to topple off the haymow is so unlike him as to be impossible. He constructed a barrier up there so his boys wouldn't fall over easily. He would have had to back up and hit it just right to even fall over. And he always watched where he was going. I don't buy it. And he was nearly run off the road a week earlier. Add all these other things after his death, and there has to be a connection."

"I can see where you're coming from, but we've got no evidence. I'll take another crack at the file just because you're asking, but I don't think I'll find anything."

The server brought Blake's lunch, and he waited until she left before he continued. "Did you hear Paradise is in town?"

Rod put his sandwich down again. "You're determined to keep me from eating, aren't you? She's working for you? Last I heard, she was in Montgomery. Had a run-in with a black panther that nearly took her arm."

Rod was Paradise's cousin, but the two had never been close. Rod was twenty years older, and his mother had refused to take Paradise in after her parents died, which had led to a gulf between them as big as Mobile Bay. Paradise might not have wanted Rod to know, but Blake felt her loneliness like a thorn embedded too deep to remove. She needed family, support, people who cared about her. His mom cared, but Blake was a big believer in the power of family. Paradise had felt abandoned most of her life, and he wished he could do something to erase the haunted, lost expression lurking deep in those amber eyes.

"I'm sure she'd be glad to see you." He took a bite of his burger and the juices hit his tongue. No one could make a burger like the Tiki Hut.

Rod lifted a brow. "She's a spitfire, that one. Last time I saw her, she told my mom off and said she never wanted to see any of us again."

"She was fifteen," Blake pointed out.

"Did she learn to temper that tongue?" When Blake didn't an-swer, Rod chuckled. "I didn't think so. Still, you might be right.

I'll let my mom know and I'll have Sheila invite everyone to a cookout one night. It might heal things. If she made peace with you, there's hope."

Blake forced a laugh, but he felt anything but happy. The way he'd hurt Paradise couldn't be undone. The damage went deep into her soul, and he saw it every time their eyes met. He finished his lunch and left Rod taking a last gulp of his sweet tea.

As Blake got in his pickup, he stared toward The Sanctuary. A curl of smoke hovered above the trees, and the wail of a fire truck rose above the chatter in the bar behind him.

Something at The Sanctuary was on fire. He stomped on the accelerator and barreled for home, praying all the way.

———

The wolf pack milled around Paradise's legs, and they seemed nervous and jumpy. This wasn't part of her veterinary job, but she wanted to step in and help wherever she could. Today they'd been short a predator keeper.

One of the wolves, a female, stared past Paradise and whined. What was wrong with them? She rubbed the animal's ears and tossed out food for the pack. They didn't immediately lunge for their meal and continued to move restlessly.

The scent of smoke reached Paradise's nose and she sniffed. It didn't smell like trash. The odor was stronger and more acrid. She gave the wolf a final pat before exiting the pen and turning back toward the buildings. She shaded her eyes from the bright Alabama sun and stared in the distance at the black smoke billowing above the structures. It appeared to be coming from the little stretch of cottages, and her heart stuttered.

Wait, was it *her* cottage?

She took off running toward the buildings. As she neared she heard shouts and saw flames leaping through the roof of her sweet little home. The flames had wasted no time in roaring through the cottage's old timber in spite of the stream of water pumping out through the fire hose the firemen held.

Blake stopped her as she neared. "Stay back."

The heat radiating from the burning structure checked her impulse to evade him and dart into the cottage to gather her things. Everything she cared about was inside. At least Rosy was safe back in the medical building. Her vision blurred as she watched the last traces of her old life vanish in the flames. The pictures of her with her parents, the necklace her mother always wore, and the tattered teddy bear she'd taken to every foster home through the years were all . . . *gone*.

She sensed a presence move closer, and she glanced over to see Blake on her left side. He didn't speak at first and squeezed her forearm as if he knew her pain. But he didn't. He'd always had roots here. She yanked her arm away and folded her arms over her chest.

"Stand back, it's going!" a fireman yelled as the roof caved in and sparks shot into the blue sky.

"I'm sorry, Paradise. All the wiring was redone when we remodeled it. The place was like new. I don't understand what happened. The fire marshal should know more when he investigates."

She stiffened and blinked back the moisture in her eyes. Was he implying she'd done something? "I didn't even turn on anything electrical this morning. I had cereal for breakfast and didn't so much as use a hair dryer."

He reached toward her, then dropped his hand. "This wasn't your fault. I didn't mean I thought it was. With everything happening around here, I have to wonder if it was set."

The thought hadn't been on her radar, but it should have been. She exhaled and stared back at the cottage. "Can you tell where it started?"

"Not really. It's a small place. Once it cools, I'll take a walk-through. Insurance will cover your belongings." His expression soured. "At least I hope it will. If it was arson, we probably won't get a payment until they find out who did it."

"Some things can't be replaced." Her voice wobbled.

He didn't ask what those irreplaceable things were, and she didn't tell him. She wasn't sure she could hold her composure if she laid out what the fire had taken today. Everything that mattered to her was gone.

Jenna approached with a little boy on each side. She kept tight hold of their hands. Tears streamed down her face. "I'm so sorry, Paradise. All your things are gone."

They all watched in silence until the flames finally subsided into smoking ruins. A small hand crept into Paradise's and she glanced down. Isaac stared up at her with a sympathetic gaze. She picked him up, and he wrapped his skinny arms around her neck.

"Are you sad?" he whispered in her ear.

"A little bit."

"Your clothes are all gone?"

She hadn't thought about the fact she had no clothes for to-morrow. "They are."

"And your shoes?"

"Shoes too."

"What about your teddy bear? Maybe it hid under the bed."

"I don't think that would have saved him. I'm sure he's gone too."

"I have lots of bears. You can have whatever you want."

She pressed her lips against his soft cheek. "You're so sweet, Isaac. I wouldn't want to take your favorite bear."

"Well, maybe not my *favorite* one. But you can have any of the others."

"Thank you, honey." She exchanged an amused glance with Jenna. "You're a good mom, Jenna. This little guy wants me to have any of his stuffed bears except his favorite one."

"He means it too. He's got the softest heart." Her attention moved from Paradise to just over her shoulder. "The fire marshal is coming over. Maybe he knows something."

Paradise turned to see a slim man in his fifties approaching. He nodded at them. "Heck of a problem to be having on the heels of finding that body."

"Can you tell what happened?" Blake asked.

"We'll know more when things cool, but I think it was arson. I saw patterns of an accelerant, and I smelled kerosene."

Arson. Why pick on her cottage? Was it dumb luck or something more?

CHAPTER 8

THE STENCH OF ASH and ruin permeated Blake's clothes and clung to his hair as he walked with Paradise back toward the main house. "I'd be glad to take you to Foley to buy a few things."

The only comfort he could offer was to try to meet her physical needs. Nothing had survived the fire—not clothing, toiletries, or personal belongings. He fully expected her to turn down the help, but her eyes held more vulnerability than he'd ever seen and she nodded. "I'd appreciate it, but I'd rather not face the hubbub of Foley. Could you take me to Pelican Harbor? I'm not sure I could focus enough to drive. I can't think of what all I need."

"I'm good at lists. I buy supplies for the park all the time. Let me tell Mom we're heading out. She's searching for the insurance papers and other documents she needs for the police." He didn't want to think about what the fire meant for the refuge. Insurance money could be tied up a long time with the reality of arson hanging over the settlement. He wanted to think no one in town would believe any of them had set fire to the cottage, but he knew how fast rumors could spread in a small town.

She stopped and put her hand to her mouth. "I started to say

I'd get my purse, but it's gone. I have no ATM card, no credit cards, no cash."

He checked the impulse to tell her he'd buy her things. Paradise had never been one to accept financial help. She was fiercely independent. "What bank are you using?"

The stress lines around her mouth eased. "You're right. See, I can't think. I would have gone to town by myself and come right back without anything." She named her bank, a national one.

"There's a branch in Pelican Harbor. You can get a new debit card and withdraw some cash from your account too."

He handed her the keys. "Start my truck and get in out of the wind." He felt sweaty and sticky from standing near the heat, but if she couldn't shower and change, he wouldn't either.

He told his mother what they were doing, and she nodded. "I think we're in trouble, Blake. We won't have funds to rebuild the cottage until the insurance money comes through. We promised Paradise lodging as part of her pay, and I have nowhere to put her."

He thought through their options. "She can have my studio over the garage. I can bunk with the boys, sleep on an air mattress on their floor."

"You could sleep on the full-size bed that's the bottom bunk, and Levi can take the top bunk. Isaac can sleep with me. He does half the time anyway." Amusement lit her eyes. "Though be prepared for them to fight over getting to sleep with you."

"True enough." They already took turns getting to stay with him in his tiny apartment.

"I'll let the boys know you'll be staying in their room as soon as I deliver the documents to the detective."

"Do you know how the policy reads?"

"Not yet." She tucked her dark hair behind her ears and turned back toward the files. "I think we can prove we had nothing to do with it. You were in town with McShea, and the boys and I were with other employees."

He hadn't thought of alibis, and a load lifted from his shoulders. Maybe it wouldn't take as long as he thought. "I'm going to take her to Pelican Harbor. There are more shops there than in Nova Cambridge, and she doesn't want to go to Foley." He left his mother digging through the files and went out to his truck.

Paradise was in the passenger seat with her head back and her eyes closed. His chest squeezed at the dampness on her cheeks. No family, no close friends here. Did she have close friends in Montgomery? She'd always been closed off with shields firmly in place. Her one friend, Abby Dillard, now a McClellan, lived in Pelican Harbor and worked at the bank. He should give her a call and let her know Paradise was back.

She opened her eyes and caught him staring. His face heated, and he went around to the driver's side and slung himself under the steering wheel. "Mom mentioned we had good alibis, so I hope insurance will kick in right away. Make sure you keep your receipts. That's one thing Mom insisted on—replacement insurance. I thought it was silly to spend the money for that, but she was right."

She leaned her head against the window. "I've got enough in the bank to buy what I need for now. I'm not high maintenance."

"You never have been. Any special shop you like?"

"I don't know what's still around. Is Island Bling still there?"

The women's apparel shop was the largest in Pelican Harbor. "Sure is. Not that I've ever been inside. Nothing tall enough."

She smiled at his pathetic attempt at a joke. "I won't make you go inside. You can sit on a park bench or go find a sporting goods place."

"I think I can manage my first visit."

She turned to stare out the window and said nothing the rest of the drive into town. The stop at the bank proved easy even with no ID. Her old school friend Abby had fixed her up with a debit card and cash in hand.

He parked in the small lot next to Island Bling and followed her inside. She went straight to the jeans stacked on tables. He wandered to the tees and took a hunter-green one with Big Al, the University of Alabama elephant mascot, on the back to show her. "This would go well with your coloring. A small, right? I think it would fit."

She eyed him. "What do you know about coloring and clothing?"

"I've got eyes and notice things." He laid the tee on the stack of jeans. "Give it a try."

She shook her head, but the hint of a smile hovered on her lips and a bit of the sadness in her eyes ebbed. With several more tops in her stack, she stepped into a dressing room while he poked through the display of purses. She wasn't the fancy-purse type, and he spotted a small bag with a zipper that opened with room for cards, ID, and money. Its brown pebbly finish felt like real leather, and the price seemed to reflect that. She'd never want to spend that much for a purse, but in an impulsive move, he took it to the cashier and paid for it. He took it out to the truck and tossed it inside. Once they were heading home, she couldn't take it back when he gave it to her.

When he returned to the store, she was at the counter paying for the new items. He counted the outfits. Three jeans, four shorts, a lightweight jacket, and seven tees. It was a start.

She handed him the large bag. "I'll meet you in the truck in a few minutes. There's a lingerie store down the street."

He took the bag with no complaint. A man could withstand only so much temptation.

Look at her—she was in the truck with Blake Lawson and she was being civil to him. The back of Blake's truck held her new clothing, toiletries, shoes, and some snacks. He hadn't mentioned where she would be lodged now that her cabin was toast, but they likely had an empty one she could claim.

"Oh, wait." She sat upright. "I forgot to buy a purse."

He reached for something on the floor and handed her a bag. "I got you one."

"What? I'll bet it's pink."

"You lose. Here, check it out."

She opened the bag and reached inside. Her hand touched leather, and she withdrew the cutest purse she'd ever seen. The brown pebbly finish was just right, and it wasn't a huge thing she'd have to tote around. "It's perfect, but you didn't need to do that. It feels like real leather."

"I didn't ask, but I thought you'd like it."

Her tongue felt glued to the top of her mouth. She hadn't expected him to do something like this. "Thank you, Blake. That was very kind."

"We can't have you toting your debit card and cash around in a plastic bag." He started the truck and pulled out of the parking lot. "Any other stops before we head home?"

What would he say if she told him the real reason she was here? "Could we go to Nova Cambridge and drive by the old neighborhood?"

"Sure. Feeling nostalgic, or is there another reason?"

She was tired of feeling she was fighting the world. Though she still wanted to hold him at arm's length, he'd be ready to fight for her. He'd always been one to take up for the underdog in school.

His listening skills should have only improved with his years in the Marines. She had to have an ally. The fire had convinced her she couldn't do this on her own. The idea of finding the man who'd killed her parents had seemed possible until she arrived and found the enemy ensconced in her childhood home. And most friends she remembered from her teens weren't around any longer. Running into her old friend Abby in the bank had been a stroke of luck, but she had no idea if it was possible to resurrect anything from the past.

Her gaze strayed to Blake's strong jaw and firm lips. Except for Blake and Jenna. They'd once been the rocks that bolstered her fragile confidence. She couldn't truly trust them, but they were at least kindred spirits. They were facing an adversary too.

She had sensed Blake's deep regret over their past, but trust came hard to her. She'd been betrayed too many times by too many people.

"Paradise?"

She blinked and found that Blake had left Pelican Harbor behind. He'd pulled into a stand of oak trees and parked the truck under lacy strands of hanging moss that gleamed white in the moonlight. "Sorry, I was thinking."

He ran both front windows down, then shut off the engine. "Tell me why you're really here. I don't believe it was because you needed a job. Accepting help from my family would have been your last choice, not your first thought. Something else drove you back here, and I don't believe it was your arm injury."

Her fingers found the ridge of ugly, painful flesh under the thin fabric of her cotton shirt. Blake had flinched at the sight of the angry red ridges marring her skin. Everyone did, and she used to keep it covered to spare the sensibilities of other people until she decided she couldn't put on a mask. Her real handicap wasn't the weakness in her arm—it was the fear that froze her in place when she least expected it.

Blake shifted on the seat. "You can talk to me."

She exhaled and slumped against the seat. "It all started three months ago, right after my injury. I was on pain pills at night so I could sleep, but they had a nasty side effect—nightmares. I thought that's all they were, but they began to happen during the day. Visions of waking in fear in a dark closet while someone whispered my name on the other side of the door."

"Memories of that night? You didn't remember much when we were dating."

"The doctors thought I blocked them out, and we all agreed it was for the best. There was no benefit to remembering that horrible night." She hugged herself and shivered in spite of the heat shimmering in the air. "I cut out the pills because I'd rather deal with the pain than with the nightmares and sudden slams of memory. But it didn't help. It was as if once the door was open, it couldn't be shut, no matter how hard I tried."

"Did you try sleeping pills?"

"No. I hate drugs, but that wasn't the reason. The things I've remembered make me feel like I did something that set this into motion. That somehow it was my fault. And I can't endure not knowing if it's true or not. I have to find out what happened that night, Blake. Ever since I arrived, I feel like someone is watching me. I think it's the murderer."

She saw the concern settle over his face. "I'm not crazy, Blake. What if the killer is afraid I'll remember something? What if he knows that's why I'm here and he feels he has to either drive me away or get rid of me? Maybe he set fire to my cottage."

"I don't think you're crazy. You're a deep thinker and the most sane person I know. What can I do to help?"

His quiet confidence calmed her heart, which had been stuttering with dread. "You and your mom know everyone. Help me find the people who lived on our street and who might remember. Maybe the more I uncover, the more I'll remember."

"I'm sure Mom will want to help too." He started the engine and ran up the windows. "I have a friend in the state police department. Maybe he can send us a copy of the murder files. You'll have to prepare yourself for the graphic pictures."

She shivered. "I'm ready." Her bravado felt hollow though. She would have to face her worst nightmares.

CHAPTER 9

NOVA CAMBRIDGE WAS A small university town four miles from the entrance to The Sanctuary. There were only a few shops, two gas stations, a grocery store, a coffee shop, and a few other places that catered to the students at Tupelo Grove University. It had seemed a safe and perfect place to live, and never once had Paradise sensed danger lurking anywhere. Her life had been idyllic until the terrible night her parents were murdered.

Blake drove slowly through town, past the old hotel that had been converted to shops and businesses. The building's lights and antique streetlamps showed people sitting at tables and chairs on the large front porch of the former hotel. She read the lit sign over the door. "University Grounds. Coffee shop?"

"It's got great coffee. Cider and beignets too. Want to stop?"

"Not just yet."

She didn't have to direct Blake since he'd grown up here in a different neighborhood from her parents' home. He was a year ahead of her in grade school, but when she was placed in foster care with his next-door neighbors, he'd started looking out for her.

She'd idolized him, and when she was fourteen, he'd started to notice her in a different way.

Their path to the old neighborhood took them past Tupelo Grove University. Tupelo trees marched in rows along the brick paths, and she spotted the little pond she used to love. The stately old buildings had decayed some since she lived here. "Seems a little worse for the wear."

"New management is working on increasing enrollment and adding new classes."

It felt right to be here with him tonight. Back when they'd dated there was no coffee shop, and they would cruise the dark streets talking for hours. Sometimes they'd make the trip to Pelican Harbor and buy beignets to eat as they walked past the shimmering waves of Bon Secour Bay. It seemed a lifetime ago and yet just yesterday. Did he ever think about those times?

She studied the line of his jaw and the strong column of his neck. If she had more courage, she'd ask why he never married. It didn't matter though—their time had come and gone. And maybe it wouldn't have lasted anyway. They'd been kids, young and in love, but still kids with a lot to learn.

"We should have gotten beignets when we were in Pelican Harbor. Petit Charms is just as good as ever. The boys beg me to buy them anytime I head to town. When I get back, they'll ask for them."

"We could stop at University Grounds and get them some. Or is it Petit Charms or bust for them?"

"They aren't picky. I'll grab some on the way out."

Did he ever regret giving up his career to help his mom? Knowing Blake, she would bet his decision wasn't something he'd had to think about. Even as a teenager he'd been selfless and had always tried to help his mom. Jenna had raised a fine son, and Paradise already saw the signs the other two boys would turn out as well as Blake.

"How'd you manage to finance college and vet school?" Blake asked.

She tensed at the thought of more revelations. "Mr. Gibson paid for it as long as I promised not to press charges against his son."

"The father of the guy who raped you?"

She clenched her hands together and nodded. It wasn't something she was proud of as it smacked of blackmail.

He touched her hand. "I'm sorry. I can tell it's all still very painful."

"Dragging the case into court would have been agony, but maybe I shouldn't have taken the easy way out. What if Scott did it again? The thought has haunted me all this time."

"There wouldn't have been good answers back then. At least you did something with your life. You didn't let it define you."

"It has though." She hugged herself and still couldn't look at him. "I don't like to be touched."

"I've noticed."

"The boys are helping me get over it. And you." She dared a peek at his expression at her admission. His blue eyes held a warmth and tenderness she hadn't seen in so long. The intensity made her uncomfortable.

The moon came out from behind a cloud, and the light touched the trees with a silvery glimmer. A memory slammed into her out of nowhere. A glimmer of moonlight slanting through her bedroom window followed by a scream. She'd bolted upright when the scream pealed again. Her mother's.

"Paradise?" Blake stopped the truck in the middle of the quiet street.

She shook off the terror of the memory and swallowed hard. "I—I remembered something. I heard my mom scream that night. There was a loud thump too, and I was too scared to move for a few seconds, then I slid off the bed and hid under it. Steps went past my door, and when they proceeded down the hall, I crawled out from under my bed and hid in the closet."

"Do you remember anything else? A voice maybe? Did someone come into your room?"

The moisture in her mouth dried up, and she shook her head. He reached over and took her hand, and she let him. The physical touch grounded her. She was fine—it was a memory, nothing more. No one was lurking in the darker shadows under the tupelo trees.

She finally found her voice. "I'm okay. You can drive on."

His hand squeezed hers one last time before he placed it back on the steering wheel. She glanced at him from the corner of her eye as he drove down the road. Her former home was lit up, and light streamed from nearly every window. She spotted the little girl she'd seen the day she arrived in town. A television flickered across the room, and the child sat entranced. Paradise remembered evenings like this one. Her mom and dad had often watched a kids' movie with her, or they would play Go Fish or a board game.

Her vision blurred, and she didn't realize she was crying until Blake parked along the road and slid across the bench seat to slip his arm around her. She buried her face in his chest and sobbed for the life that had once been and would never come again.

———

Paradise would think he was a total slob. Blake glanced around the tiny space above the garage and tried to see it through her eyes. A couple of books on fly-fishing lay open on the sofa, and his fishing rod, tackle box, and waders occupied too much space in the corner behind the brown tweed sofa. A distinctly fishy odor permeated the air too.

He grabbed up his fishing gear. "I'll stash this stuff somewhere else, and you can air out the room. Mom changed the sheets, but she didn't get a chance to clear out my belongings. Give me fifteen minutes to grab it all."

She didn't seem perturbed at the state of the place. "I'll help. I hate taking your apartment. Are you sure there isn't another cottage available?"

"Everything else is occupied."

"This is occupied too. Where are you going to stay?"

"I'll be in the main house. Mom has it all planned out." He didn't mention he'd likely be bunking with one of his brothers. "I'm used to being in a barracks, so I can sleep anywhere. It won't be much of an adjustment for me."

"I appreciate it."

Though she didn't mention it, he knew she had no real choice. The Sanctuary didn't have the funds to increase her salary, and she wouldn't be able to pay rent with what they could pay. Now that they'd talked, he understood why she'd taken the shoestring wage they could afford.

She headed to the closet and began to pull out boxes. "I'll start with these."

He whipped around. "No, I'll get those. Some of them are heavy." *And personal.*

Before he could move her out of the way, one of the boxes tilted and slid off the top of the other one in her hands. The top opened, and the contents spilled onto the floorboards. Blake froze as everything he'd hoped to hide from her rolled into view.

The set of Harry Potter novels she'd given him for Christmas that last year peeked out the top of the box along with the other items he'd kept all these years.

She dropped to her knees and tugged the books the rest of the way out of the box, then lifted out the other items. The snow globe she'd given him for Christmas the first year, notes she'd written him in class, tickets to the school play when he'd kissed her for the first time. All the memories he sometimes pulled out with regret lay exposed in a pathetic little pile. If she didn't already think he was a total loser, she would now.

Her guarded expression dropped away. Her amber eyes held the old softness he hadn't spotted in years. This wasn't the time to air old feelings. But were those feelings gone, or had they just moved underground?

His face burned as he knelt and began to toss the items back into the box. "This stuff has been stored up here forever. I'll take care of clearing out the closet if you want to pack up my books in the bookcase."

Her fingers brushed his hand as she took the globe from him. "You still have this. My dad gave it to me when I was a kid. I'd forgotten I gave it to you." She shook it and the white snow swirled down on the boy and girl skating by a red barn and a two-story farmhouse. "His parents gave it to him when he was ten. He always said it reminded him of growing up in Indiana. My grandparents lived on a farm like this."

"I remember. You should take it back."

"I wanted you to have it."

"But your mementos burned up. It's a piece of your dad." He pressed it into her hand. "Please take it, Paradise."

She hesitated before her fingers closed around it. "It might help me remember." She turned back to the items in the box and picked up the ticket stubs for *Harry Potter and the Deathly Hallows*. Her eyes went misty.

Did she remember their first kiss as vividly as he did? He cleared the huskiness from his throat. "I reread the series sometimes." He stuffed more things in the box while she continued to examine other items. If he got it all out of view, maybe she wouldn't realize he'd kept every one of the notes she ever sent him.

She held up the Angry Birds plushie. "You hated this thing. I can't believe you kept it."

And it was better if she didn't know how many memories he'd packed in this box. He plucked it from her hand and caught a whiff of the plumeria scent she wore even back then. The fragrance heightened the tightness in his chest. He tossed the plushie in the box, then closed the lid. He doubted she'd even kept the class ring he'd given her while he'd treasured every minute he spent with her. It had been a waste of time and energy pining for someone who hated him.

And he couldn't blame her for the way she felt.

CHAPTER 10

EVEN WITH CLEAN SHEETS, the bed pillows smelled of Blake—his cypress-eucalyptus soap blended with an earthy scent from working in the barns. Paradise resisted the impulse to leap from the bed. She couldn't lower her guard around him. Seeing the mementos he'd kept all these years had turned her insides to mush. She'd spent the past two hours downstairs with his family eating beignets and playing games, but her thoughts kept returning to the things he'd treasured.

The time spent together tonight had shattered her defenses, and it would take time to rebuild them.

The only reason she'd come back was to find the truth. Romance wasn't on her agenda. Especially with Blake Lawson. She'd tried to get over him and thought she'd succeeded. But even still Blake made her heart sing, and she couldn't allow it. After she uncovered the truth, she had to escape to someplace where she could start over without the past staring her down every minute. Somewhere her glances didn't stray to Blake's thick hair and understanding smile.

She gazed over at the snow globe on the bedside table. At least something was left of her parents. Her phone vibrated with a message, and she glanced at the time. A little after eleven. She read the text from her cousin Rod's wife, Sheila.

Hey, Paradise, I heard you're back in town—long time no see. I'm having a cookout on Sunday afternoon and it would be great to catch up. Rod's mom and siblings will be here too and all the various kids. No need to bring anything. Rod is smoking ribs and Mom is bringing corn casserole and baked beans. I've got dessert duty. Feel free to bring a plus one. Maybe Blake?

Paradise's finger hovered over her phone. How did she answer? Her family had washed their hands of her long ago. Her second cousin Lily, Rod's mother, could have saved her from foster care, but she'd said she couldn't handle her own two and didn't want to add to the chaos. The rejection had left Paradise scarred. Was it time to try to bury the hatchet? Maybe her cousin would have some insight into who murdered her parents.

Sure, she texted back.

Great! See you at one.

Paradise put her phone back on the nightstand, but there was no way she could fall asleep now. She sat up and slid her legs over the edge of the bed. Blake's deep voice calling the name Cody came from the front yard. She was decent in sleeping shorts and a tee, so she went down the garage stairs and stood on the bottom step, watching Blake in the moonlight for a minute. He was ready for bed in red TSU athletic shorts and a white tee. The light outlined his strong biceps and square jaw. If anything, he'd grown even more virile and handsome over the past fifteen years. The stiff night wind carried the scent of his soap to Paradise and mingled it with the fragrance of the roses in the front flower bed.

She made a movement and he stilled as he turned toward the house. "Paradise? What are you doing up so late?"

She descended the last step. "You're the one out here yelling at someone."

"Not someone." He gestured to a dog. "He was supposed to do his business and come back in, but a bunny caught his attention. I had to give him a little redirection."

She eyed the dog. He seemed to be made out of leftover parts from random breeds: Chihuahua legs, Great Dane ears, greyhound body, and an elegant—but crooked—Chesapeake Bay retriever tail. He had wispy brown-gray fur with several severe cowlicks.

The dog lifted his muzzle and she took a step back. "Is he snarling at me?"

"What? No. Cody is only dangerous to himself. That's his crazy snaggletooth."

The incisor stuck out of his lower jaw and made him appear slightly rabid. "I didn't know you had a dog."

"It's my cousin Hez's dog. He asked me to watch him for a few days while he's on a short trip." Blake studied her expression. "You still haven't said what you're doing up."

"Want to go to a picnic on Sunday afternoon?" She started to retreat to the garage stairs. "You know what? Forget it. It was a dumb suggestion."

He reached toward her with one hand. "No, wait! I'd love to. Where do you want to go?"

Did he think she was asking him to be alone with her? They'd often explored the swamp and woods around the area. Being together in nature had been their favorite pastime. Every minute she'd spent with Blake back then had created the best memories she had. Ones she still clung to when life got hard. Had those memories played a part in her decision to pursue the truth? Maybe subconsciously she wanted to see if Blake lived up to the memories she treasured.

She hugged herself against the night breeze. "Rod and Sheila want me to come to a family picnic. I suspect you had something to do with the invitation, so I thought it only fair you had to endure it with me."

He took another step her way. "Maybe it won't be awful. They're family, Paradise. There are kids you haven't met, and they've probably changed since you left town. They might be trying to make amends."

She noticed how adroitly he'd dodged the question of whether he was responsible for the invitation. "I want to see what Lily remembers in the weeks leading up to my parents' murder."

And why she didn't want to take me in.

Her gut roiled with an awful thought. Was it because she knew Paradise was somehow at fault?

Saturday afternoon Blake didn't have to bang the fence and call for Serena. She grunted and stood at the sight of him and Paradise, and her cubs nosed toward them. The woman in jeans and a tee that read *Have Pencil Will Travel* had introduced herself as Gwen Marcey. Blake liked her based on her T-shirt alone, but her open, sunny expression cemented it.

"So we were here in the bus." Blake gestured to the safari bus they'd brought to the grizzly enclosure. "We got out to feed Serena on the encounter tour when the shooting started."

Gwen headed back that way. "Let's sit on the bus to chat. It might help your memories."

He and Paradise followed the forensic artist back to the vehicle. The safari vehicle was equipped with long rows of seats in a giant U along the perimeter of the bus and two long benches back-to-back in the middle.

Gwen slid onto the middle bench facing the bear enclosure. "Since you have both been separately interviewed by the police, it's fine to do this together. It will probably be easiest if you sit next to me."

Paradise settled beside Gwen, and Blake sat by her.

Gwen patted Paradise's hand. "Sweetheart, I'm not feeding you to the lions." When she coaxed a smile from Paradise, she continued. "That's better. Let me start by saying this sketch won't get anyone falsely arrested. It's simply a tool for the police to use in finding people who have the features you remember. They could find several suspects who resemble this sketch, but no one is arrested without actual evidence. We can rest if you become tired—in fact, we will likely take several breaks. I brought granola bars and water with me in case we get hungry. And if you really press me, I'll dig out my stash of peanut M&M's."

"I'd take a handful of those now," Blake said with a grin.

Gwen pulled out a jar of candy from the plastic tub she'd brought, and he dug out a handful. He offered the jar to Paradise, and after a hesitation, she took a handful too.

"Is this going to be a party?" Paradise asked. "Here I thought it would be uncomfortable."

Gwen opened the cover of her sketch pad and took out a pencil. "The only thing uncomfortable here is my prosthetic bra, and when I get home, it's coming off. Now which suspect do you remember best?"

"The man," Blake said in unison with Paradise. "They were necking there." He pointed to the bench seat across the back of the bus. "I only saw the woman's side view."

"I was at an angle where I saw her face from the front once when I was exiting the vehicle," Paradise said. "But I saw the man better. I'm not sure I would even be able to describe her."

"So we'll start with his drawing." Gwen pulled out a batch of photos. She separated them into two piles and handed one to each of them. "I want you to study each picture and make two piles. One for people who are nothing at all like the shooter and one for people who remind you of the man in some way."

"Got it." Blake went through his stack. He put the discards—men who were not like the guy at all—in one pile and the others who had a similar nose or haircut or facial shape in another pile.

Paradise was slower than he was, but her maybe pile was bigger.

"You're flipping through yours quickly, Blake. You sure about all the discards?"

"I was a Marine paramedic and I tend to make snap decisions, but I'm sure." When Gwen nodded, seemingly content with his answer, he went back to the task.

One picture held him up. It was a white male in his thirties with blond hair and a sneer on his stubbly face. The guy on the tour didn't sneer, but he did have stubble. His had more of a red hue though. Blake placed the picture in a third pile to talk about.

"These are fresh stacks." Gwen handed them more photos. "These are the pictures your cohort in crime here already went through. You know the drill."

They switched stacks and went through the process again. Blake kept catching whiffs of Paradise's plumeria scent, and it brought back distracting memories he had to keep pushing away.

When they were finished, Gwen took their maybe stacks and began to go through them. She laid multiple photos in her own pile until she'd examined every picture. "These are the pictures you both chose. Let's go over why you put them in your pile. Age, haircut, other things that caught your attention. We'll see if you both set them aside for the same reason."

With her skilled coaxing they finished a composite of a man in his thirties with longish hair that curled over his collar. His broad face had bold brows over wide-set eyes. He wore jeans and a green tee with a ball cap that covered the top of his head.

Paradise tapped the picture. "That looks just like him."

"One small thing." Blake reached for the picture he'd put in a third pile. "Did you see this guy?"

Paradise studied the photo. "He was in my discard pile. I thought about putting him in the maybe one though, but I couldn't figure out why."

"It's his hair." Blake didn't want to feed her any information in case his slight niggle of familiarity was wrong.

"The stubble," she said finally. "The guy had a five o'clock shadow. Only his was kind of reddish, wasn't it?"

"That's what I remembered too." He handed the picture to Gwen. "Book 'em, Danno."

They went through the same procedure with the woman but with much less success. Finding the man would have to be the focus.

CHAPTER 11

TEENAGERS AND ADULTS PLAYING volleyball spilled across the yard suffering from the drought. On the right side of Rod and Sheila McShea's house, smaller children played in a sandbox next to a swing set. Blake stayed close to Paradise as they walked toward the group of adults gathered around the smoker and grill. A lavish spread of food covered a long folding table, and outdoor chairs sat ready for use. The smoker vied with the scent of fresh-cut grass for dominance.

"Steady," he whispered to her as they approached. "Just smile and stay close. I can start the conversation until you feel more comfortable."

The scent of her hair, that sweet plumeria fragrance, made him want to move closer, but he checked the impulse. She was skittish enough without him making her feel cornered. His fingers on her elbow guided her toward Rod. Some chatter about the incidents at the refuge might help put her at ease. If there was one thing Paradise hated, it was conversations that got too personal. She'd been that way as long as he'd known her.

He'd known the McShea family all his life. Small-town life was like that. He lifted his hand in greeting when Rod spotted him.

Rod glanced from him to Paradise and his eyes widened. "Paradise." He put down the tongs and wiped his hands on the towel hanging from his belt before heading to greet them. He enfolded her in a bear hug. "What's it been? Fifteen years? You're as pretty as ever."

Yearning glinted in her eyes. "Something like that." She stepped back and moved closer to Blake. "You look great, Rod."

"Thanks." He turned and gestured. "You could mosey over and say hi to Mom. She's here somewhere."

Paradise's smile slipped a little. "I'm sure I'll run into her shortly. I think Blake wanted to talk to you, and I'll hang around for now."

Blake recognized his cue to steer the conversation away from the personal family direction it had taken. "We were both wondering if any new evidence has turned up on the shooting or the fire? And do you know yet how Danielle Mason died?" The activist had been at the top of his concerns.

Rod's smile vanished, and he was all cop. "We found a little blood evidence in some trees outside the paddock of Dillard Ranch, probably when she was loaded into the trailer. I'm working through alibis now and trying to find the murder site itself."

Rod was known for being open with his constituents, and this was the first murder in the area in years. He hadn't revealed anything a ranch employee didn't know as forensics combed over the area.

"And the shooting?"

"I personally talked to the group of activists camping out near the swamp. They claimed they were trying to free the animals, but no one would tell me who had the gun. They admitted they fired the shots though. The sketch you two did of the man was recognized right off, but he was long gone by the time we interviewed everyone. Neither of you could identify the woman, so that was a wash. I told them to leave the area or I'd arrest the whole lot of them. Not that I have anywhere to house that many." His frown deepened. "But they packed up and headed out of town."

"What about the Mason woman's death? One of them might have been responsible," Paradise put in.

"Maybe. I got addresses and phone numbers from all of them before they skedaddled, and I'll follow up. I wanted to avert any further incidents by disbanding them. They seem to be a menace when they're together."

Blake supposed they couldn't stay around forever, and if the department had no evidence, Rod couldn't order them to stay anyway. "What did the Dillards have to say about the murder?"

His dad had been friends with old man Dillard years ago, and the older rancher had always been kind to him. And violence from the family wasn't something he could envision. His wife, Stacy, had been Blake's babysitter on occasion when he was growing up. Still, the ranch employed five hands, some of whom were newcomers to the area.

Rod's mouth twisted. "About what you'd expect. They had no idea the body was in the trailer with the horse. They didn't see it."

"How could they load the horse and not see it?"

"Dillard said they loaded the animal first and left the trailer unattended for about half an hour. He thinks someone put the body in during that time."

The sick horse likely wouldn't have been any trouble to someone stashing the body in the trailer. "But why put it there where it would be found right away? I don't get it."

"I don't either," Rod said. "Maybe whoever killed her wanted to throw suspicion on you. Rumors in a small town can destroy a business."

Blake knew that only too well. Their earnings were already suffering. "Or it was a threatening gesture to us maybe."

"Possible."

"And the fire? Any idea who set it?" Paradise asked.

Rod glanced at her before turning back to his smoker for a moment to check the temperature. "The group at the campsite all claim it wasn't them, and I'm inclined to believe them."

It wasn't much, but at least Rod didn't seem to be hiding anything. Blake glanced at Paradise. Should he ask about her parents' murders? She might not be ready to ask yet.

Her amber eyes darkened with intensity, and she gave him a slight shake of her head before she took a step toward her cousin. "I'd like to see the evidence gathered from the murder of my parents. I could examine it in a conference room or something so you don't have to make copies."

"Why would you want to do that? There are graphic crime scene photos, girl. Leave it to the professionals."

"The killer is still out there. The professionals haven't made any headway. Maybe I'll remember something."

"You were nine years old, and the sheriff had a child psychologist talk to you. You didn't see anything."

"Maybe I blocked it out."

His brows drew together. "You remembering something?"

She hesitated and stared down at the grass. "Not yet, but I'd like to try."

Rod lifted the smoker lid and began to pull meat from it. "I'll think about it."

Blake felt the tension radiating off Paradise, and he led her away. "Don't go ballistic and burn any bridges. Hez is trying to acquire the records, and I made that call to my state police friend. I think we'll get them." He nodded toward the group of women watching the children play. "You want some company when you talk to your cousin for the first time?"

She shook her head. "I have to face her sometime. Might as well be now."

"I'll hang close. Look my way, and I'll be there in a flash."

Her grateful smile warmed him, and he watched her walk across the plush grass toward her cousin. There might be fireworks. He sensed Paradise's impatience to get to the truth, but these things often couldn't be pushed.

———

Paradise walked on lead feet as she went toward the relatives talking in groups by the kids' sandbox. The thumping of her heart made her slow to catch her breath. She did not want to be here. Catching up with family who had turned their backs on her wasn't her idea of a good time. She forced herself forward and heard the animated voices sputter and stop when the women realized she was there.

She focused on Rod's sister's face. Molly's willowy frame looked like she could be blown over by a stiff wind, and her hazel eyes lit when she spotted Paradise. "Paradise Alden, you come here right now. I've been dying to see you since Rod said you were in town."

Paradise allowed herself to be enfolded in a tight embrace. She'd forgotten how kind Molly had always been to her quiet younger cousin. "You haven't changed a bit, Molly. I think Emily was five when I left. Did you have any more?"

Molly released her. "Four of those hoodlums are mine. Emily

is twenty now, and the others range from eight to fourteen. The youngest will kill me yet." She pointed out a gangly towheaded boy playing volleyball with the bigger kids on the other side of the house. She linked arms with Paradise. "Come along and say hi to Mom. She's in the kitchen taking apple dumplings out of the oven."

Paradise's chest squeezed, but she allowed her cousin to drag her into the two-story house and away from any help she might expect from Blake. "Nice house."

"Rod had it built three years ago. Sheila loves it, and if she's happy, everyone is happy." The acerbic note in Molly's voice told of vague disapproval.

Paradise gawked at family pictures lining the entry and sitting on tables as Molly dragged her to the kitchen.

"The kitchen is this way. Mom, Paradise is here," Molly announced as they crossed from the oak flooring to the kitchen tile.

Paradise pinned a smile to her face. "Hello, Lily." The years had been kind to her older second cousin, and even in her seventies, Lily had smooth skin and thick and lustrous salt-and-pepper hair that touched her shoulders. "You're just as pretty as I remember."

The sincerity in her voice teased a grin from Lily's stern expression. "I see you never tamed that hair. Your mother never tried either. You could have been a model if she'd straightened the lion's mane."

Paradise was thankful Lily made no move to embrace her. Hypocrisy had never been something she liked to indulge. "Those apple dumplings smell great. I remember you made them for Mom for her birthday every year. She loved them."

Lily's expression softened even more. "I still miss your mother. We were more like sisters than cousins."

Paradise's face felt frozen in place. Lily had rewarded Mom for her kindness by turning her back on her only child. "What do you remember about that night?"

Lily turned briskly toward the oven, and she bent to remove the dumplings. "Let's remember the good times and not that horrible night." The pan clanked on the stove as she set it down.

"I can't do that, Lily. They've never received justice, and the longer it's denied them, the worse it feels. I can't sweep it under the rug and forget it happened."

Lily banged the pan on the stovetop. "You don't even remember anything, Paradise. This is your usual melodrama. Life is too short to stew about things we can't change. Move on with your life. Get married and have kids. They'll keep you so busy you'll forget all about the sad past."

Tears burned Paradise's eyes. She should have known her cousin would dismiss her desire to bring justice to her parents. "I can't do that." She gulped down the angry words that would get her nowhere. Softening her tone, she took a step closer to Lily. "You were the first person on the scene. What do you remember? Who called you?"

"I don't like to think about it."

"Please, Mom," Molly said. "Can't you see how important this is to Paradise?"

Lily pressed her lips together and sighed. "Your mother called me a little after eleven that night. She said someone was trying to break in the back door. I called the sheriff's office and headed there myself."

Gerald Davis had been the sheriff at the time. "You found me in the closet." She remembered that much.

"You were in the far corner rocking back and forth and singing."

Paradise didn't remember that detail. "What was I singing?"

"No song I'd ever heard. Something about monsters under the

bed and angels watching over you. I always thought you made it up."

"Where were Mom and Dad?" She'd been too young to ask questions at the time and too distraught and rebellious from the rejection in her teens.

Lily winced. "Your mom was in your bedroom, and your dad was in the backyard with his pistol. He probably had it because he'd seen or heard the intruder. The sheriff thought he'd been killed first. The glass in the back door had been busted in from the outside, and the killer had reached in and unlocked the door."

My bedroom. The memory of screams echoed in her head, and she wanted to slap her palms over her ears to drown out the noise. She had to have heard those screams in real life when she was nine.

She swallowed. "Was there ever a viable suspect?"

"I never heard of one, but Rod would know. He was on the department then, though not a detective. Still, I'm sure he followed it since it was family." Lily grabbed hot pads and lifted the plate of apple dumplings. "We'd better get outside before they eat without us."

The relief in her voice touched Paradise. This couldn't have been easy for her.

CHAPTER 12

PARADISE'S DAY WITH HER family hadn't gone as well as Blake had hoped. The winter sun had begun to sink quickly over the tops of the live oak trees even though it was only five, and there was a distinct chill in the air through the air vent.

A big truck barreled past them, and it backfired as it drew alongside Blake's pickup. He jerked at the loud sound before he could cover it, and his heart rate accelerated. He hid the calming breaths he took before Paradise could notice. Noises like that took him right back to that last ambush.

His phone dinged with a message as he pulled into the drive at The Sanctuary. "Hez has news."

Paradise unfastened her seat belt. "Can you call him and put it on speakerphone?" Her voice vibrated with hope.

"Let's take the Gator over to the pond and watch the sunset. He said to give him a couple of minutes."

They got out, and he led her to the Gator. They always left the key in the utility vehicle so it was ready for use by any of the staff, but it was universally acknowledged that no one but Blake used it. He'd drive it on the road to town if he could. The green beast ate up the mile out to the pond, and he could sense Paradise's tension build as they passed the tiger enclosure.

"Still scared of them?"

"I'm working on it."

He took that as a yes. "You could always specialize in smaller species."

"I'm not going to let fear keep me from following my dream of working with wild animals. The big cats were always my favorite, and I have to get past this. I *will* get past it."

She settled on the bench under a big tupelo tree, and he pulled out his phone and called Hez. "Hey, buddy, got your text. What's up?" He put it on speakerphone. "Paradise is here with me."

"Hi, Paradise," Hez said in his deep voice.

"Nice to 'meet' you, Hez. I've heard a lot about you."

"Same. I wanted to let you know I was able to obtain copies of the investigation into the murder of your parents. I'm sorry to report I don't feel it was thoroughly examined. They didn't talk to many neighbors, and the few leads they had seemed to go nowhere. The notes reveal a very lackadaisical approach to finding the killer."

"Why wouldn't the sheriff's department investigate?"

"I wondered the same thing and did a little poking around on my own. I apologize if the information I'm about to tell you is upsetting, but it's part of getting to the truth."

"I want to know," she said.

"Very well. First of all, there's a rumor the old sheriff, Gerald Davis, was having an affair with your mother."

Paradise gasped, and her hand went to her throat. "Do you think it's true?"

"I do. I spoke to your mother's neighbor, and she reported

seeing the sheriff visit late at night when your father was out of town."

"Dad was out of town a lot. He sold sound equipment to churches and music artists and was gone several nights a week. Much of the time he was only home on weekends."

"That's what the neighbor reported. She saw your mother and Gerald kissing at the door many times."

The color washed out of Paradise's cheeks. "I never saw or heard anything."

"Kids sleep hard," Blake said. "My brothers never wake in the night. Mom has vacuumed the hall while they're sleeping, and they never stir."

Paradise twisted her wild hair into a knot on top of her head and poked a stick from the ground in it. "You think the sheriff had something to do with the murders?"

Hez's voice came through the phone again. "It's possible. In fact, I'd say it's likely. Sex and money are the most common reasons for murder. Maybe your dad found them together and the sheriff killed him. Your mom might have objected, and he was afraid she'd tell, so he killed her too. You remember nothing, Paradise?"

"My cousin said Dad was in the backyard with a gun, and Mom was found in my bedroom. I was hiding in the closet. H-how did they die?" Her voice wobbled.

"Bludgeoned with a ball bat."

"But Dad had a gun."

"It wasn't loaded. The hair and blood on the bat confirmed it as the murder weapon."

Blake felt Paradise quiver, and he took her hand. Surprisingly, she let him keep it. This had to be hard to hear. The pictures in her head of the scene would be horrific. If only she'd let him hold her.

"I have the crime-scene photos, but the box of actual evidence hasn't been located."

"How'd you get the files, Hez?" Blake asked.

"Let's just say I have a friend in the Pelican Harbor police station. They're the actual files, and I made copies. I'll return the packet to my friend tomorrow. I'll have the folder for you whenever you want to pick it up. And my friend is still searching for the box of evidence."

"Could we come now?" Paradise asked.

"I'm about to head out on a dinner cruise with Savannah. How about I leave my condo unlocked? You can grab the file off the kitchen counter."

"We'll be there in half an hour," Blake said.

"Brace yourself, Paradise. The pictures will be shocking and hard to see."

"I have to. There might be a clue that no one but me would recognize. I was in that backyard and that bedroom."

Blake squeezed her fingers. She wasn't only beautiful but strong too. But then, he had always known that. It took a special kind of inner strength to soldier through what she'd experienced. She was the same girl he'd fallen in love with when he was sixteen and yet somehow even more interesting now. Ever since she'd arrived his emotions had been in turmoil.

He ended the call with Hez and stood, pulling Paradise up with him. "I can get the file if you'd rather stay here."

"No, I have to go. I want to see it right away. Hearing about the sheriff tells me no one is going to bring justice to my parents except me."

"And me. I'm with you on this quest, Paradise. You don't have to face it alone."

She lifted her chin, and her eyes glistened with moisture. "This isn't your fight, Blake. If the sheriff's family hears about this, we might be facing more than a fire and a few stray gunshots."

"I'm battle hardened. I don't even flinch at the sound of gunfire anymore. You can't do this alone."

Indecision flickered across her expression, but she nodded and squeezed his fingers. "Let's get that file."

———

Paradise spotted the red folder on Hez's marble counter immediately, but she held back instead of rushing to it. The details inside were sure to be disturbing, and she wanted to prepare herself. The faint scent of confectioners' sugar and frying pastry rose from Petit Charms downstairs, and she was tempted to turn tail and run for fortification in a beignet.

Blake stepped past her and picked up the folder. "Want me to pull out the pictures first? You can read the details without being assaulted by the photos."

She wanted to shake her head, but she found herself nodding instead. "Maybe just arrange them so the pictures are behind everything else."

His eyes softened and he flipped open the folder. From her spot near the door, she caught a glimpse of a glossy photo, though she couldn't make out any details. If not for Blake's quick intervention, she would have seen them first.

He pulled out a stool for her at the breakfast bar. "It's quiet here, and Hez won't be back for hours. We can take our time."

The red folder both drew and repelled her, but her feet made the decision and took her to the seat. She perched on the barstool and pulled the evidence toward her with a suppressed shudder. All her nightmares centered around the contents, and for the first time, she wished she was a drinker. She'd take some Dutch courage right about now.

She inhaled, then finally opened the cover. The responding officer had filled out a detailed report of what he found upon entering the home: the back door unlocked with broken glass on the kitchen floor, signs of a struggle, and the coppery stench of blood.

Paradise stopped at that detail and smelled it herself in her memory. The memories of her childhood home had grown vague over the years, but the pictures in her head sharpened into focus. She remembered the navy sofa and the area rug under it. Her new Polly Pocket had been on the floor by the fireplace the night of the murders, and she saw a mention of it in the report. What had happened to all her things? They had vanished along with her home and parents.

She read through the clinical descriptions of her mother's wounds and moved on to her father. It took tight focus to read for clues and not to see the horrific details in her head. She went back to the list of items taken as evidence: a ball bat, presumed to be the murder weapon, hair and blood evidence, two cell phones, a computer, items of clothing, a hair clip, and an onyx cuff link.

Blake was beside her, and he moved in closer to touch his finger to the list of evidence collected. He was so near she could see the flecks of gray in his blue eyes. A shiver of attraction slipped down her spine and curled in her belly. Blake's charisma wasn't so much that he was strong and handsome—it was his kind manner and the way he seemed to skim past her prickly exterior and see *her*. The real Paradise who hid behind a stony expression. He was a deep thinker yet thoughtful of others.

Resisting his pull was going to be tough. When his pupils dilated, her pulse leaped. Had he sensed her moment of weakness?

She cleared her throat. "Do you think Sheriff Davis hid the evidence, and that's why it's missing?"

He edged away a few inches. "I wouldn't be surprised."

"If we had it, we could retest the DNA."

"The office is shorthanded. Maybe it's misfiled."

She turned back to the file. The photographs would be next, and she steeled herself to flip the page.

Blake's hand came down on hers as she wavered. "You don't have to do this, Paradise. Let me and Hez study them. You have enough nightmares."

"I have to see," she whispered.

"I know." He lifted his hand out of her way.

She bit her lip hard enough to taste blood, then moved the evidence report out of the way. The first photo slammed into her brain, and she flinched. Lights illuminated her father's body in the backyard. She couldn't look at his head, so she focused on the area around him. The grass was pressed down by footprints, and a sneaker lay discarded a foot away from his right side. Both feet were bare.

She studied it. "That's not his shoe."

"You sure?"

"Positive. He always wore Converse with the star on the side. I think those are Nike. And he had *big* feet."

"That might be the perspective of a nine-year-old girl."

"Mom always called his feet canoes. I went with her to buy them before, and we had to go from store to store. I think he wore a fifteen."

Blake came closer. "Those are definitely smaller than that. I'd guess a ten. Do you see anything else out of place?"

If she took her time, she could do this. She returned to her inspection of the picture and finally dared to examine her father's clothing. "He's got his suit pants and button-down shirt on. Usually the first thing he did when he got in off the road was change into jeans and a tee. He'd often go putter in his shop. He liked woodworking. I remember his onyx cuff links. He must have lost it in a struggle inside, then come outside."

"Do you remember if he'd been gone that day?"

She pressed her palms to the sides of her head. "It's all locked up inside. I've tried to remember, and I just can't."

His warm fingers pressed down on her shoulder. "Easy, babe. Don't get upset. When you're ready to remember, it will come. It sounds like it's possible he came home and found your mom with the sheriff in a compromising position."

"I wish we could confront the sheriff."

"We can't talk to him, but his wife is still alive. Maybe she suspected something. She lives here in Pelican Harbor."

At least they had some direction. She closed the red folder. "That's all I can stand right now. When can we go see her?"

"Maybe after work tomorrow."

It would have to do—for now. She glanced at the time. "My first educational session with students is tomorrow. I'd better go study up."

"How about some beignets first? Petit Charms is right below us. We can hardly walk past without a taste."

She didn't want to smile, but her lips took over the reaction for her and lifted. "Beignets, then work."

CHAPTER 13

THE REFUGE HELD LECTURES every Monday morning at ten, and the room contained about twenty people—more than Paradise expected for her first educational speech. Speeches were easy for her. She was able to distance herself from the audience and focus on facts. And it would provide distraction from the images in her head from the file last night. They hadn't found the Aldens' neighbor at home and had discovered she was away on vacation the next two weeks.

She set Rosy's cage on top of the table in front of her and coaxed the fox out. "This is Rosy, one of our fennec foxes. She doesn't like being touched, so she will hang close to me." Several children were in the room, and she suspected they'd be her most active participants. "What do you know about fennec foxes?"

A girl with brown pigtails shot up a hand. She appeared to be about ten, a prime age to know at least something about an animal. "They are the smallest of all the foxes, and they live in the Sahara Desert and North Africa. They're related to dogs."

"Very good. They range all over the Sinai Peninsula in Egypt, and the Arava and Negev Deserts in Israel. Their desert habitat has helped them adapt to going long periods without any water. Anything else?"

"Um, they're nocturnal, I think?"

"Correct. Are they solitary?"

When the girl didn't answer, a boy about the same age raised a cautious hand. "I think they live in family units."

"You're right. Even young adults stay with their parents until they mate and establish their own families and territories. Rosy here is about two. She recently had an injury to a paw, and I had her stay with me at nighttime." The audience gasped, and the kids leaned forward. "She has a mate, and they will stay together for life. While she was with me, she roamed the house searching for her family. She had three kits waiting for her at home."

"Didn't she poop on your floor?" a little girl asked.

"She's litter trained and was a perfect guest."

"What does Rosy eat?" the boy asked.

"She's an omnivore. Do you know what that means?"

He nodded. "She eats lots of things, animals and plants both."

"Her main diet is insects, rodents, snails, lizards, geckos, plants, fruits, roots, and eggs. She has long claws for digging below the surface to find insects, and those big ears give her excellent hearing to hunt down her prey."

She talked a few more minutes about Rosy and her clan before dismissing the group to go wander the preserve.

As the people filed out of the room, Blake poked his head in the doorway. "Got a minute?"

"Sure." She coaxed Rosy back into her cage and carried it toward him. "Let me return her to her family. She's getting antsy. We can talk on the way."

The warm breeze lifted her hair, and she could feel it soaking up the humidity. She should have put it in a ponytail. Blake held the door for her, and they walked along the path to the fox's habitat.

"Creed Greene wants me and Mom to come into the office for more questioning about the Mason murder."

She stopped. "You think they suspect you and your mom?"

His grim expression answered her question before he spoke. "He made it clear we are his top suspects. And I can't blame him. I had the altercation with her. Her behavior has impacted our bottom line, and we clearly wanted her gone and out of our hair. She was from California, so there aren't any family members around they could target. We're low-hanging fruit."

They reached the fox habitat, and she released Rosy. Her kits ran to meet her. "When are you going?"

"They want us at three."

"You want me to watch the boys?"

"If you don't mind. I could ask another employee, but they like you."

"I like them too, and besides, I live right there. Creed is a bad man. Be careful what you say, Blake. I get the impression he wants to close the case and doesn't care how he does it."

"I'll be careful. I asked Hez to meet us there too."

"That's a good idea."

His tight voice and jaw showed his worry. "I think you're right about Creed. I might need to start investigating the murder on my own."

"I'll help," she said quickly.

"You're already knee-deep in finding out what happened to your parents."

"This is a more immediate threat. The neighbor won't be back for two weeks, and we don't have any good leads to follow right now. I want to help."

"I could use the support." He ran his hand through his hair. "The refuge is already on shaky ground, and if word leaks out that we're the prime suspects, I don't know what that'll do to the business. It could be our death knell."

She knew how a rumor could torpedo a business. "You'll probably be gone awhile. Tell your mom I'll handle dinner with the boys." Paradise didn't know how it happened, but she found her hand on his arm. "I know you're worried, Blake. This is all still fresh. We can figure it out."

His hand covered hers. "You don't know how much that means."

The moment stretched between them because she didn't want to move unless it was to step closer to the faint whiff of his cypress-eucalyptus soap. She forced herself to pull her hand away, but it was an effort. This was not good.

~

The Bon Secour sheriff substation was a small block building that featured three offices, an evidence-processing room, a holding area, and an interrogation room. Blake had thought he and his mom would be interrogated together, but they were separated as soon as they arrived. He'd volunteered to go first, and Hez had accompanied him to the room, a small space with a long table with enough chairs to seat six. He'd never expected to find himself at the center of a murder investigation. A stench of despair mingled with some kind of strong disinfectant.

An expressionless Creed Greene dropped into a chair on the other side of the table and tipped back the chair. "Let's get to the bottom of this, Lawson. The autopsy pinpoints Danielle Mason's death between 10:00 p.m., January 8, and 2:00 a.m., January 9. Where were you?"

Blake glanced at Hez, who gave a small nod. "I usually go to bed around ten thirty, but I was tired and hit the sack just before ten. Nothing awakened me, and I got up at six like usual, showered, and joined my family for breakfast in the house. My little brother Levi slept with me. He's the seven-year-old."

"You live over the garage? Does it have a separate entrance?"

"Yes, it's got its own staircase inside the garage."

"Can anyone see you coming or going from the house? Can anyone corroborate your statement?"

"Not the actual staircase. My mother would have been able to see me enter the garage if she happened to be looking. I'm sure she didn't though. She goes to bed earlier than me, and she's usually busy with the boys. But like I said, Levi stayed with me."

Creed frowned but didn't answer. "What time did you enter your apartment?"

"After dinner I played Uno with the boys, and we watched cartoons for a bit. Levi and I went to my place around eight so Mom could get Isaac bathed and in bed. Levi showered at my apartment, and we went to bed at nine and watched a few cartoons. Again, that's my usual schedule. I turned the TV off at ten."

"You don't go out with friends?"

"I left the Marines to help my mom with the boys after Hank died. My brothers need a male role model they can depend on, and it's something that's important to me. I see a friend on occasion for lunch, but evenings are devoted to the boys."

Creed blinked, and his nose curled. Maybe that sounded pompous, but it was the truth. Mom couldn't do everything by herself. She would try, but The Sanctuary was a lot of work, and there would be little time left for the kids. They deserved more than the leftovers.

"So you have no real alibi."

"I have Levi."

"Who could have slept through you sneaking out."

"We have video around the house. I didn't go anywhere. Check it and you'll see."

"Would you be willing to take a lie detector test and give us DNA?"

Hez cleared his throat. "Do you have evidence my client committed the crime?"

Creed brought the front legs of his chair down with a thump. "I have plenty of suspicions. The bad blood between them was well known."

"We both know lie detector tests are notoriously unreliable, and they're not admissible in court. I will allow the DNA test to help you out, but hear me clearly: I won't allow my client to put himself in a situation where he's accused of something he didn't do. We're done here unless you can come up with some actual evidence." Stern-faced, Hez leaned forward. "Do your job, Detective. The real killer is out there, but you're wasting time digging in the wrong hole."

Creed's eyes squinted to slits in his enraged face. "He knows more than he's admitting, and I'm going to nail his butt to the wall. You defense attorneys are all alike—you don't care about justice. All you want is to let the guilty go free. Wait here for the tech to take the DNA." He rose and left the room.

The harsh words didn't change Hez's expression. He shook his head. "He's out to get you, Blake. I think I'll put a bug in Jane Dixon's ear. The sheriff's department works closely with Pelican Harbor's techs and resources in this area. The police chief needs to be aware of Greene's vendetta. Any personal reason he seems focused on you?"

"I have no idea. I'd called the sheriff's department when the

activist group blocked the entrance, and he came out and ordered them away. He seemed fine then."

"Maybe it's career oriented. He wants to clear the case and add
a notch to his belt."

The brunette tech came in. She spoke to Hez before opening
the swab package and rolling the cotton tip around the inside of
Blake's mouth. When she left, Hez rose. "That was Savannah's
best friend, Nora Craft. She's good, so you don't have to worry
about her tampering with the evidence."

Blake followed him out the door, where they found his mother
waiting for her turn, and he hugged her before Hez led her off
to the room. They had nothing to hide. Danielle Mason's determination to shut them down had been an annoyance but hardly
worth killing over.

Blake wandered back out into the late-afternoon sunshine to
clear out the stink of accusation still clinging to him. He found
the coffee shop and ordered a black Americano, then went back
outside to wait. It seemed an eternity before Hez and his mother
exited the building. From Mom's somber expression, he knew it
hadn't been fun.

He joined them at the foot of the concrete steps. "At least he
didn't throw you in jail. Did he want to give you a lie detector
test too? And take your DNA?"

Hez answered for her. "He knew better than to ask about the
polygraph, but I allowed the DNA. You both did great, but I
don't think this is over. He's got a vendetta. Didn't you say you
had a developer ask to buy the property for a lot of money?"

Blake's mother blew a strand of dark brown hair out of her
eyes. "We did. I said no, of course."

"I'm going to poke around and see if the guy has a connection
to the activists."

The thought hadn't crossed Blake's mind. "Whoa, that's wild. You seriously think Frank Ellis could be behind the activists?"

"It happens. The work you guys do is amazing and necessary, so there's no reason to try to shut you down. The animals are well cared for and happy with plenty of space to roam. They're safely contained too. It makes no sense why you'd be the activists' target."

"Thanks, Hez." His mother hugged him and turned toward the truck. "That's what we thought, but I never dreamed there could be a nefarious purpose behind it. I'm exhausted and hungry. Let's get out of here before they haul us back in."

Blake couldn't wait to tell Paradise about Hez's suspicions. Could Frank Ellis be the culprit?

CHAPTER 14

PARADISE GLANCED AT THE clock. Nearly five. Jenna had put a pork roast in the Crock-Pot first thing this morning, and the aroma made her mouth water. All Paradise had to do was come up with side dishes and dessert. Finishing supper had helped occupy her hands and her mind.

The boys had been her constant shadow, and so far they'd played Uno and made cookies together. She'd enjoyed it more than she'd expected. She'd been on edge for two hours, knowing what Blake and Jenna must be going through. How could Creed suspect them? It was so unfair.

Isaac sidled up with a pan dotted with various sizes of cookies. Chocolate smeared his mouth. "See my cookie."

Levi pointed to one that had a hat made of chips. "That one's mine. And that one—the zombie with the teeth."

"Very nice! Chocolate chips for eyes and the teeth are perfect. You boys are great cookie makers." They'd doubled the amount of chocolate chips, but they would be tasty even though they were lopsided and a little too moist. "Let's pop them in the oven." She took the pan and slid them into Jenna's second oven.

She checked the potatoes au gratin, and they would be ready in another half hour. Homegrown green beans from Jenna's freezer waited in a pan with bacon for her to warm up. When was the last time Paradise had prepared food for other people? Probably years. It made her feel part of the family here, which was dangerous.

The front door opened, and Jenna called out, "We're home in one piece."

Paradise wiped her hands on the red gingham apron she'd donned and followed the boys, who dashed off to meet their mother and brother.

Isaac was already on Blake's shoulders when they entered the kitchen. "Smells good."

"I helped!" Isaac said. "We made cookies. Since we were so good, could we use Daddy's telescope tonight?"

"I'm sure Blake could be talked into that," Jenna said.

Levi clung to his mother's slim form like a spider monkey. "Mine is a zombie with chocolate chips for teeth." He bared his own teeth and growled.

Jenna gave a mock shudder. "You might have to eat that one."

Levi shook his head. "Blake is brave enough to bite its head off."

Suppressing a smile, Paradise flipped on the burner. "I'll cook the green beans."

She checked the cookies and the potatoes again. Just a few more minutes. She grabbed forks and shredded the pork, then checked the oven again. The cookies were perfect, and so were the potatoes, so she pulled them out.

Blake's presence filled the room. "I'm starved. I don't think I got lunch."

"It's ready." She'd already set the table. "Want me to fix you a plate?"

"I can do it."

"How did the interrogation go?"

"It's clear he's out to pin this on me or Mom. Maybe both of us. He took DNA, but Hez told us to refuse the polygraph."

"I'll bet that fired up Creed."

Blake snagged a hot cookie and juggled it from hand to hand. "It did." Gooey chocolate clung to his fingers after he popped pieces in his mouth.

Her gaze lingered on the chocolate around his firm lips and she imagined the taste. She gave a slight shake to her head to reprimand her stray thoughts. "Creed's attitude cements what we have to do. We'll have to find the culprit."

"I'm game."

He gave her a warning glance when his mother came into the room, and she understood he didn't want to worry Jenna. She'd likely tell them to let the police handle it, but it didn't appear that would happen.

Jenna prepared plates of food for the boys. "I hadn't thought about Frank's offer to buy our land until the interrogation." She set their plates on the table and called them in to eat.

Blake heaped food on his plate and sat between the boys. "I hadn't either. Are you reconsidering selling, Mom?"

"No, I didn't mean that, but I'm surprised Frank hasn't returned."

"We were emphatic we weren't interested. Hank had turned him down too."

"What do you know about Frank Ellis?" Paradise asked.

"He was born and raised in the Gulf Shores area. His houses

are top-notch and sell for big bucks. I don't really know him though."

The boys scampered from the room and ran to get their iPads for their allotted evening time.

"I do," Jenna said when they were gone. "I dated him in high school."

"You never told me that," Blake said.

She rose and began to clear the table. "It was a long time ago."

Blake carried his plate to the sink. "Do you think he'd do anything underhanded?"

"Back in high school he was a straight shooter. Time changes people. So many wear masks. Maybe it was always that way, but it seems worse now. So I don't know."

"Hez is on it, and he'll find out."

Levi came back into the kitchen. "Blake, it's dark. Can we look at the moon tonight? Mommy said it was okay," he said.

Blake ruffled his hair. "I think that can be arranged."

He never seemed impatient with his brothers. Paradise had forgotten how even-tempered he always was, and she liked that quality just as much now as she did back then.

———

Paradise waved away flying insects as she surveyed the hippo submerged in the pond. Her wild mane of curls blew in the light breeze, and the heat brought pink to her cheeks. Blake forced his attention to Bertha. Only her eyes and nostrils showed above the murky water.

Paradise put her hands on her hips. "How are we going to get her out?"

The hippo was Blake's favorite animal in the preserve. He'd spent many happy hours fishing beside her. Hez had joined him on occasion as well. "Bertha, I brought something for you." He got out of the Gator and went around to the back. He held up the out-of-season watermelon he'd paid a ridiculous price for, and he could have sworn he saw the hippo's eyes light up.

"Look at her," Paradise marveled. "She's leaving the water for the melon."

"And watch how she limps. I noticed it yesterday."

Bertha lumbered toward them, and he backed away with the melon. She followed the lure of her favorite food, and the limp started almost at once. "See?" He let her walk a few more steps before approaching her with the melon. No need to cause her more misery. As he approached she opened her huge mouth, and he deposited the melon inside.

Paradise approached with a thermal tool. "Most hippos are aggressive, but she seems pretty mellow."

"Bertha came to us as a calf, and I've never known her to charge."

Paradise knelt by the affected right back leg and checked the temperature on the thermal-imaging camera. "The heat in the joint above her foot is elevated by two degrees. She might have a stress fracture in a toe or in the joint. I'll give her an anti-inflammatory, and we should make sure she doesn't use it much until the temperature reading goes down."

"So more food and less foraging." He patted the hippo's head. "You'll like that, you lazy girl."

Paradise started to stand, then stopped. "Wait a second, what's this?" She peered closer at Bertha's foot. "There's something wrapped around her toes here. I'll have to sedate her to remove it. I doubt she would be accommodating enough to lift her hoof off the ground for me."

"Probably not." And he wouldn't want to run the risk of the hippo injuring Paradise.

She injected Bertha with the sedative. It took several minutes for the medicine to take effect. The hippo staggered toward the water, then crumpled to the mud before she reached it.

He joined Paradise beside the animal, and when she struggled to lift the heavy hoof, he reached in. "Let me get that. You see if you can figure out what's wrong."

It took all his effort to hold Bertha's leg up while Paradise fiddled with whatever was causing the hippo's lameness. "It's some kind of wire," she muttered. "There, I think I've got it. You can put her leg down."

"Gladly." He lowered the hippo's leg and straightened. "Maybe it's not a fracture at all that was causing the pain."

"Probably not. The wire could have cut off blood flow, which affected her mobility." She rose from beside the sleeping hippo and held up the wire.

His stomach bottomed out, and he took the wire from her fingers. This type of thing was a common sight when he was in war zones. "Blasting cap wire."

"You're kidding."

He shook his head. "Let's do a sweep of the area around her enclosure. Someone could have planted an explosive device."

Paradise put her bag of medical supplies away, and he grabbed boots for both of them from the back. "Here, put these on. Most of the area around here is marshy, and you're liable to sink in mud to your ankles."

She paused and slid her feet into them. "Let's split up. What am I looking for?"

"Maybe more wire attached to a long metal insert. Maybe blasting material. Call me, and don't touch anything dangerous."

"Got it."

He walked toward the north side of the pond while she went the other way through a straggly stand of trees and marsh grass. Mud tried to suck a boot off, and he paused to yank it back on. Bent over, he saw the ground from a different angle and spotted a flash of something red sticking up out of the mud. He pulled at it and discovered another length of blasting wire about three feet long.

This wasn't good. Who had been out here with this kind of material? He wiped the mud from his hands onto his jeans and grabbed his phone to call the sheriff's department. When he explained what he'd found, he was passed to Greene, the last person he wanted to talk to.

"Another fire?" Greene asked when he came on the line.

Blake could hear the smirk in his voice. The guy should be fired. "No, worse than fire. Explosives." As he explained what he'd found, he spotted Paradise walking his way holding a beer can. "Hang on." He jogged to meet her and saw the blasting cap wire sticking out the top. "You shouldn't have touched that. It could have blown up. Set it gently on the ground and back away." He wanted to yank it out of her hands and protect her, but that might set it off. "Put it down, Paradise. Right now and very gently."

Her amber eyes went wide, and she set it on the mud gingerly, then they both backed away. "Greene, you there?"

"Yeah. What's going on?"

"Paradise found an incendiary device in a beer can."

"A beer can?" His voice rose a notch. "We recovered one of those from the fire at your cottage."

"You never mentioned it."

"We're still investigating, and you and your mom are still suspects in that fire."

"We have alibis," he reminded the detective.

"There was a timer on it."

Blake didn't need the detective to explain what that meant. It changed everything, and the attention from the police would be squarely back on him and Mom. He ended the call with Greene.

Paradise wore a worried frown. "He's not taking it seriously?"

"Worse than that. Mom and I are under suspicion. They found a similar device in the house, and it had a timer. Our alibis mean nothing now. Creed seems certain we torched our own property for the insurance money. And with that suspicion hanging over our heads, the payout to replace what was lost will be delayed. We're stuck until the real culprit is found."

"I'm sorry. What can we do?"

He checked the time on his phone. Four o'clock and his duties were over for the day. "I doubt Hez has dug up anything yet, so there isn't much we can do about stuff here. How about we try again to catch the prior sheriff's wife?"

She smiled, and he spotted the gratitude in her face. It would help him to focus on something else for now. Something other than how he could have lost her just now, and he'd realized just how deep his emotions still went.

CHAPTER 15

THE HOUSE WHERE GERALD Davis had lived was down a quiet street in Pelican Harbor. Paradise peered through the passenger window as Blake pulled his truck onto the freshly raked oyster-shell driveway and shut off the engine. The ranch had been built in the seventies but had been updated with dark paint and white shutters. She had a vague memory of visiting here with her mother once. Was her mother friends with Bea Davis?

An older woman straightened from a squat at the flower bed by the porch and shielded her eyes from the sun. A wide-brimmed straw hat covered the top of her salt-and-pepper hair that curled around her face in the humidity. Paradise didn't really recognize her, but then, she was just a little girl when she'd last been here.

Paradise got out of the truck and approached. "Mrs. Davis?"

"Call me Bea, honey. Even though I'm seventy, Mrs. Davis will always be my mother." Her soft drawl held a hint of southern sweet tea and black-eyed peas. She removed cloth gloves stained green at the fingertips. "You seem familiar." She took off her hat and wiped the perspiration from her forehead. "But you're with the handsome Blake here, so you're automatically a friend. I could use some sweet tea, how about y'all?"

"We wouldn't say no," Blake said. "And this is Paradise Alden. We'd like to chat a bit if you don't mind."

The warmth faltered on Bea's face. "You don't say. It's been a minute since you were around these parts." She motioned for them to come with her, and they followed her into the cool interior that held on to the sweet aroma of some kind of treat— maybe cookies.

Bea gestured to the tan sofas facing each other. "Gerald remodeled it for me before he died. He didn't hang around long enough to enjoy it though."

"It's lovely," Paradise said.

And it was. White walls contrasted with wide plank floors in a light color. The living room held comfortable tan furniture that created a neutral vibe with the decor in different shades of white. Pictures of white-haired Bea with young children hung on a wall. "Your grandchildren?"

Bea beamed. "I have eight. Each of our four had two. They are my world." She turned toward the wide opening into the dining room. "Have a seat and I'll be right back with tea."

Paradise sank onto the comfortable sofa and Blake joined her. She glanced around at the pictures, barely remembering the burly sheriff who grinned out of the frames beside Bea and two daughters who were carbon copies of their mother. The tinkle of ice came from beyond the dining room as she gathered her thoughts about what to ask. Gerald might not have been the type who talked about his cases with his wife. Still, the murders had affected the whole town. Bea should have picked up something about it all.

"Here you go." Bea approached with a tray of glasses and a pitcher.

Paradise accepted a frosty glass of sweet tea and took a sip. "You could give lessons on how to properly prepare sweet tea."

"It's all in the steeping and the simple syrup." Bea settled on the sofa across from them. "Now, what can I do for you?"

"For years I didn't remember much about the murder of my parents, but I-I'm starting to have dreams about it. I'd like to know what you remember of that time."

Bea sipped her tea and didn't answer for a long moment. "What good will it do, little Paradise? You can't bring them back."

"Their killer was never found," Blake said. "Justice has never been served."

"Justice is capricious. That's what Gerald always said."

Was there a reason Bea was dodging the question? "Did Gerald ever have a suspect in mind? It seems like someone murdered my parents and got clean away."

"He wasn't much of one to talk about cases, but I heard rumors."

"What kind of rumors?" Blake asked.

Bea stared at them without expression before her shoulders sagged. "Guess it doesn't matter now. I always wondered if Gerald did it."

"Why would you suspect your husband?" Paradise asked.

"He was going to leave me for your mother," she said flatly. "Your mama planned to get a divorce too. Then it all changed. He came home early the night of the murders, while I was still at work at the surveyor's office. He seemed strange with a stiff expression and told me he'd decided he still loved me and didn't want to leave me."

"Were you suspicious?"

"Not then. I was just overjoyed to hear he still loved me. It was later, the next day, when I heard about the murders. I wondered—oh yes, I wondered. And when he begged me to give him an alibi if anyone asked where he was that afternoon, I wondered even more. But I didn't want our two teenagers to have the stigma of a father in prison."

Bea's expression held no trace of guilt. "So I was prepared to lie. I didn't have to though. Gerald was never under suspicion. I'm not the blabbing type, so I never even told my mother when Gerald first told me he was leaving. I never told a soul. And our marital problems never came out, and as far as I know, no hint of an affair was ever written in the case files."

Paradise struggled to take it all in. "I remember my parents fighting a lot."

"I'd guess your dad never knew. Men don't tend to stay quiet about things like that. I have no idea why I'm telling you all this, other than to say maybe justice has been served. Gerald's final days of liver cancer weren't pleasant. He paid dearly for his sin."

Could it really be that easy? Had the sheriff killed them? And if so, did Paradise need to prove it so she knew for sure?

———

The lions were getting closer. Paradise cowered in the closet with the scent of her mother's perfume wafting around her. She used to love to hide in here and play with Mama's shoes. Sliding them on her small feet made her feel as tall and elegant as her mother. And just as beautiful.

Another roar came, and she tried to make herself even smaller in the corner with the shoeboxes heaped like a fence around her. She smelled the lion's hot breath right outside the door. Its teeth would clamp around her arm before he dragged her all the way into his mouth. There was nothing in here for her to use to defend herself—no way for a little girl to battle something that large.

Sheriff Davis laughed. "Get her, lion. Once she's gone, everything is mine."

Paradise shook her head. She didn't like the sheriff. He came to see Mama and they made her go outside to play. She didn't want him here.

All she could do was scream, "No, no!"

She opened her mouth and piercing screams erupted from her throat. They pealed out, one after another until she was hoarse from it. But the lion had her now, and she couldn't escape.

"Paradise." A warm hand touched her arm. "You're okay, babe. It's Blake."

She blinked and realized she was in the garage loft apartment. Moonlight streamed through the window and gilded Blake's strong jaw and cheekbones with a glimmer of gold. "B-Blake? Where's the lion?"

He raised her to a seated position and sat on the edge of the bed before he pulled her against his chest. "There's no lion. You're safe."

Her heart still tried to pound out of her chest, and she could *smell* the lion's acrid odor. It had to be in here. "It's here somewhere," she whispered. "Don't you smell it?"

"My jacket might smell like lion. I wear it into the predator enclosures. There's nothing here, babe. Just you and me. You had a nightmare."

Her tongue dried in her mouth, and her throat constricted. A nightmare? It was only a nightmare? She turned her face into the soft material of his tee and put her arms around him. His pulse under her ear accelerated and his embrace tightened. She burrowed closer, not wanting to face the fear again. His hand smoothed her hair and she closed her eyes at the blissful sensation of such a tender caress.

Blake had always made her feel safe and protected. He was such a caregiver still, stepping in to be a dad to his brothers and a helper to his mother. There weren't many men like Blake Lawson out in the world. She'd checked out a few frogs, and Prince Charming always revealed his warts.

Except for Blake. His steadying presence calmed her like nothing else ever had.

She lifted her head and stared into his face, trying to read his feelings. His blue eyes smiled in such a gentle, accepting way. He never made her feel less-than or like she would never measure up to some impossible, perfect goal. He'd always seen her for who she was and had loved her anyway.

Her lips parted, and she wanted nothing more than to feel his lips on hers again after all these years. It was crazy and she should move away. But she slid her hand up to his neck and pulled him closer.

A flash of joy sparked in his gaze, and his arms tightened around her. When the kiss came, it was everything she remembered. Tender but masterful. Gentle but passionate. And she felt it all the way through her being.

She slipped her other arm up to join the first and kissed him back with all the yearning she'd suppressed through the years. Her temperature gauge went from freezing to red hot in seconds.

She'd never gotten over him. Not really. She'd tried to tell herself she had, but it was a convenient story she'd told herself in the midnight hours when she yearned to call him. His kiss drove all thoughts from her head for several long minutes, until he gave a shaky laugh and pulled away.

But he kept his arms tight around her. "Okay now?"

She nodded and made a slight motion to pull back, and his embrace dropped away, leaving her feeling cold and bereft. "Thank you for rescuing me from the lion. Sheriff Davis was in my dream too, and this time I remembered how he used to come see my mother. She would make me go outside to play until he was gone." She rubbed the gooseflesh that had erupted on her arms. "I think his wife might be right and he killed them. It would explain why the investigation never seemed to lead any-where. No one really cared."

The furnace kicked on with a rattle and a wheeze that seemed so normal. That wheeze was the lion's breath she'd heard in her dream. The last of her fear seeped away. "I think I can sleep now. How'd you get in?"

"Your door was ajar. I heard something in the yard, then heard you scream. I came running up the steps and was sure someone was in here when I saw the door. You didn't hear anything? That latch can be tricky."

Cold shuddered down her spine. "I know I locked it, Blake."

"I'll check it."

She wasn't going to stay here by herself when someone could be in her apartment. Barefooted, she padded along behind him as he flipped on lights and checked behind furniture and in the closet. No one was inside, but Blake stopped and took a sharp inhale.

"What is it?" But he didn't have to answer because she saw the muddy footprints on the kitchen floor herself. "Those aren't yours?"

"Nope." He showed her his clean-soled sneakers. "I think you'd better stay in the main house tonight. You can take the bottom full bunk as long as you don't mind sleeping with Levi. It was his turn tonight. I'll sleep on the sofa."

She doubted she'd sleep anyway, not with her lips still burning from his kisses and her heart still hammering from knowing someone had been in here with her.

CHAPTER 16

THE HUMID NIGHT AIR held the taste of menace. Blake stalked the perimeter of The Sanctuary fence and watched for movement in the trees and buildings. Who had been in the garage apartment? Before the Mason woman's body was discovered, he would have said he trusted every one of their employees, but too many things had happened in the past two weeks.

What if he hadn't heard Paradise? Would someone have attacked her? He didn't like admitting to himself how she seemed to be a target. And that kiss had left him craving more. Where did he want their relationship to go now? He feared examining that question too closely. One thing he knew for sure—a piece of his heart still belonged to her and maybe always would. Tonight she'd been frightened, and he feared tomorrow she'd have her shields firmly in place again.

A shadow loomed in the barn doorway. "You okay, Blake? You're out late." Lacey Armstrong moved into view. Her sleek brown hair was up in a topknot.

"We had an intruder in the main house. Muddy footprints in

my apartment. You're up late." He eyed her bike shorts and tee. "You're out exercising at this hour?"

"They're comfortable for sleeping. It was my turn to man the animal hospital overnight. The hyenas were making a ruckus, and I came out to see what they were hot about."

He turned in the direction of the hyena enclosure. "You see anything?"

"A rabbit had wandered in, and they were fighting over the carcass."

While Blake liked animals, the hyenas were a breed he would have been happy to send off somewhere else. He didn't dare turn his back on one, and they could be vicious. "Did you hear or see anything else?"

She shook her head and came close enough he caught a whiff of a light scent she wore, something sweet and enticing. Lacey had been working here a year, and when he arrived to help out, they'd become friends. Though she'd made it clear she was happy to entertain a closer relationship, Blake wasn't ready for anything romantic. He'd never made a move to go beyond a casual friendship.

She put her hand on his arm. "What do you make of all this? It feels like we're being deliberately targeted, doesn't it?"

He didn't want to offend her, so he didn't move away. "Yeah, it does. The murder, the fire, constant intruders. There's a purpose behind all of it, but I can't see who would stand to gain anything by harassing us." He shifted when the hyenas snarled again, and her hand fell away. "I think I'll check out the hyena enclosure myself."

"I'll walk with you." She fell into step beside him.

He used his key at the first gate. "How's it going with Paradise? You enjoying working with her?"

"She's okay. A little reserved but pleasant. She's good at what she does. Serena had a cracked paw pad, and Paradise spotted the problem. She dosed her with an antibiotic, and Serena thanked her for it."

Serena was the best grizzly and reciprocated their affection by showing off for them. "Sounds like she's settling in well."

"How are you dealing with her being here?"

Blake heard the personal curiosity in her question. The fact he and Paradise had dated once must have made its way through the employees. "She's a good vet, and I'm glad she's here. She's going to be an asset and will help out anywhere we ask her."

Lacey didn't probe further, and they reached the back of the hyena enclosure as the vocalizations grew louder. He approached the fence and peered through the dark into the corners of the space. The clan of three stood staring toward a dark corner where a tupelo tree loomed. The dominant female, Clara, ruled the pack with a steel will and decided who ate and who was driven off. The male ate last, and Blake often had to separate the sexes to ensure he got enough food.

He studied the odd behavior of the animals warily, watching that dark corner. Hyenas usually only feared lions, so he couldn't puzzle out what type of animal hid in the darkness of the big tree. Maybe it was another hyena.

He walked the length of the enclosure looking for breaches in the perimeter and found one low in the fence. He shone his phone flashlight at the small hole and frowned. "I think this has been cut." He squatted and studied the metal links. Drops of blood clung to the blunt edges of the fence as if something had been forced through. Had the rabbit been pushed into the enclosure? If so, for what reason?

He stood and continued to search the perimeter. The hyena habitat had several enclosures where they were able to segregate the clan when various areas required cleaning or the animals had to be separated. In the last space, he spotted a gate lock left open.

Someone had come through here. Had they distracted the animals with a rabbit while they sneaked through? His gaze went out over the vast expanses of The Sanctuary, and it clicked. The other side of the hyena enclosure made for an easy access from outside the park. Zebras and wildebeest roamed in their large grazing habitat. There was no danger in walking through the animals there. The hyenas were the danger, and if they were distracted, an intruder could access the buildings.

The intruder had entered here.

~

A lion roared in the distance, and Paradise sat up with adrenaline racing through her. She swallowed past the constriction in her throat and forced herself to lie back on a pillow that still held the all-too-enticing scent of Blake. Levi muttered in his sleep and rolled closer. The warm little bundle of boy relaxed her, and she snuggled him closer.

When she was in the last foster home, the family's two-year-old daughter used to creep into her bed in the middle of the night. Paradise had forgotten how comforting a child could be. She hadn't allowed herself to dream of having her own little boy or girl, but this little boy made the idea more appealing than she'd imagined.

She drifted in a state between sleep and waking with the thought of a little boy with Blake's blue eyes and intelligence. A sound roused her and she opened her eyes again to find Levi had his foot in her face. She touched it tenderly and flipped him around before thinking about the dream of children. It was only

in that kind of twilight wakefulness she let those kinds of long-
ings seep through. In the daylight she didn't think a family would
be in her future. It was too hard for anyone to get through and
see the real her under the prickly surface she projected.

She touched her lips. Kissing Blake had felt like coming
home. Even after all these years, he'd vaulted over the walls she'd
erected like they didn't exist. And maybe they didn't where he
was concerned. They never had.

She sat up at the distant sound of a door closing. Had something else happened? She slid her legs over the side of the bed and
checked to make sure Levi stayed put before tiptoeing out of the
room. She found Blake, his forehead creased with worry, in the
kitchen pouring a glass of orange juice. Did the man ever sleep
or relax? It was after one.

He turned toward her and stilled. "You should be sleeping."

"So should you. You're just now getting in?"

"I think I found out how the intruder got into my apartment.
We have cameras at the entrance, and I think he wanted to avoid
being seen. Someone distracted the hyenas with a rabbit and
walked right through."

He offered her his glass of juice, but she shook her head. "Any
idea who it was?"

"No."

His penetrating gaze unnerved her, and she crossed her arms
over her chest. "That was who was in my apartment."

"I think so. It disturbs me that someone seems to be targeting
you."

"Or maybe he was targeting you. He might not know you gave
up your place for me. There's no way to know for sure."

He absorbed her statement before nodding. "Okay, true."
His frown deepened. "I don't think you should stay there alone.

We're better to stay in a group. If you're okay with a little boy or two invading your space on occasion."

"The boys are fine, but I don't want to displace you a second night."

"I'll rest better if I know you're not up there alone."

"Why do you care?" The question erupted before she could stop it. "I feel like I've been nothing but trouble. You probably wish your mom had never emailed me."

"I don't wish that at all." His gaze dropped to her mouth, and he took a step toward her.

"Why not?" She held her breath. Would he tell her the truth or guard his words? If her life depended on it, she didn't think she could untangle the knot of her emotions. Maybe he knew how he felt, but she wasn't sure she could name the things that made her mouth go dry and her heart begin to gallop. She wanted to blame physical attraction for all that, but her heart knew better.

He set the juice on the counter and came closer still. "You have upended my life again, you know. Something has always bound us, Paradise. You might not want to admit it, but you know it, don't you?"

She didn't want to agree with him, but the words spilled out anyway. "You were always kind to me, even back in high school."

"I always felt way more than kindness, and you know that too."

He wasn't saying what he felt now, but he didn't have to. She knew. They both knew. And her reserve had never fooled him. He had laser vision into her soul. The man she didn't know as well as the teenager, but she wanted to.

She should flee to the bedroom, but her feet stood rooted in one spot as he took a step closer. Then another until he was standing close enough to kiss her again. And she couldn't think of anything she'd rather experience than another brush of his lips on hers. She might just suffocate waiting for him to make a move, so she did. She placed her hand on his chest and stared into those gentle eyes.

His fingertips came under her chin and nudged it up a bit. "I don't want you to trample my heart again, Paradise, but I'm afraid you might."

His words were a dose of cold water over the heat rising in her chest. He was too good and kind, and she didn't want to hurt him. Could she move beyond the pain of her past rejections? Did she even want to try for a new start with Blake? Part of her did, but could things be different when she was the same broken person inside?

She pulled back her hand. "I'd better let you get some sleep." She fled before the disappointment on his face collapsed her resolve.

CHAPTER 17

HOW MUCH HAD SHE slept last night? Paradise guessed it wasn't more than three hours. And Blake would have gotten even less. She arrived at the clinic and found a light schedule waiting, but the lingering chemical odor inside had her head throbbing in half an hour. Fresh air might help. She opened the windows, and while the room aired, she headed outside to take a walk around the grounds.

She'd been here nine days, and she hadn't forced herself to see the jaguar enclosure. The population report had revealed they had a black jaguar, and it was time she tried to face her fear.

Her steps lagged as she walked across the scruffy winter grass toward the predator section. The distinctive jaguar nasal grunting came from her left, and she froze. She barely turned her head and saw the black panther's yellowish eyes fixed on her. The greeting came again, but at least it wasn't the more aggressive roar. This jaguar simply wanted to say hello.

All she had to do was put one foot in front of the other and move toward the enclosure. She could even grab some meat from the nearby shed and feed her, but Paradise's legs refused to move.

She rubbed her throbbing shoulder. "She's behind the fence. She can't hurt me." The whispered reassurance did nothing to calm her racing heart, and she still couldn't move.

A male voice spoke from behind her, and she whipped around to see Detective Greene bearing down on her with an intent expression. She turned on shaky legs, and for once she welcomed his appearance. She could delay confronting her nightmare for a while.

"Lacey pointed me in this direction." His gaze raked her from head to foot before focusing on her face. "I wanted to pick up the blasting materials the two of you found."

"I think Blake has those."

"And he's out on a safari tour, so I hoped you could help me. I'd hate to make a wasted trip."

"I think he put them in the barn. This way." She led the way back toward the main entrance to the row of buildings where supplies were stored.

Her back prickled between her shoulder blades, and she had no doubt Greene was watching the sway of her hips as she walked. If she could have had him go first, she would have. She unlocked the barn door and left it open. "There's a locked cabinet here on the right."

Going inside the dim barn with a lech like Greene didn't seem like a good idea, but Paradise had no choice. All she had to do was hand over the evidence, and he'd be out of her way. Dust motes of hay danced in the dim sunlight streaming through the door, and she held back a sneeze.

The cabinet where Blake had left the evidence stood open, and she peered inside. "It was on this shelf." She touched the now-empty spot on the second shelf. "Someone's taken it."

"Or Blake has hidden it. I doubt he'd want me to have a chance to examine it."

"Deputy Greene, Blake is not behind the crimes that have happened. Your blind determination to pin this on him is going to backfire on you."

He stepped into her personal space. "That sounds like a threat." The fingers of his right hand twined around a lock of her hair. "You're really quite beautiful. I might see my way to going in another direction if you'd let me take you to dinner. I'm sure I could show you a good time."

She knocked his hand out of the way and took a step back. "You're disgusting. What would the sergeant think if he knew you were behaving this way?"

She'd thought her implied threat would have an effect since he'd seemed worried about her tattling to her cousin a few days ago, but Greene scowled and reached for her hair again.

"It wouldn't be good for your long-term health for you to complain about me. I've got connections over McShea's head."

She turned to run from the barn, but he caught her by her left upper arm, and the too-painful spot flared into raging pain. A moan tried to escape and she bit it back. She wouldn't give him the satisfaction of knowing he'd hurt her.

She whipped around and knocked one leg out from under him. He let go of her arm on his way down, and she took the opportunity to rush into the sunshine.

She slammed the door behind her to slow him down and ran for the safari bus in the distance. As she reached it, the first bit of sanity returned to her head. She couldn't let Blake intervene in this—Greene would increase his attacks. And if the two men got into a fight, Blake could be arrested for attacking an officer. The felony accusation would be difficult to overcome.

She stopped and controlled the panic raging in her chest. As long as she was away from Greene, things would be okay. He'd never try anything with people around.

Blake slowed the safari vehicle and leaned out the window. "Need something?"

"A ride back to my facilities."

"Hop aboard."

She went up the steps to the seats. As she settled at the bench seat in the center, she spotted Greene running toward them. She bit down on her lip hard enough to taste blood, but she couldn't tell Blake to accelerate away. He'd know something was wrong.

Greene reached the bus. "There you are, Lawson. I wanted to pick up the evidence you found."

"I took it to the substation first thing this morning before I started work. McShea has it."

Greene's angry gaze wandered to Paradise, and his promise of retribution pierced her. She'd have to do everything in her power not to be alone with him.

———

Blake dropped Paradise and the other riders off, then put away his vehicle before he went to make cleaning rounds. His first stop was the hyena enclosure.

The cackle of hyenas was three hundred yards out from the fence in their enclosure, and their pungent scent carried to Blake on the wind. A secondary fence and gate stood between them and the area he needed to access. He pulled out his black key and inserted it into the outer lock. A quick *click* and he was inside the perimeter space where he could toss food to the animals.

Cleaning up after the animals was a task he routinely performed, and he set to work with a pitchfork and wheelbarrow. Once the work was done and he'd given the animals their nutritional supplements, he intended to check out the area now that it was daylight. Someone had gained access through here, and he had to shut down that possibility.

The leader moseyed to the fence and watched him work. Clara hated his red hat, so he had left it in the shed when he grabbed the shovel and wheelbarrow. Hyenas were the one predator none of the keepers liked interacting with. It wasn't their scrappy fur and hunched backs that put most of them off. A keeper might think he had a bond with one of them only to find the animal stalking him as food. While he gave them scratches and rubs through the fence, he never went inside the enclosure with them. And anytime his fingers were through the holes in the fence, he watched their faces and snatched his hand back when their eyes indicated their disposition might change.

He ignored Clara and the rest of the cackle. They were probably ready for their supplements since it meant more meat, but that detail would come once Blake cleaned the enclosure and let them back in.

His thoughts lingered on Paradise and the spectacular way she'd kissed him back last night. Did she regret it now? He hoped not, because her response had stirred to life deeper feelings he thought had died long ago. The morning's sunrise brought the hope he'd see the expression in her eyes he used to watch for when they were dating. Her tender and loving gaze used to make him feel like he was Superman. Would he ever see that again?

He flipped the last of the excrement into the wheelbarrow before turning and facing three hyenas lined up in single file.

In stalking mode.

On his side of the fence.

He froze, and his pulse accelerated so quickly he felt dizzy. How did they get past the lock on the fence?

He kept his gaze on Clara's laughing, drooling grin as he expelled the air from his lungs. She edged closer, and he straightened into a commanding stance. "Clara, are you ready for your supplements?"

The alpha female's eyes flickered with interest. Hyenas were crazy smart, like monkeys. They appeared doglike but were a member of the mongoose family, which meant they were more closely related to a cat. If he could reach the cooler with the meat and supplements, he might make it out of here alive. Hyenas could completely consume a zebra in thirty minutes.

Keeping his posture rigid and in charge, he backed toward the wagon where he'd left the rest of his equipment. Clara matched him step-by-step. As long as she didn't decide he would make the better snack, this might work. Another three feet and he'd have his hands on that cooler.

A noise caught Clara's attention, and she turned her nose to Blake's right. He spotted Lacey in the Gator. She was making a big racket as though she wanted to attract them. The Gator made an abrupt stop near the perimeter fence, and she got out with a bucket of meat.

"Hey there, cutie." Lacey's manner was easy and confident as she stepped to the fence and began to toss pieces of meat over the barrier.

Clara grabbed the first piece of meat while her pack waited their turn. None of them would eat until Clara was satiated, and that could take a while since this wasn't a regularly scheduled feeding.

Blake moved noiselessly to the gate, unlocked it, and began to slide through. In the same moment he felt the brush of teeth along the back of his slacks. He leaped the final few inches and slammed the gate shut behind him. The lock clicked into place, and he sagged with relief.

The hyena on the other side of the fence, Clara's sister Maisie, turned laughing jowls his way as if to say, *I almost had you.*

And it wasn't a lie. A few seconds and he would have had a nasty bite. Shaken, he exhaled and walked to join Lacey, who stepped away from the fence. "You got here at the right time."

A frown crouched between her brown eyes. "I saw you were in trouble. They get you at all?" She stopped to wipe her bloody hands on the grass.

He shook his head. "How'd you know I needed help?"

She turned and gestured toward the nearby shed. "I was grabbing some straw and saw them circling you like in *The Lion King.* Did you go in there with them?"

"No. They were in the outer enclosure, and I went in to clean. They got through the gate somehow."

"They're smart. Did Clara manage to open it?"

"I don't see how. It's got a black-key lock. It's not like she could perform her usual trick of opening an S lock."

She reached into the Gator and pulled out a set of binoculars she fitted to her eyes. "The lock is off, Blake. Have a look."

He took the binoculars she offered and focused them. The lock hung open, but he knew it appeared locked before he entered through the outer gate. Something had happened here last night, and it seemed someone didn't want him to discover what. That person had risked their own life by tampering with the lock so the gate appeared secure yet allowed the clever hyena to get into the perimeter enclosure.

Blake lowered the binoculars and turned around, nearly coming nose to nose with Lacey. "Oops, sorry." He stepped back, but she moved with him, staying close enough for the heady fragrance of her flowery perfume to follow.

Her lush lips were parted invitingly, and she ran a pale pink nail across his chest. "If you'd really like to thank me, a kiss would do."

The blatant invitation in her voice and body language was impossible to misconstrue. "Uh, how about a heartfelt thank-you?"

"You can do better than that."

Without warning, her slim arms snaked around his neck, and she reached up to plant her lips against his. Her soft body pressed against him, and he opened his eyes wide with alarm. He reached up and took her arms to try to pull them away from his neck, but she tightened her grip.

"Don't fight it," she murmured against his mouth. "I've seen the way you watch me."

He managed to gently wrench her arms away and blocked her with his arm when she made a move to engage in another clutch session. "I'm sorry, Lacey. I, uh, I don't want to hurt you, but I'm sorry if I gave you the wrong impression. I'm not looking for a romantic relationship."

Over her shoulder he spied Paradise, mouth gaping and eyes wide as she took in the scene. She'd clearly misread the situation. And why wouldn't she? From her perspective she'd just broken up a romantic liaison.

She whirled and, hand to her mouth, raced down the dirt road toward the fennec fox enclosure. Lacey grabbed at his forearm as he leaped past her to follow Paradise, but her fingers slid off.

"Paradise, wait!" he called.

She gave no indication she heard him, or if she did, she only picked up her pace to escape. She'd been as skittish as a new fawn when she got here, and he feared every inch he'd gained was about to be lost forever.

CHAPTER 18

PARADISE COULDN'T BREATHE, COULDN'T think. *Stupid, stupid.*
What had made her think anything would change? Blake had
betrayed her once, and she should have expected he'd do it again.
Seeing him in that embrace with Lacey was a stab to the heart she
didn't think she'd recover from. She'd spent last night daydream-
ing about what could be, only to fall off a cliff of reality today.
The sight of Lacey in his arms after her own run-in with Greene
was especially painful—were all men only after one thing?

But Blake had always been different, and he deserved much
more than someone like her. Maybe Lacey was that someone
special who would make him happy. What would it take to get
it through her thick head that no one had ever wanted her for
herself—and no one ever would? She never should have come
back here. Even digging out the truth about her parents' murders
wasn't worth the pain clawing at her chest right now.

"Paradise!"

Blake's voice calling her name was as discordant as nails on
a chalkboard—and just as unwelcome. She wanted to be alone
to lick her wounds. Her first instinct had been to run to little

Rosy, the fennec fox she'd spent so much time with. Rosy was like her—softer inside than people realized but too prickly to make into a pet. Rosy didn't like to be petted, but she would sit and listen with her intelligent and sympathetic eyes fixed on Paradise's face. Her kits were just as sweet.

Once Paradise hit the door into the small shed housing Rosy, tears leaked from her eyes and scalded her cheeks. She shut the door behind her and clicked the lock to keep Blake out. How did she even face him after showing how much his betrayal had wounded her? She wasn't going to talk to him no matter how much he begged her to open the door.

The little fox's enormous ears pricked in her direction, and the sorrowful vocalization told her Rosy already detected her pain. Rosy trotted to join Paradise and curled into a ball by her feet. Her kits held back at first, then they, too, sidled over to join their mother. Their father, always the more skittish one, peered at her from a far corner. She checked the impulse to scoop up Rosy and snuggle her to her chest. Rosy's long nose settled onto Paradise's shoe, and Paradise squatted beside the small animals and tried to block out the sound of Blake's voice on the other side of the door.

"Paradise, I know how it appeared, but it isn't what you think. Uh, Lacey has a crush, that's all. She made a move I wasn't expecting, and you saw it at the worst possible time. I wasn't kissing her. I was trying to remove her arms from around my neck."

"You expect me to believe that?" Her shout made Rosy cower and whine, and the kits ran to the corner. Paradise touched Rosy on the head, then drew back her hand before she caused the little fox more distress. "Go away, Blake. Just leave me alone."

The lock clicked and the door swung open. She dashed the tears from her eyes and hoped he wouldn't realize how distraught she was from his behavior. She should have realized he'd have a key to every lock on the property.

Blake's face was ashen, and his eyes held desperation. "I'm not going away. We're going to face this and talk about it. I think Lacey recognized how I felt about you and was making a desperate attempt to snare my attention. I didn't want to hurt her after she'd just saved me from a very bad situation."

Paradise put her hand to her throat. "What situation?"

"A very dangerous one with the hyenas." He told her about the unlocked gate and being circled by the animals. "A bad bite was imminent."

"Or worse. Such carelessness doesn't sound like you."

"It isn't. I checked out the inside lock before I entered the perimeter, and it appeared secure. Someone tampered with it."

With anyone else she might not have believed he'd followed safety precautions. "Sabotage?"

"I didn't get a chance to examine it yet. Lacey made her move."

What had happened with Lacey would have to wait for her to assess later. Paradise rose and brushed the dirt and straw from her hands. "We'd better check it out. If someone exposed you to that much danger on purpose, we need to know why." The rejection on his face told her he'd taken note of the distance in her voice and stance.

She brushed past him and marched toward the hyena enclosure. Was it wrong she was almost relieved to find a reason to stop her headlong rush into his arms again? What a fool she was.

———

Blake's chest ached at the sight of Paradise's pale, set face. Talking more about it would get nowhere. He'd have to show her he had no interest in Lacey. One thing was sure—he intended to avoid being alone with the vet tech if he could. She'd made no secret of her interest, but he'd thought he'd managed to make it clear it wasn't reciprocated.

The sun beat down from a blue sky, and he backhanded the moisture from his forehead as they reached the hyena enclosure. The humidity shimmered in the air and heightened the odor of the dominant females crowding the fence line and watching their approach with laughing faces.

He'd only allowed himself to consider a nasty bite, but it could have been worse—much worse. If Lacey hadn't been there, he could have been a bloody stain on the grass right now. Though she'd caused him personal grief with Paradise, she'd saved his life.

The gate between the inner and perimeter enclosures stood open. He stopped and grabbed a pail of food from the food shed. "I'll coax them into the other enclosure with food."

Paradise put her hands on her hips and studied the fencing. "But even if you coax them over there, how can you shut and lock the gate? Is there a pole around here somewhere? I could push it shut while you distract them with meat."

He gestured to her right before he started toward the back enclosure. "There's one in the utility shed by the food hut."

The cackle moved closer to the fence as he skirted it. They paced him step-by-step until Clara stepped through the open gate and led her group into the back enclosure. Where was Paradise? He didn't see her with the long pole yet, but maybe she was having trouble finding it. There was still half a pail of food left, but he doled it out slowly, piece by piece.

She should have been here by now. The shed wasn't that large. Foreboding shivered up his spine. "Paradise?" Clara snarled and sprang back at his loud voice, so he tossed her another piece of meat.

When Paradise still didn't answer, he set the pail on the ground and headed toward the shed. What could have delayed her? He paused to rinse the blood from his hands at the outside spigot, then wiped his hands on the grass before touching the entry handle. The metal hinges complained as he pushed open the heavy wooden door. It only opened six inches before it resisted his shove as if something was in the way.

He spied a hand stretched out on the cement floor, and his pulse shot up. "Paradise!"

Shoving the door hard might hurt her, but there was a window on the back side of the building, so he went that way. Had she tripped and fallen? He reached the window and peered through the fly-speckled glass.

Fear seized his muscles. Paradise lay stretched out on the floor with one leg crumpled under her.

He shoved the window open, though it was a tight squeeze to maneuver his wide shoulders through the opening. He let his arms dangle, and when his fingertips brushed the cool concrete, he lowered the rest of his body onto the floor. The coppery scent of blood was in the air, and he crawled to her side. "Paradise?" He ran his fingers over her head and found blood oozing from a lump on her scalp. He checked her pulse and breathing and found them reassuringly steady.

A quick assessment of her limbs didn't indicate any broken bones. He touched her cheek. "Paradise, can you hear me?" She had to be all right. He couldn't lose her.

She moaned and reached a hand toward her head with her eyes still closed. "Hurts. Something hit me."

"I'm going to call for an ambulance." He whipped out his

phone and called 911. The dispatcher promised to send one out immediately. Blake ended the call and placed his hand on her forehead. "Help will be here soon. Try not to move."

She opened her lids in a squint and reached for his hand. "Something hit me on the head when I opened the door. That was the last thing I remember."

Her grip on his hand was just shy of painful, but he relished it. At least she needed him right at this moment. He held up two fingers. "How many fingers?"

"Two."

He changed to four. "Now how many?"

She squinted. "Four."

All good signs. "Did you hear anything? Was someone in here?"

"I don't think so." Her soft gaze was fixed on his face, and the shield she usually wore was completely down.

He gazed into those gorgeous amber eyes and saw a glimmer of the way she used to stare at him. Maybe there was still an ember or two of what had once burned deep inside her heart where she tried to keep it hidden. He wished he could trust it, but she was likely to have her defenses fully in place as soon as all her senses returned. All that tenderness shimmering in the depths of her eyes would vanish. But if he was patient, maybe he could smash those defenses forever.

Her lids came down and shuttered the vulnerability again as she struggled to sit up. "Whoa, whoa," he said. "You need to be still until the ambulance gets here."

"I'm okay. My head hurts, but I want to see what clobbered me."

Her words were steady and so were her movements, so he gave in and helped her sit. "You stay here while I see what happened."

Once he was sure she wasn't trying to stand, he rose and glanced around the shed. Pitchforks, rakes, buckets, and various other tools were neatly organized on hooks and shelves. He stepped closer to the door and a gleam caught his eye. A shiny wire snaked around the top of the doorframe and then across the ceiling. It had been attached with staples, and he followed it to where it ended. An antique iron had been attached to one end, and it hung down near the center of the room.

He frowned and gave it a swing. If it had been attached to the ceiling and let loose, it would have hit whoever came through the door in the head. In this case it had struck Paradise, but she wasn't likely the target since he was the one most likely to use this shed.

It had been a planned attack on Blake.

CHAPTER 19

AFTER A CT SCAN and a thorough checkup at the hospital, Paradise was released to go home. She rested amid a mountain of pillows atop the bottom bunk bed. Her jaw ached and so did her head. The boys curled at her side like puppies. Levi had a book, and Isaac scribbled with his crayons in a coloring book. The scent of wax from the crayons was somehow homey and soothing to Paradise.

Her dark hair in a messy bun, Jenna poked her head inside the door. "How's your headache?"

"Lurking in the background but not bad."

"Want me to scoop these hoodlums out of here?"

"They're fine. I like having them with me. I—I don't really want to be alone." Paradise still trembled from the memory of that iron coming toward her from out of nowhere. The malevolence of such an action was unbelievable. Who would want to hurt Blake like that?

Jenna's expression softened, and she headed toward the closet. "I'll put some lavender essential oil in the diffuser. That should help your aching head. I don't mind sitting with you either."

"You have a lot to do. I'm fine with your boys taking care of me."

Her expression still doubtful, Jenna pulled out a diffuser and a box of essential oils. The hiss of the machine started, and the scent of lavender began to swirl around the room. "I have to order food, but I'll check in later."

"Wh-where's Blake?" Paradise hated the way she sounded so needy. She was fine—really. Just shaken.

What if that iron had killed Blake? The thought of those gentle eyes being closed forever stole her breath, and she closed her eyes briefly.

"You okay, Paradise?" Jenna asked.

Paradise opened her eyes and nodded. "Fine." She was relieved her voice sounded normal.

"Blake said to tell you he'd check on you after he was done with the investigation. Detective Greene is out there now assessing the attack." Jenna's voice wobbled. "I'll admit I'm worried about my boy. He's usually the main person to access that shed. Someone seems out to get him. I-I've lost two men I love now, and the thought of losing my oldest son is overwhelming."

Paradise should have thought of Jenna's fear in this situation. "Of course you're scared. It feels like the answer to who's behind all this is lurking just out of sight. Does Blake have any enemies?"

"Not that I know of. He makes friends wherever he goes."

"What about when he was in the Marines? Could he have made an enemy there?"

The troubled expression in Jenna's blue eyes intensified. "I hadn't thought of that, but I suppose it's possible. We can ask him. There's an incident that happened in Afghanistan that he doesn't like to talk about. I've thought this had to be related to the preserve, but it could be something else."

The determination to get to the bottom of the danger pushed Paradise's headache to the back of her consciousness. Or maybe it was the sweet scent of lavender essential oil filling her lungs. She sat up and grabbed the notebook on the bedside table. *Check Afghanistan, other jobs.*

"You have more color in your cheeks," Jenna said with a lilt in her voice. "I'm glad you and Blake have buried the hatchet. He's beaten himself up for years about how things went down with you. I think your coming back will be healing for you both."

The pen stilled in Paradise's hands, and she glanced up to glimpse speculation in Jenna's face. Did she secretly hope they would resume their relationship? The thought wasn't as terrifying as it had been before that kiss. Was Jenna right and her heart was healing? Paradise hadn't thought it possible for that to happen.

When Jenna left, Paradise glanced at the boys. Levi was on his back with both legs bent. One leg was suspended by the knee of the other one. His foot swung back and forth as he read, and he had the cutest bedhead she'd ever seen. Isaac wore a frown of concentration as he colored the sea a gray color. The sky was black, but the area had recently undergone a tropical storm, so he might be easing the trauma of it with the colors. Maybe that's what she should have done—poured all her stress and pain into some kind of art to drain the power it had held over her heart.

Instead, she had bottled it up inside where it had festered and soured for years. What would it feel like to let it all float off her shoulders? Could she even do it? For so many years she'd guarded her heart and feelings, never letting anyone get too close.

Isaac put down his crayon and crawled over to nestle against her. She snugged him against her side and rested her chin on his tousled head to inhale the scent of his shampoo. His hair smelled of eucalyptus, just like Blake's. The little boys mimicked Blake in everything, even their toiletries. Blake took his role of surrogate father with great care. The boys were lucky to have him in their lives.

Was it too late for Paradise to turn her life around? Did she dare hope for her life to change so dramatically?

⌣

Blake shook his head in disgust as Greene drove off in a plume of red dirt. It was clear nothing would convince the deputy to actually investigate the incidents. The guy already saw Blake behind bars for orchestrating it himself. In what universe did that make sense?

Eager to see how Paradise was doing, he jogged toward the main house. As he reached the porch, his phone sounded with a call from Hez. Blake dropped into a rocker on the porch. "Hey, buddy. I was hoping to hear from you today. We've got more trouble." He launched into the morning's events as well as the hyena incident.

"You think both incidents were targeted at you?" Hez's deep voice rumbled with concern.

"At least the shed trap had to be aimed at me. Most of the time I'm the only one in there. And we have a schedule for who is cleaning what enclosures. It was my turn." He told his cousin about the detective. "He had the place dusted for prints, and of course, most will be mine. He asked me if I had that kind of wire in my supplies. Of course I do. And we also have old homesteading artifacts used as decorations around the sheds and houses. I just checked and the old iron that had been in the family restroom was missing."

A long pause followed. "I see," Hez said. "Step-by-step, someone is setting you up."

"Yeah. I'm swinging in the dark trying to figure it out. If I had some idea who was behind it, I might make some progress. You have any luck with the developer?"

"I checked into Frank Ellis pretty thoroughly. I thought he was clean until I heard a complaint about a finder's fee he paid to a guy for help in acquiring a property out on Fort Morgan Road."

Blake knew his cousin well enough to catch his guarded tone. "And that's problematic how?"

"Someone in the community might be desperate enough to do Mr. Ellis a favor by running you off."

"What did the last guy do to help him out?"

"Several people said he started a clandestine online smear campaign against the business. It was never proven, of course, probably because the business owner didn't have the money to file a lawsuit and find the proof."

Blake frowned. "A smear campaign using the protests would be about the same thing, but taking it to murder, arson, and personal attacks is a whole new level."

"True. And very concerning. It might not be an Ellis accomplice at all. In fact, it sounds like someone with a vendetta against you personally."

The door opened on his right and Paradise stepped out onto the porch. Her curly hair was down on the shoulders of her tee, and he spied a bruise on one of those gorgeous legs, about six inches above her ankle. He gestured to the rocker beside him, and she nodded before settling in it.

She tucked a thick curl behind her ear, and the light revealed the dark circles under her eyes and the bruise spreading out from her hairline on the left side. At least she was alive.

He realized Hez had said something. "Excuse me?"

"I think you should start thinking about anyone who might have a grudge against you or your mom."

"Why Mom?"

"What better way to get back at her than to take her oldest son? There's no greater pain than losing a child." Hez's voice went husky.

Blake winced. He'd walked that painful road with Hez when his little girl died, and that was a never-ending pain. "True. I'll talk to Mom. Thanks for all you're doing, Hez. I appreciate it."

"You'll get my bill."

Blake laughed. "Like the last one?" Hez had yet to bill them for any of the work.

"Just like that. Talk later. Give my best to everyone."

Blake put his phone away and examined Paradise's expression. "How's that headache?"

"Not too bad. Your mom diffused lavender, so I apologize if the boys' room smells girly when you get to sleep here again."

He grinned. "You think I made it to thirty years old without having essential oils rubbed on my chest and that air diffuser going? I'm used to it."

She chuckled. "How'd you get so easygoing? Was it losing your dad at such a young age?"

"My mom would tell you I came from the womb without a wail and she never heard me cry until I fell off the bed at six months old." He shrugged. "I think she's exaggerating. I remember a lot of times growing up when I was watching her struggle to make ends meet and I wanted to make things easier somehow. I thought if I never complained or cried, it would be easier for her. I'm not sure that's true, and it probably set me back some in life. The squeaky wheel gets the oil, you know? I might have moved up the food chain in the Marines if I'd been the type to be career focused.

"When I became a Christian at twelve, I started on a journey of trying to be truthful about everything. There were some conflicts during those years until I figured out Jesus didn't need me to tell Mom she was getting lines around her eyes or to tell my best friend he was a blockhead." He barked out a laugh. "Live and learn."

She stared down at her hands. "I think you're pretty perfect, you know."

He almost didn't hear the softly spoken words, and he wasn't sure how to answer. He was far from perfect, but he wanted to be that way, at least in her eyes. "Hardly perfect. Think back to your fifteen-year-old self and channel that earlier rage. You'll remember all the ways I failed you."

She gave the chair a gentle rock and didn't look at him. "Teenagers don't need to be taught stupid. Their hormones do the talking."

What did she mean by that? Did she mean their teenage obsession with each other was only hormones? It hadn't been on his part. Even if she hadn't realized it yet, they were bound together in their teens, and that bond had never really been severed.

CHAPTER 20

A TIGER ROARED IN the distance, and Paradise turned her attention that direction. She couldn't see the big cats from the porch, and that was a good thing. The sun touched the landscape with a warm glow of orange and gold. Her headache was mostly gone, but she still felt a little dizzy and disoriented. The doctor had said that sensation would pass.

"That was Hez on the phone," Blake said.

She listened to him recount the news about finder's fees and questionable practices. "So it could be anyone in the area doing this."

"Maybe. Hez is concerned about the attacks being so clearly targeted at me. He wanted me to think about any enemies from my past."

"Your mom and I were talking about that too."

He sent a crooked grin her way. "Uh-oh. It's always dangerous when the women in a guy's life gang up on him."

Warmth spread up her chest. He considered her a woman in his life. "She said there was an incident in Afghanistan that still bothered you. Could you have an enemy from there? I don't know details, and maybe you don't want to talk about it, but I thought you should at least consider it."

He rubbed a crease between those clear blue eyes. "She knows I don't like to talk about it. I lost my best friend that day."

"You don't have to tell me."

He turned a vulnerable gaze her way and said nothing for a long moment. Then he sighed, hunching his shoulders. "Maybe it would help to talk about it. Kent was a fellow medic. He was on his way to attend to injuries in a car crash. He was tending to a woman and a bomb went off in a vest she wore under her clothes."

Paradise winced. How could a suicide bomber look someone in the eye and detonate a bomb?

Blake's eyes were haunted and in a faraway place. "He wasn't killed but extremely critical. He was going to lose at least one leg, but he required plasma as soon as I got the bleeding stopped. He was blood type O positive and I gave him AB negative. He had a major hemolytic transfusion reaction. His kidneys failed, and he died." Blake released a pained sigh.

Tears filled her eyes, and she reached over to hold his hand. "You were trying to save his life. It could have happened to anyone in the frantic push to save him."

"Another medic had brought the bags of blood to me, but I should have double-checked labels. It wasn't until I was removing the bag to give him another unit that I realized the error. I did everything I could to save him but failed."

"It sounds like he might have died no matter what you did." She wished she could offer more comfort than holding his hand.

"There's no way of knowing for sure, but he was my friend and I failed him." He squeezed the bridge of his nose.

She clung to his hand more tightly. "I'm sorry, Blake. I can tell you loved him. It doesn't sound like you made any enemies from that."

He lowered his head and shook it. "His twin brother would fit that bill. He was there and saw what happened. I receive angry letters from him about every three months. He's still in a lot of pain."

"Have you ever talked to the medic who brought you the wrong bags in the first place? Does he get letters too?"

"I've never asked. Ultimately, it was my fault. I don't blame him for making a mistake in the heat of the battle."

"And you shouldn't blame yourself either. The same circumstances apply to you too. I wish you could forgive yourself as easily as your God forgives you."

He lifted his head. "The unbeliever is advising me on God's nature?"

She freed his hand. "I know there's a God. I'm just reluctant to trust him after the things he let me go through."

"I wish you could see yourself the way I do. Those struggles you've endured have made you strong. A warrior really. You've been able to stand on your own and forge your course. That's remarkable when you think about the challenges you've overcome to do it. I believe God was loving you, steering you, even when you didn't sense him there."

"Why would you say that?"

"Because I prayed for him to be with you all these years."

Her eyes filled with tears again. She'd blamed him, raged inside at his betrayal. Yet he'd kept her in his heart and had prayed for her. Was he right? Had God been there waiting for her to hear his voice, sense his love for her? She wanted to believe that, but something in her warred with lowering her guard enough to accept it.

"Thank you for praying." She rose. "I'm going to grab my computer and try to find Kent's brother. Do you know where he lives?" Ignoring the disappointment in his face, she rushed inside and grabbed her laptop from the bedroom before rejoining him.

She plopped beside him again and opened her laptop. "What's his name? I'll check socials first."

"Clark Reynolds."

Her fingers paused. "You're kidding. Clark and Kent for twins?"

He grinned. "Kent said his dad was a huge Superman fan. The twins always liked it."

She resumed her search. "This has to be him. Superman Clark Reynolds." She turned the laptop around for Blake to see the guy's picture.

His gaze clung hungrily to the photo. "That's him. He and Kent were identical."

She went back to the profile. "He lives in Mobile."

"They were originally from Indiana. The last I heard Clark was in Atlanta."

"Well, he's right down the road now. He could be behind all this. I think we need to talk to him. You game?"

Blake's nod was slow in coming. "I should do it alone in case he pulls a gun. I don't want you in harm's way."

"You're not going alone, and that's final. Tomorrow is Sunday. Let's go after church."

"You going with us tomorrow?"

She hesitated before giving her own slow nod. "If you prayed for me all this time, I think I'd better say thank you."

What had she just gotten herself into?

———

The aroma of fried chicken made Paradise's mouth water. "I'll go help your mom with dinner. I'm a little sore but I'm feeling much better." She stopped and tipped her head to one side. "Have you seen the boys? They sure are quiet."

Blake frowned and leaped up. "That's never a good sign."

She followed him inside where they found Jenna, face red and perspiring, standing at the stove flipping chicken in the skillet. "Dinner will be done in a few. You might get the boys to wash their hands."

"Where are they? I haven't heard a peep," Blake said.

"Still in their room."

Paradise went to the wall of cabinets while Blake left the room. "I'll set the table while Blake grabs the boys."

Jenna shook her head. "You just got clocked by an iron, Paradise. You're supposed to be resting."

"The lavender made me good as new." She touched the lump on her face. "Well, except for my face."

"You're beautiful. No bruise can change that."

Paradise shook her head at Jenna's comment and focused on her task. The chicken would go nicely with the blue plates, so she took down the plates and put them in their places around the table.

Blake reappeared. "Levi is reading, but Isaac isn't there. I checked all the bedrooms and the bathroom."

"Check the back. Maybe he went out to play in the new sand I had delivered for their sandbox. They're supposed to tell me if they're going outside, but sometimes they forget, especially Isaac." Jenna turned off the burner.

Paradise went to the back door and out onto the deck. Jenna and Blake followed. The green space was empty of a towheaded little boy, and her gut clenched. She and Blake had been on the front porch for an hour, and Isaac had been on the bed coloring. He hadn't gone out past them.

She spied an upside-down pail by the fence and went to check it out. A child-sized bare footprint marred the top with traces of red mud. "Blake, I think he climbed the fence."

The boys were never allowed out of the yard alone. While the protocols for the enclosures were tight, Jenna rightly didn't allow them too close to any of the animals without adult supervision. Paradise tried to assure herself the little guy couldn't wander into danger, but her heart didn't believe it. The sabotage Blake had discovered was probably targeted at him, but it left everyone vulnerable—especially the children.

"Let's split up and find him," Blake said. "He loves the otters. I'll check there first."

"And the beavers," Jenna said. "Paradise, would you stay here with Levi in case Isaac comes back on his own?"

Paradise wanted to be out searching too, but she nodded. "I'll take care of him."

The darkness swallowed up their figures as they raced off calling Isaac's name. Paradise jogged back inside and peered in on Levi, who closed his book. "Want to help find Isaac? Does he hide in here anywhere?"

Levi scrambled off the bed. "Sometimes he likes to play in Blake's apartment. He likes to watch out the window. I'll show you."

They hadn't checked the apartment, so she followed the little boy out the front to the garage and climbed the stairs to the apartment. The door was closed but not locked. A thorough search didn't turn up Isaac.

She took Levi's hand and went back down to the porch. "Any other ideas where he might hide? Did he say anything before he left you?"

Levi thought for a moment, then frowned. "He said he was working on a present for Tigey."

The white tiger was named Tigris but called Tigey by the staff. She was a sanctuary favorite, but the little guy wouldn't go to the tiger enclosure by himself, would he? And even if he did, there was no danger. The security around the big cats was extensive, and he'd never get past the gate.

"He said Tigey had babies, but I told him that was silly and not true. You don't think he went to see for himself, do you?"

Her heart sank. "I sure hope not." She pulled out her phone and tried to call Blake, but his phone went off on the porch. He must have laid it down without thinking. When she tried Jenna, it went to voice mail. She sometimes had her phone switched off and she might not have realized it.

She took Levi by the hand. "Let's just walk that way. Maybe we'll find him along the route."

But hopefully, Jenna had found him gawking at the beavers and just hadn't been able to call. Levi held her hand as they walked through the landscape lights along the path. As they neared the tiger enclosure, she heard a tiger chuff, a typical welcoming sound they used in various ways. Sometimes it was a welcome to a trainer, sometimes it was a noise asserting their right of territory when they were swapped out of enclosures.

She hoped the tiger was reacting to their approach, but a fist formed in her gut at the soft sound. "Isaac!" she called.

"I'm here, Paradise." His small voice came from ahead. "Levi was right—Tigey doesn't really have any babies."

The bottom dropped out of her stomach. *He's in the tiger enclosure.*

She gripped Levi's shoulder. Blake was likely the closest. "Levi, go to the otter enclosure and get Blake. Don't stop along the way anywhere and don't try to go in any gates. Get Blake and bring him back."

"Is the tiger going to eat Isaac?" His voice trembled.

"No, I'm going to go get him, but I need Blake." She gave Levi a quick push. "Run as fast as you can."

He sprinted away from the big cat enclosures toward the river enclosures. The white tiger tensed and watched him go as if she would like to leap. Paradise couldn't breathe, could barely think as she approached the enclosure and studied Isaac sitting in the dirt near the big white tiger.

The tigers here had been raised from kittens and socialized with the trainers who went in with them every day, but Isaac was small. He was prey size and a succulent morsel for the tiger, whose tail was lashing back and forth.

Not a good sign.

And she had to go into the inner enclosure and save him. "Isaac, I want you to get up. Don't run and don't try to play with Tigey. Keep your face turned toward her and back away toward the gate. I'm coming inside the perimeter gate. I'll open it and grab you, okay?"

"Okay. She won't hurt me though. She likes me."

A desperate prayer surged into her heart. *God, if you're there, we need you big-time here. I need you. Please, please help.*

———

When Blake hadn't found Isaac at the otter enclosure or heard that his mother had located him, the first niggle of concern shivered up his spine. Where could he be?

He thought to call his mom, then realized he hadn't brought his phone. Maybe she'd found him but couldn't call. They should have coordinated. He cupped his hands around his mouth when he reached the bird aviary. "Isaac!"

A startled flutter of wings from the aviary was the only answer. He'd circle back to the house in case his mother hadn't taken her phone with her either. Maybe they were all safe and sound waiting on him.

He stopped and shook his head. No, she would have rushed home to call him if she'd found Isaac and didn't have her phone. If she tried his number, it would have rung on the front porch, and she would be out searching for him now so that he knew.

He turned back to the otter enclosure. Could his little brother have gotten inside the otter building? It was all locked up, but Isaac was resourceful. Blake patted his pocket for his key and approached the low-slung concrete building. He inserted the key but stopped and turned at the sound of a small voice calling his name. "Isaac?"

The figure came into view under a wash of lights. "It's me." Levi's eyes were wide with horror. "You have to come now! Isaac is in with Tigey, and Paradise is going inside after him." His brother threw himself against Blake's legs and sobs erupted from him. "The tiger will eat them both!"

A shot of pure terror shot down Blake's spine. He scooped up Levi and raced toward the tiger enclosure.

CHAPTER 21

PARADISE'S HANDS SHOOK AS she reached the outside gate. *It's unlocked.* How had Isaac gotten a key and entered? Was this another case of sabotage? Her throat closed as she eyed the tiger with its tail lashing. Tigris's eyes gleamed in the moonlight as she turned her head to stare at Paradise's movements.

Paradise held her breath as the tiger turned her way at the scrape of the gate opening. The high fence rose way above her head and angled slightly in with metal mesh over it to keep an animal from climbing it. Where was Blake? The tigers knew and liked him. If she had him here, this sheer and rising terror wouldn't be quite so bad. If there'd been time, she would have gotten food from the shed, but the tiger could pounce on Isaac at any moment.

She stared directly into the tiger's eyes. "Hey, girl," she said in a soothing, conversational tone. "How are you tonight?" She should have been making an effort to get to know the big cats in her care, but she'd let her stupid fear keep her from doing her job.

The big cat's tail ceased its lashing, but the tiger continued to watch her every movement. "That's right, we're friends."

She walked through the empty first enclosure and reached the inner gate that stood wide open. Her muscles were tense, and she had to force herself to walk through the opening. The musky odor of the big cats intensified, and a wave of nausea nearly took her down as her fear heightened. She'd hoped never to be this close to a big cat again.

"Isaac, move very slowly." She kept the same tone so the tiger would think she was addressing her. "Keep staring at Tigey in case she looks your way. I'm going to try to keep her attention on me."

"Okay."

Out of the corner of her eye, she saw him rise from the ground and start backing toward her. "That's it. Just a few more feet and you can go through to the outer enclosure. Once you get through the first gate, keep backing up until you're out. Don't make any sudden movements that would startle her."

"It will be okay, Paradise. God will take care of you."

Such trust from the little boy shook her. She wished she could believe the way he did. The way Blake and Jenna did. God hadn't done such a great job of helping her in her life, but just in case he was listening, she shot up an awkward prayer again.

God, if you're there, please, please help me. Isaac doesn't deserve this. If the tiger attacks, let it come for me.

Tears sprang to her eyes, and she licked her lips before trying to speak to the tiger again. She couldn't let fear translate to her tone. "Good girl, Tigey. We can be friends, right? You're so beautiful."

Isaac had reached the gate and slipped through. Another minute and he would be safe outside of the perimeter enclosure too. She'd conquered her fear enough to face down this big cat.

A sense of peace began to replace the trembling in her knees. Warmth filled her chest, and she saw how beautiful the tiger truly was. Those dramatic markings and her blue eyes were stunning. And the power in those muscles wasn't just for killing and eating but for leaping and stretching. Every movement the animal made was a work of art. God had made the tiger as well as her, right? Even if she died right here on this red dirt tonight, she had this incandescent moment of recognition that God had heard her just a little bit.

A deep voice spoke from the tiger's left. "Why, there you are, Tigey. How's my sweet girl?"

The massive white head moved toward Blake's voice, and the tiger stretched out her front legs and moved toward him. Blake reached through the fence wires and rubbed Tigris's side. Jenna, her face white, stood just past him with both boys in her arms.

"Such a pretty girl," Blake crooned. His gaze flickered over Paradise, and he made an almost imperceptible motion toward the gate.

She swallowed hard and nodded before backing away as quietly as she could. Her hand touched the hard surface of the gate, and she changed course enough to exit the opening. The gate creaked as she shut it, and the tiger turned back toward her momentarily until Blake spoke again. "Look at me, Tigris. I'm here. Want to play ball?"

The animal's ears flickered at the word *ball*. Paradise had heard she was particularly fond of large balls. Though Blake had no toys at hand, the big cat gave him her rapt attention.

Paradise whirled and raced for the other gate. She opened it and dashed through before closing it and locking it tight. Her knees didn't support her, and she sank to the grass with her arms clutched around her.

Then Blake was there, holding her and crooning in her ear. "You're safe and Isaac is fine. You saved him."

Jenna knelt down too, and the family surrounded her on every side. Small hands patted her face and hair, and the heat from Blake's body radiated around her in a comforting embrace.

Jenna was sobbing, though she clearly was trying to suppress the cries pouring from her throat. "Thank you for saving my baby. I don't know how I can ever repay you."

Paradise closed her eyes and let them touch her, heal her with their honest love and gratitude. She opened her eyes and stared at Jenna, then at Blake. "It wasn't me. God was in that enclosure tonight. I couldn't have done it on my own. I—I felt him."

And while she had much to learn, she felt the boulder she'd been carrying for so many years roll off and vanish. Maybe she wasn't beyond hope.

———

None of them could have lived here if they'd lost this little guy. The animals would have been a constant reminder of the danger that had suddenly stolen him away. Blake's arms tightened around Isaac, and he rested his chin on the boy's head against his chest. Isaac had fallen asleep as soon as they'd gotten home, even though dinner was ready. None of the rest of them could force down a morsel either. The near tragedy had stolen their appetites, and Mom had put the food away without comment.

Blake couldn't tear his gaze away from Paradise's beautiful face. She'd managed to compartmentalize her fear and save his little brother. If he wasn't already crazy about her, her bravery tonight would have sealed the deal.

"This has gone too far." Blake choked out the words past the fear that had lodged in his throat for the past hour. The solid weight of his little brother on his lap on the sofa reinforced how badly this could have gone. "If the gate was unlocked, someone left it that way on purpose to try to hurt me. I hadn't made my rounds yet tonight, but I would have gone in there and been vulnerable to an attack. I ordered some additional cameras a few days ago, and they should be here soon. We have to find the culprit."

"And why would he think Tigey had cubs?" his mom asked. "Someone had to tell him."

"He said he heard some visitors say there were tiger cubs," Levi said from his spot nestled against Paradise. "He was sure it had to be Tigey with the babies."

Paradise sat beside him with her feet curled under her. The faint scent of plumeria wafted from her. They should move the boys to bed, but none of them wanted the boys out of their sight. Blake studied her serene expression. She seemed different after having just faced down a white tiger to rescue Isaac. He'd been shocked by her mention of God being with her, knowing what he did about her struggle with faith.

His mother carried in a tray, and the aroma of strong coffee wafted toward him. "I thought we could all use some brain fuel. It's a given that none of us are ready for bed and won't be for hours. I don't think I can sleep tonight at all, and I'm going to have both boys sleep with me."

"I'll take them and let you get some rest," Blake said.

His mom shook her head. "I need them with me."

"I get it," he said. She'd laid two men in the dirt, and tonight's awful incident had made terror rear its horrifying head.

"We need help to figure this out," Paradise said. "Could we hire an investigator? I have a little bit of savings I could throw into the pot."

"They're expensive," he said. "And Hez is digging for us for free. He never sends me a bill."

"This might take up more time than he can spare for free," his mother said. "But we aren't helpless. We're all smart. Let's start with interviewing all our employees. Someone had a key, Blake. This wasn't some random person off the street. That lock wasn't broken, right? It had been left open on purpose."

Blake shifted Isaac's small form. "It wasn't broken, just unlocked. I examined it after everyone was safe."

"Can we make everyone account for their keys?" Paradise asked. "Do you know how many keys have been made for black locks? What's the color mean anyway?"

"Black is the highest security," Mom said. "We use them for the big cats and other predators. Green is for animal habitats, and blue is for generic gates like the front entrance. A key that opens the black gates will open anything in the park. I have a list of who has what keys on my computer. Let me go check it." She rose and went down the hall, and her office light came on.

Blake reached across the sofa and took Paradise's hand. "Doing okay?"

Her fingers closed around his. "I'm not even shaking. I think maybe God really was in there with us."

He squeezed her fingers. "I'm sure that's true." Her full lips were slightly parted, and he checked the impulse to kiss her. They were still reeling from the events of the evening, but he wanted nothing more than to pull her onto his lap and bury his face in her hair.

His mom came back in. "There are eleven black keys out, most of them with the predator keepers. Tomorrow I'll personally talk to every employee who has one in their possession and ask to see it. I want to make sure they haven't lost a key."

"Maybe it would be better for me to talk to them. You tend to be too sweet, Mom. They might snow you."

His mother wrinkled her nose. "This mama bear has her teeth bared, Blake. I want to do it. I promise I'll be fierce without a trace of sweetness."

The fire in her blue eyes convinced him and he nodded. "Okay, Mom, it's all yours. You want me to be there too?"

"You and Paradise go to the police station tomorrow and tell them what nearly happened. They *must* help find who did this. Surely even that idiot Greene will know you wouldn't do something like this and put your little brother in danger."

"We can try." Blake had his doubts Greene would listen. "I might go to McShea. Paradise is his cousin, and he might listen if she comes along to tell how it all went down."

And he wouldn't mind being with her on the drive anyway.

CHAPTER 22

THE AROMA OF BACON and eggs filled the kitchen as Paradise wheeled in a whiteboard on a stand the boys used for home-school. The wheels squeaked on the kitchen tile, and the noise brought Blake's gaze to her as she maneuvered it into place by the kitchen table. "I thought we'd lay out what we know and where our investigation should go next."

She'd had the best night's sleep she could remember since forever last night, and she was ready to tackle the seemingly insurmountable question of who was targeting Blake.

She picked up the marker and wrote *Events* at the top, then drew lines to the next spots down to the attacks they knew about—*Murder of Danielle Mason, Shots Fired at Bears, Break-ins at Apartment and House, Arson at Cottage, Beer-Can IED in Field, Hyena Incident, Iron Attack in Shed, Tiger Incident.*

Blake joined her at the whiteboard and held out his hand for the marker. "That's *nine* incidents. I didn't realize there were quite so many. The attacks just keep coming." He drew connections down the white surface. "Danielle and the shots fired at the bears are connected by the activist group."

Paradise nodded. "At that time we didn't know if it was activists trying to shut us down or something else. Then the other attacks happened, and the focus seemed to laser in on you."

Jenna set a bowl of scrambled eggs on the table. "But maybe not. All of the attacks have brought havoc to the park. If the sabotage at the hyena or tiger enclosures had resulted in injury or death, the media would have been all over us. We would have had no choice but to close."

"Good point." Paradise studied the board a moment. "I think our next step should be to at least take this list to the police and see where their investigation stands, but let's talk to Rod and not Greene. He might not tell us anything, but Greene would brush us off."

Blake reached over to fill his plate with bacon and eggs. "I reviewed the video camera footage too, but none of them picked up anything unusual. The idea of someone targeting me specifically is something I need to check out. I laid awake thinking about it last night. I want to follow through on our idea to see Clark Reynolds."

"Reynolds? The twin brother who hates you?" Jenna asked.

He nodded. "Paradise brought up the revenge idea before Isaac went missing. Mom, he lives in Mobile. That elevated the possibility in my mind."

Jenna picked up her fork. "While you do that, I'm going to talk to the employees this morning. I didn't sleep much last night."

"I'm sure Levi was sideways all night," Blake said.

Jenna's smile was a ghost of its usual joyful one. "It was more worry than anything else. I couldn't stop hanging on to my boys."

Paradise reached for breakfast and winced. Her shoulder was sore from her PT this morning. "The ordeal must have exhausted them. They're usually up by now."

Jenna poured coffee for all of them and carried the mugs to the table. "I'm glad for it too. We have to figure this out. I came to the conclusion last night that I can't keep fighting when my boys are in danger. I love the preserve, but the boys are more important to me than anything. We have to make some traction on resolving the danger or I'm going to sell."

The stark words hit Paradise in the gut, and Blake flinched too. "What would you do if you sold?"

"I could do anything. The land is worth a lot of money. I could just raise my boys in peace. I mean, I wouldn't be happy with nothing to do, but I could open a bookstore or some other business where I could have them with me. Nothing is worth what we went through last night." She glanced at Paradise. "I hate that I got you here to work and might be pulling the rug out from under you."

"Whatever you decide will be fine. I realized last night that I don't have to live in the past. What happened to me is over, and I'm going to move on. I won't live under that cloud anymore. I can find a new life here and be content." She glanced at Blake out of the corner of her eye. He was staring at her, and she thought she saw hope shining in his eyes.

Hope ballooned in her chest as well, and she couldn't remember a time when she'd felt this good, this positive. Maybe when she was a kid. Was that what faith brought to a person? She had a lot to learn, and she didn't know where to start, but she wanted to begin. "Do either of you have a Bible I could borrow?"

Blake straightened and went wide-eyed. "I do. I'll get it."

The thought of reading a Bible that meant something to him warmed her. Blake was the kindest, most faith-filled person she'd ever met. If there was a chance she could learn from him, she would take it. But she was also a little scared. What would it mean for her life to move forward this way?

She snagged a piece of bacon and a spoonful of scrambled eggs and dug in. The thought of barging into her cousin's office should have been daunting, but things couldn't continue this way. If they had to shake a few trees to release the fruit, she was ready to do it. And seeing Jenna's set face and Blake's tight jaw, she knew they were just as determined.

Blake returned holding a Bible. The navy leather was worn in spots, and the yellowed pages had been touched many times over the years. "Mom got this for me when I turned sixteen. She got me a study Bible for Christmas a few years ago, and I use that now." He placed it in her hands.

Paradise smoothed the soft leather with shaky fingers. This was the Bible he'd been reading when they were dating. She could tell from his expression it meant something special to him. "I'll take good care of it."

"I'm not worried about that. I want you to have it."

The boys wandered in with sleepy eyes, and Levi ran to climb onto Paradise's lap while Isaac scampered over to his mother, who scooped him up and held him tightly against her shoulder.

Levi patted the Bible in her hand. "That's Blake's. Did he give it to you?"

"He did. For now."

"It's got maps in the back with north and south. Blake always calls the Bible our North Star. Have you ever seen the North Star?"

"I haven't. Maybe you can show me sometime."

"Okay." Levi clambered down and climbed onto his own chair to eat breakfast.

Isaac slipped off Jenna's lap and came to stand by Paradise. "I have a North Star card. You can use it to hold your place."

"I'd love that."

Isaac ran off and returned a couple of minutes later with the card. The star shone brightly in the center. "Here you go. Jesus is our North Star, you know. And he'll be yours too."

Tears pooled in Paradise's eyes as she stared at the card, and she touched his soft hair. He looked so much like Blake. Did he ever wish he had his own family? He was thirty now, just a little older than her, and she could no longer deny the longing she felt for more stability, for a place to settle in and belong. For a man who loved her in spite of her faults.

Was Blake that man? Did she dare voice to herself how much she hoped it might be true?

Something had definitely changed with Paradise. After church Blake kept stealing glances at her contented face as he maneuvered his pickup through the construction clogging the street to the main sheriff's department in Bay Minette. He'd called the Bon Secour sheriff substation and had been informed McShea was at headquarters.

Blake parked in the lot, and they got out to walk inside. "You want to lead with the questions or have me do it?"

"He's my cousin, so I'll give it a try first."

He held the door open for her, and they stepped into a quiet front office. Several people sat in chairs by the window and stared at them as they went to the front desk.

A uniformed woman in her thirties with weary, jaded eyes

studied them. "Can I help you?" Her tone indicated she wasn't ready to help anyone.

"I'm Paradise Alden, Sergeant McShea's cousin. Is Rod free?"

The woman's brows went up. "I'll let him know you're out here. He was off today, but then he had to come in. I think he's free now, so hang on."

That changed her attitude. Maybe Paradise was right and she'd get somewhere today with Rod. Even deputies cared what their relatives thought of them. Paradise's return to town might have impacted Rod more than they knew. The past had been so tragic and ugly. If she could find redemption and peace after all these years, Blake was all for it.

The woman returned. "You can go on back. First door on the right. I'll unlock the entry door." A beep sounded and the door latch clicked.

Blake opened it and let Paradise go through first. The building smelled like fresh \paint. Rod's door was closed, but she rapped her knuckles on it and he called for them to come in.

They stepped into a large office that was surprisingly clean. The big desk held only a computer and a single manila folder. Several framed commendations hung on the wall behind Rod's desk.

"I hope we're not intruding, Rod," Paradise said.

He leaned back with his arms stretched up and his hands behind his head. His toned muscles bulged under his tan shirt. "My meeting is over. I always have time for my little cousin. Coffee? I just made it fresh, so it's not sludge."

Blake shut the door behind them and followed Paradise's lead to settle in one of the four chairs facing the desk. He planned to stay quiet unless he was asked a question.

"We'd both love a coffee," Paradise said.

Blake admired the way she'd made it almost a social call. It might put Rod at ease. He watched the sergeant stroll to his coffee bar and pour coffee into real mugs. Blake recognized the aroma of good coffee from Serda's in Bay Minette. He accepted the hot mug with a barely murmured thanks. Best to slide into the background.

Paradise took a sip of her coffee. "This is really good."

"From Costa Rica. It's my favorite. Oh, and before I forget, your DNA came back, Blake. It didn't match, just as we suspected. And thanks for the evidence you dropped off. The blasting material matches what we found in the burned cottage." Rod resumed his seat and set his mug on the desktop. "What brings you to town?"

"Something very distressing happened last night, and I wanted to tell you myself." Paradise launched into the incident in the tiger enclosure.

Rod's eyes widened with what appeared to be genuine shock. "That's terrible." He glanced at Blake. "The boys are both okay?"

"Yes, other than being a little clingy this morning from the trauma. Levi ran to get me, and he was nearly hysterical at the thought of his little brother being eaten. It's not something he'll soon forget. Me either, for that matter." He swallowed and his dry throat clicked. The memory of seeing his little brother and Paradise in the enclosure with the tiger would haunt him too.

"Someone left the gate unlocked." Paradise's voice snagged Rod's attention again. "And it wasn't the first time. The same thing happened in the hyena enclosure a few days ago."

"And there was that iron that hit you in the head," Rod said.

Rod must have been paying attention to everything that had happened at The Sanctuary. "We suspect it might have been targeted at me. I'm most apt to go into the enclosures, and hardly anyone uses that shed where the iron was placed."

"Interesting premise. Have you mentioned it to Detective Greene?"

Blake caught a warning glance from Paradise and shut his mouth against the truth. No sense in antagonizing McShea by pointing out his detective was biased. Better let Paradise use her diplomacy and relationship.

"Not yet. I knew you'd care about how a little boy could have died yesterday, and I knew you'd have every piece of what was going on at your disposal."

Rod nodded and reached for his coffee again. "That was wise. There have been several incidents out there. It's very troubling."

"Nine incidents to be precise."

Rod ran his finger around the top of his coffee mug. "That many?"

Paradise ticked through them on her fingers. "Someone either wants the refuge to close down or they're seeking revenge against Blake for something."

"Anyone special we should focus on?"

Paradise nodded. "Blake has received threats from a man in Mobile. Clark Reynolds. We plan to talk to him, but any background information you could dig up would be helpful."

"It would be best if the two of you stayed out of the investigation. Let our officers handle talking to Reynolds."

Blake's fingers curled into his palms, and somehow he managed to keep quiet. Paradise nodded as if she agreed with Rod, but Blake knew that glint in her eye was from her efforts not to challenge her cousin.

They rose and thanked Rod for his time before exiting into the bright Alabama sunshine. "Think that was a bust?" he asked when they were alone inside the truck.

"Maybe." Her lips flattened and she consulted her phone. "We're thirty miles from Mobile right now. Are you thinking what I'm thinking?"

He started the truck and put it in gear. "Yep. We'll get to Clark before Greene spoils it all."

CHAPTER 23

THE MOBILE ADDRESS BELONGED to a decaying trailer set back from a gravel road among maple and birch trees. The grass was nearly a foot high, and weeds poked through what was left of the gravel. The whole look of the place gave off a bad vibe.

She leaned forward. "Does anyone live here? The grass shouldn't be so high if Reynolds is driving on it."

"One way to find out." Blake turned the truck into the drive, and the tires thumped along the potholes to the trailer. "I'll take the lead on this one."

She left her hand on the door after he parked and stared at the front door, which stood open a bit as if the latch didn't work. "I don't think he's here, Blake." She opened her door and stepped into the high weeds in the drive.

Blake got out and approached the trailer. Paradise crowded close behind him. She could almost hear the dueling banjos from *Deliverance* echoing on the wind. She shivered and pushed away the thought. It was an old abandoned trailer and nothing more.

The metal steps canted to one side amid the weeds, and several discarded beer bottles poked their necks up through the vegetation. Blake mounted the steps and rapped on the door, which opened a few more inches. "Clark? You in there?" He rapped again, and this time the door opened another foot.

Paradise peered past his shoulder into the gloom of the trailer's interior. It wasn't as disheveled as she expected from seeing the exterior. A brown tweed sofa was in view, and the coffee table in front of it held only a single beer bottle. No debris was scattered on the brown carpet either.

"Clark?" Blake called again.

"You looking for me?" A gruff voice came from behind them, and two German shepherds charged toward them.

Paradise stepped forward. "Good boys." She kept her tone friendly and light. The dogs stopped their forward momentum and pricked their ears in her direction. "Such a beauty," she crooned. She held out her hand and prayed for a sniff or two and not a bite.

Clark was a big guy with hunched shoulders weighed down by life. His shaggy brown hair curled on his neck. He was clean-shaven and his clothes were wrinkled. He eyed her. "Huh. How'd you do that? They don't like anyone." He glared at Blake. "You got some nerve coming here, Lawson. Get off my property before I sic my dogs on you."

Blake stuffed his hands in his pockets. "I wanted to see how you were doing, Clark."

The man swept his hand over the property. "How do you think I'm doing? No family, no friends, no brother, thanks to you. My mom killed herself after you murdered Kent."

Blake's jaw clenched, and he took his hands out of his pockets. "If I could take his place, I would. He was my best friend, Clark."

Clark balled his hands into fists. "You should be in jail. I'd like to see you strapped into the electric chair. I'd pull the switch."

"I can't disagree with that."

Paradise couldn't hold her tongue a moment longer. "Clark, it was an accident. Have you never made a mistake? Failed to check something? It was a terrible tragedy, but you have to know Blake loved your brother."

Clark swept a glare over her and snorted. "You're letting him off too easy. It's not your brother who died."

"No, it's not, but we're both sympathetic to your pain. Blake carries it too. How would you feel if a mistake you made harmed someone you loved? How would you be able to make amends? If there was a way, Blake would do it. But Kent is dead and nothing can bring him back. Instead, Blake has dedicated his life to helping other people. What more do you want him to do?"

Tears glimmered in Clark's eyes. "I might find peace if he was as dead as Kent."

A few weeks ago she was as tormented as Clark. Would this have been her fate if she'd kept on the same path of anger and revenge? "You wouldn't. Two wrongs don't make a right. You'd still be angry and hate filled. The only thing that will help is for you to forgive him."

"Forgive him? Did you pick some weed out of my patch? I will never forgive him."

"Then your life won't change, Clark. You'll die a lonely man with no friends because you've pushed everyone away. We can't control what happens to us, but we can choose how we respond."

He sneered. "What do you know about my kind of pain?"

"My parents were murdered. Bludgeoned to death." His eyes widened but he didn't answer. Enough of this though. She couldn't make him see what was in front of his face, just like no one else could have gotten through to her. "Your driveway is all overgrown. We nearly missed it."

"My truck died a month ago, and I don't have the money to fix it. Transmission. Not that anyone cares."

Pay it forward. She had some savings, but the inner voice warred with her logic. The guy didn't deserve anything from her. She pushed the urge away for now until she could examine it later.

"So you've been stuck here for a month? How are you getting groceries and other necessities?"

He shrugged. "I got good legs, so I hoof it." Her questions seemed to have drained his defiance. He brushed past them. "I've said all I'm going to say." His voice was tired and hopeless, and he didn't look at either of them as he went up the steps with his dogs into the trailer. The door slammed but then cracked open again as the latch didn't hold.

Blake took her hand. "You are amazing. I think he could tell you cared, and somehow that defused his anger."

She curled her fingers into his and leaned against him, the strength running out of her legs as her adrenaline crashed. "If he'd sicced those dogs on us, we'd have been in trouble. But the bigger news is he can't be behind what's going on. He doesn't have transportation."

So they were back to square one.

Paradise's silence filled the truck cab, but Blake let her stare out the window with her thoughts. He had plenty of his own as well. Like how completely he'd ruined Clark's life. To have someone wish him dead was a new experience, and he wished he could heal the man's pain somehow. The worst thing was he deserved it.

Paradise pointed out an auto repair place on the outskirts of

Mobile only a few miles from Clark's trailer. "Can we stop there a minute?"

Blake glanced at the busy lot. "Sure." He pulled in beside the tow truck. "You having car trouble? There's a closer place in Pelican Harbor."

"Not me. I want to get Clark's truck repaired."

Jaw slack, he stared at her for a long minute. "Why? I mean, he just threw us off his property."

"I've done worse. Didn't you get a sense of how alone and desperate he felt? I've been in that spot so many times. How do you think he will feel when that tow truck pulls up and tells him his truck will be repaired at no cost to him?"

"Paradise, it's his transmission! That's not a cheap fix."

She opened her door. "We'll find out how much."

No wonder thoughts of her filled his every waking moment. She was still an enigma. He shook his head and followed her inside to an aging space painted a dingy beige. Cracked vinyl tiles the same color covered the floor. A waiting room with two guys watching TV was to the left through an open door.

A woman behind a long green counter glanced their way. "Can I help you folks?" Her dark eyes gave them a once-over in a curious but friendly way.

Paradise approached her with a smile. "Do you know Clark Reynolds down the road?"

"Matter of fact, I do. He's a regular, or he was until that old truck of his died on him."

"How much would it cost to fix his transmission?"

The woman's brows winged up, and she quoted a price that made Blake's eyes widen too. It was much less than he'd expected. The woman must have noticed his surprise because she glanced his way. "Our owner, Glen, is Clark's third cousin and they go bowling sometimes. He was trying to help, but Clark didn't have the funds even for a discount rate."

"I'd like to pay for it," Paradise said.

"He your boyfriend or something?"

Paradise handed over her debit card. "No, but I think he needs a hand."

"He's going to ask how this happened." The woman took the card and went to her computer. "What do I tell him?"

"Just tell him a friend wanted to help."

Warmth flooded Blake's chest, and he wanted to wrap Paradise up in his arms. Something deep had happened last night. He'd loved the old Paradise, but this new one was more intriguing in a lot of ways. He had thought of offering to help with the repair, but he saw her deep desire to do this herself.

The woman returned the card, and Paradise signed the receipt. "You're a good person," the woman said. "Thank you."

"I'm not good at all, but other people have helped me. And God did too." Paradise slid the pen back across the counter and headed for the door.

"I wish we could be mice in the corner to see his reaction," Blake said once they reached his truck. He stretched his arm across the seat and touched her shoulder. "That was a terrific thing to do, Paradise."

He could get lost in those amber eyes she turned his way. They'd always been full of mystery and secrets, but today they were clear. And content, definitely content. He'd never seen contentment in her before.

She reached up and put her right hand on top of his. "I had a good teacher. You never gave up on me, Blake. Even when I showed up here angry and distant, you were kind. Always. I caused a lot of upheaval in your life, and I'm sorry for that."

"Most of us can use having a little shake-up in life. We get into a rut." He didn't move until she dropped her hand back onto her lap and turned her gaze away. Even then, it took a few seconds for him to start the truck and put his attention on driving back to The Sanctuary.

They might have struck out on their investigation, but their lives had taken a turn for the better. At least he hoped so.

CHAPTER 24

JENNA WAS IN THE office with the boys when Paradise and Blake returned from talking to Clark. Levi's face brightened when they came in, but he stayed at his mom's desk where he was sharpening pencils in her electric sharpener.

"Hey, Levi," Paradise said. "That's a super-fun job."

He nodded. "Mommy told me I could make all of them as sharp as they can get." Isaac left his job of organizing paper clips to run to Paradise, and she picked him up. "Hey, little man."

He scowled. "I'm a big guy now, Paradise. Let's go see the tigers. I think Tigey misses me. I heard her calling me before you got here."

A lion roared in the distance, and Paradise waited for the fear to creep in, but it never happened. This little guy's escapades had made her face her fear and conquer it. Or maybe it was all God. She hugged Isaac tight. "We'll go see how she's doing after scaring me half to death yesterday."

Isaac palmed her face and stared in her eyes as if willing her to listen to him. "She didn't mean it. I could tell she likes you. She might even love you like I do." He planted a kiss on her cheek.

She nuzzled his neck and inhaled the scent of little boy and patchouli soap. "You're the best, Isaac." When she glanced at Blake, she found him staring at her with a longing expression. She wet her lips and focused her attention back on the little boy. "Who's game to go see Tigey?"

"Me," Levi called. "I have to finish two more pencils."

Paradise set Isaac back down. "And Blake and I want to talk to your mommy a minute."

"Aw, man." Isaac wrinkled his nose before going back to pick up more paper clips off the desk.

Blake touched her back to guide her toward where Jenna sat at her computer, and his touch made her pulse hammer in her throat. When this was all over, she wanted to drive out to the very tip of Fort Morgan Road and stick her toes in the sand while they talked for hours. She wanted to hear everything about the years since she'd left him, and she wanted him to hear the things she'd never spoken to anyone else.

The job in front of them was daunting and required all their attention, but how she wished they could grab a lazy day and unravel the tangle of misconceptions and misunderstandings that had wrecked them back then. They couldn't go forward without backing up and releasing the pain they'd been through. Clear it all out and start fresh.

She gave her head a slight shake and refocused. After a quick peek at the kids, she pitched her voice low. "How'd the employee interviews go today, Jenna?"

Jenna turned from the computer and beckoned them closer. "There's a key missing. Evan can't find his."

Blake's hand fell away from Paradise's back. "What did Evan have to say about it?"

"He laid down his key ring after unlocking the barn door and forgot about it until the next day. When he went back, it was gone."

Paradise struggled with the rising animosity she felt at Evan's name. He lived in her old house, and she still wondered about his involvement in the murders even though the old sheriff was almost certainly the killer.

Her animosity was irrational, but she couldn't help it. "When was this?"

"Four days ago. And he took some vacation time for a few days right after. Today was his first day back at work, and he came in my office first thing to ask if anyone had turned in his black key."

Black meant access to all the gates. Whoever had his key could go anywhere on the property. Paradise was tempted to talk to him herself. She hadn't done that since she started work here.

"And there's no camera back there," Blake said.

"Oh, your new cameras came today." His mother pointed to a pile of boxes just inside the front door.

He glanced that direction. "I'll install them today. Did you get any sense that Evan knew more than he was saying?"

"Not at all, especially since he came to me before I could ask about his key."

"What about the other employees?"

"No one gave off suspicious vibes. Any one of them could have taken it and used it, even gift shop employees with no top access. All they had to do was grab it and keep their mouth shut."

Blake glanced at Paradise. "You went radio silent. Was it the mention of Evan? You want to talk to him yourself?"

He knew her so well. She hadn't been sure he remembered her suspicions. Paradise nodded. "I'd feel better if I finally faced him. We've somehow managed to miss each other on this big place.

I haven't come face-to-face with him yet. Maybe it's time to lay that suspicion to rest."

She glanced over at the boys. "But first, I have a promise to keep." And it didn't hurt her a bit that the delay would give her time to form what she wanted to say to Evan.

⁓

The jaguars were the first big cats on the predator side of The Sanctuary. The distinctive nasal grunting they used to greet the keepers rumbled from the big black jaguar, and Blake expected Paradise to flinch. When she paused and glanced that way, she grabbed her shoulder as though it had begun to ache.

"You okay?" he whispered.

She swallowed and nodded, but she didn't move closer for several long moments. Her feet finally shuffled toward the tall fence with the wire canopy confining the big cat. "Hello there." Her brow creased, and she glanced at Blake. "I've forgotten its name."

Levi stepped forward. "Darth is a boy. Mom says he's handsome. I love his shiny coat. And you can just barely see his jaguar spots in his black fur. He's my favorite."

Blake blocked the boys from getting closer. "Remember not to poke your fingers through the fence." He wanted to help Paradise make this first move, but he couldn't force her.

"He's very handsome." Paradise took a couple of steps closer, and the color came back to her face. She gave her shoulder a final rub before she dropped her right hand back to her side. "Hello, Darth. Maybe we can be friends."

The jaguar's greeting rumbled again like a saw, and his tail lashed the air before he turned and went to the door into his shelter.

"He's done with us," Blake said. "I hear Tigey calling us."

Paradise's smile had returned, and he put his hand on her back and leaned in close. "Good job. How do you feel?"

"Relieved. It wasn't as hard as I'd thought it would be to see a black jaguar up close and personal again."

He'd never met anyone with a more beautiful soul than Paradise Alden. Blake started to lean down and kiss her, but Isaac tugged on the pocket of his shorts.

"Carry me, Blake."

Blake scooped up his little brother. Levi held up his hands for a ride too, but Paradise nabbed him. "You're mine, big guy." Levi wrapped his gangly arms and legs around her and smirked as if that had been his plan all along.

She was so good with the boys. How did she feel about having kids herself? He was getting ahead of himself and it was a question for the future, but he couldn't help thinking of a little girl with her wayward curls and extraordinary eyes.

He corralled his errant thoughts and walked toward the tiger enclosure. Tigey chuffed her usual greeting and approached them. The big cats had already received their evening meal, so she wasn't hungry. Blake started to pet her through the fence, but he didn't want to do that in front of the boys. They were already way too familiar with the white tiger, as the escapade with Isaac had proven.

"Beautiful girl," he crooned.

She rubbed up against the fence and chuffed another greeting. "I told you she likes you," Isaac said. "You're not scared now, are you?"

"No, but you must promise never to go inside with her again,

Isaac," Paradise said. "She could hurt you without meaning to. She's very big and has powerful muscles."

"And long claws like this." Levi curved his fingers into claws. "I thought she'd eat you even though it would've been an accident."

"Mom already told me," Isaac said in a sulky voice. "And so did Blake. I won't do it again."

"Can we see the zip line?" Levi asked. "Mom said it was going to be done soon."

"You bet. It's this way." Blake walked with the group along the oyster-shell path that led back to the entrance to the new attraction.

Another company owned the zip line attraction, but Blake had insisted on overseeing it to make sure it was safe. They climbed the wooden steps to the top platform that looked out over the predator area.

"It's really high," Levi said, his voice quavering. "I don't like it so high."

"You're a little young to go on it anyway, big guy," Blake said.

"I can do it. I'm not afraid." Isaac puffed out his chest. "You can lift me clear to the ceiling and I'm not scared."

"This is a little higher than the ceiling. And people will have to be eighteen to ride the zip line."

Blake planned to be the first to test it, and now that Paradise was recovering from the trauma of her mauling, he might be able to talk her into going on it with him. There was no real danger. The harnesses and lines were rated to carry several thousand pounds, and they'd made sure it was overengineered.

He glanced at her. "I don't remember you being afraid of heights. Does it seem scary to you?"

"Not the height, but what if something goes wrong, and we're dangling over the big cats? Or even worse, maybe it drops us right into the middle of the hyenas."

"It couldn't happen. The engineers made sure it was much safer than required. And we'll test it well without animals out there before they open it."

She gazed off into the distance where the setting sun glowed red and gold over the trees and the lake. "It's really beautiful out here. I bet it'll be a big hit. What about a night ride? You could set up special lights that don't disturb the animals but illuminate enough for the viewers to see them in their natural state. They're night prowlers. It might prove really popular."

"That's a great idea—I'll see what I can do with the lighting. Shouldn't be a big deal to figure out. We'd have to change our hours, but it might be worth it."

Darkness began to fall quickly. "Guess we'd better find Evan before he leaves for the day."

CHAPTER 25

AFTER DROPPING THE BOYS at the house for their baths, Paradise and Blake found Evan in the lion enclosure cleaning up excrement. She'd seen him from a distance during her time here, but she hadn't been close enough to speak since she'd avoided the big cats as much as possible. After a glance to make sure no lions lurked unseen in the area, she used her key to unlock the gate and slipped into the enclosure.

When the acrid stench of the big cats hit her nostrils, she froze for a moment. *You are not afraid anymore.* She would not go back to that fearful, cowering person.

Blake touched her hand. "You okay?"

She nodded. "I'm fine." She tipped up her chin, then strode toward Evan. "Hi there, Evan."

He turned into the sun to face them, and his eyes widened when he spotted her. "Paradise, I heard what happened with Isaac yesterday. Good thing you were there."

New lines had fanned around his brown eyes since she'd seen him last. He was a little taller than her, maybe five-ten, and his stocky build was all muscle and no fat. She caught the glint of a wedding ring on his left hand. His open, friendly face drained her animosity. Had she been wrong all these years, or was he just good at hiding his true nature?

She felt a crawling sensation up her back and knew it was her desire to be away from that smell of lions. "I'm very thankful the little guy is okay. We wanted to chat about the missing key situation."

His smile vanished. "I'm so sorry." He directed his apology to Blake. "The thought of what might have happened makes me want to throw up. I'm usually very careful with my key, but I had a sick kid at home, and my wife had just called with an update while I was unlocking the door."

"Is your little girl all right?" Blake asked.

Evan nodded. "It was appendicitis and she had surgery, which is why I took some vacation time. She's right as rain now though, bouncing around the house and driving Honey crazy. Any clue who took my key? I was sure someone would have turned it in."

"We haven't found it," Blake said. "And with the incident in the tiger enclosure, it's a very ominous sign. I think I probably need to change the locks."

"Good idea." Evan's gaze went back to her. "Um, this might not be the right time to say anything, Paradise, but I found a plastic tub of things in the attic recently. It had *Alden* on a piece of tape on the lid. I was cleaning things because we're going to put up drywall and make it into a play area for the kids. There was a panel to an area over the porch, and I backed out the screws and opened it up. The tub had been shoved in there."

"Did you open it?"

"I glanced through it. There was an old jewelry box, some

letters, and a baby book as well as some clothing. I thought you might want it."

"I would, thank you." Myriad questions flooded her mind—mostly, *why* was it hidden?

"You'll be interested in seeing what we've done with the place. You won't recognize it. I put in a new kitchen and opened up the wall between the living and dining rooms. We found good hardwood under the carpets too. I'd love to show it to you." He hesitated. "Unless coming back would be too painful for you." He paused, looking her in the eyes. "I don't have a clear memory of breaking into your house when you were a kid, but I know I scared you. It's bugged me over the years, and I want to apologize again."

So plausible. Too plausible? "Thank you. I'd love to see the house. Could I have a tour when I pick up the box?"

"You bet. How's Saturday? The kids are home, so it might be chaotic, but I'm off work. It gets dark so early, I didn't think after work would be a great time to see everything."

"I like kids. What time is good?"

"How about nine?"

"Perfect. We'll be back to the park before things get hectic. Thanks so much."

The cat stench made her eyes water, and she backed out of the enclosure, then took in a deep breath of fresh air.

Blake thanked Evan and followed her. "That smell got to you, didn't it? Your eyes were watering."

"Maybe I'm not completely over my phobia of big cats."

"You're a good seventy-five percent better."

He took her hand as they walked back toward the house, and she let him. The warm press of his fingers brought comfort.

"Why would my parents hide a tub like that? It didn't sound like anything important."

"You haven't seen it yet, so it's hard to say what might be in there. You'll want to go through all the clothing pockets and examine everything. Did it bother you to talk to Evan?"

"A little, but he wasn't as suspicious as I remember. He seems like a really nice guy. A family man."

"I've always liked him."

She stopped a few feet from the house. "You're not a good judge of people. You took me in and cared about me when you shouldn't have."

"Of course I should have. I didn't have any trouble seeing past that tough-girl exterior. You only think you hide your feelings well. A trained interrogator like me busts right through your defenses." He grinned, but his eyes were serious. "You have to let go of feeling like you're inferior to other people. You have so many gifts and special qualities."

Part of her wanted to hear what he thought, but she wanted to wait until they had time to talk about the future. This conversation could spin into a deeply personal direction that might make her tell him how she felt. And neither of them was ready for that.

———

On Wednesday after work, Blake went in search of Paradise and found her at the capybara habitat. The giant guinea pigs had a placid pool to enjoy and lots of room to meander around and climb on the rocks. Their habitat was a park favorite. He stood and watched Paradise return Hazel to her family after she'd been injured in a fall from a rock. The other family members chirped, whistled, and purred to welcome Hazel home as she lumbered out of the crate and onto the grass undulating through the area.

Paradise had tamed her hair in a bun that revealed the sweet curve of her neck and shoulders. The day was warm for late January, and she wore a sleeveless top that showed her shapely arms. Blake couldn't get enough of drinking her in.

She turned and caught him staring, and a flush spread across her cheeks. Her right hand strayed to the scars on her left forearm. "Where'd you come from?"

"I was looking for you." He grinned and reached out to snag the pin anchoring her bun and watched as her hair tumbled to her shoulders. "There's my Simba."

Her smile emerged. "You haven't called me that since I got here. I thought you'd forgotten."

"I was afraid of being smacked, but I couldn't help myself. Hey, I had a great idea. We should talk to Mrs. Steerforth."

"She's still around here?" She wound her hair back up and secured it in place.

He nodded. "After her husband was killed, she bought a place out on Fort Morgan Road. I'd like to find out if she felt threatened at all or if anyone tried to buy them out. I called to ask if I could stop by with a box of things I found in one of the sheds—a bunch of old children's books. Anyway, she told me to come by. Want to come with me?"

"I'd love to." She walked with him toward the parking lot and paused to wash her hands at the spigot attached to the gift shop. "She and her husband were always very kind to me. It will be good to tell her how sorry I am for her loss."

They resumed walking toward the truck. "She was badly mauled by that tiger. I hope that's not too upsetting for you."

Her fingers crept again to her left shoulder. "I'll be fine."

On the way south to the Gulf, Blake thought about asking Paradise on a real date, then tabled the idea. Their unspoken agreement to keep things casual until The Sanctuary was out of danger put the brakes on that possibility.

Traffic was light, and when they reached the address along the Gulf side of the peninsula, Mrs. Steerforth's porch and yard lights welcomed them.

She lived one house back from the beach, and the tranquil turquoise house sat on stilts in case of storm surge. Blake guessed it had been built about the time they moved away from The Sanctuary. He got the box of books from the back of the truck and followed Paradise up the steps to the back deck and entry door.

The door opened before he could knock, and Mary Steerforth stood holding it open for them. "Blake, so nice of you to bring the books." Her gaze went over his shoulder, and her brown eyes widened. "And Paradise? I didn't know you'd come back to the area." She stepped out onto the deck and opened her arms to embrace Paradise.

Mary was in her sixties but seemed older with the scars on her face and arms. Blake had to work at not glancing away from the damage left by the tiger. "Where do you want these?"

Mary released Paradise and limped to a deck chair. "Oh, just set them down anywhere. I'll probably take them to the used bookstore. I only had you bring them because I was lonely. I don't get much company these days. People wince when they see me." She touched her scar and glanced at Blake. "You did a good job of not showing any distaste."

"You've always been beautiful, Mary." And in spite of her scars, she was. Her lovely spirit shone through in her eyes and smile.

Mary gestured to the Adirondack chairs on either side of her. "Have a seat, kids, and tell me all about how The Sanctuary is doing. I don't get much news out here. Most of these places are rented by tourists, and they don't know any good scuttlebutt."

Paradise pulled a chair closer to Mary and perched on its white wooden slats. "I came on as vet and fill-in keeper wherever I'm needed. Jenna and Blake are doing a great job out there." She touched her shoulder. "You're not the only one scarred by a big cat, Mary. A black jaguar nailed me."

Mary's face softened. "Oh, honey, I'm so sorry. Are you afraid now?"

"I was, but I'm getting much better. I'm so sorry to hear about Allen."

"They killed him, you know. I suspect Hank was killed too, wasn't he?"

Blake gaped, then recovered his composure. "We have suspected his death wasn't an accident, but we've had no proof so we let it go. Who killed Allen? You think he was run off the road?"

"He was drugged. His blood showed a high methamphetamine level, and he *hated* drugs with a passion. Our only child died of a drug overdose, and he would rather be tortured than do any kind of drug. But of course no one listened to me, and I sit out here stewing about the lack of justice. I have to leave it in God's hands though. His justice is the best kind anyway."

"Who do you suspect?" Blake asked.

"Frank Ellis. He tried to buy the property, and when he couldn't, he killed Allen and planned to swoop in at the auction. But his funding got messed up, and your family slipped in before he could square it away. I'm sure he's ready to remedy that situation."

"We've suspected he might have something to do with the attacks at The Sanctuary too." Blake listed the different incidents.

Mary's expression grew more somber. "You kids will have to be on your guard. I don't know why he's so desperate to have it—there are other tracts of land for his subdivision, but he seems determined to acquire it."

And Blake was equally determined to prevent that acquisition.

CHAPTER 26

PARADISE AND BLAKE FOUND Jenna in the living room with her feet up on the sofa and a novel in her hand. The living room was neat and orderly, and Paradise sniffed the aroma of pizza hanging in the air.

She dropped her purse on the table by the entry. "I'm glad to see you relaxing."

"There's leftover pizza if you're hungry."

"I'm starved," Blake said. "Want some, Paradise? I'll nuke it."

"I like it cold."

He nodded and headed for the kitchen while she settled beside Jenna, who obligingly moved her feet away. "We went to talk to Mary Steerforth. Jenna, we're still reeling from what she told us."

Paradise launched into Mary's suspicions. "Blake and I talked on the way home. You used to date Frank. Would you want to have a little chat with him and see if you can feel out his involvement?"

"I wouldn't mind at all, but I need a ruse to contact him. I don't want him to think I'm about to cave and sell him the property."

"I wasn't sure where you were on those thoughts. After the tiger ordeal, you seemed to be willing to reconsider the idea."

Jenna put a bookmark in her novel and set it aside. "It was sheer fear talking. If people don't stand up against evil, what kind of world will we be living in? I still want to turn tail and run so I don't endanger my family, but what am I teaching the boys about having courage and facing down the wicked who want to destroy us? I would be cementing cowardice into their hearts. At least death isn't final, but cowardice is on a whole other plane."

Paradise's spine lengthened just listening to her friend. She'd always heard courage was not lack of fear but acting in spite of fear. Jenna was doing that now, and Paradise had done the same when she faced the tiger. Being courageous led to more courage, while being afraid led to more and more fear. She'd have to remember that.

She stood as Blake returned with paper plates of pepperoni pizza. "Yours is cold, crazy person that you are. The cheese on pizza should be all melty and gooey." He handed her a plate and a piece of paper towel. "I've never eaten cold pizza and never will."

"Have a bite?" Paradise tried to get him to open his mouth, but he kept it firmly clamped. When she persisted, his hand shot out and grabbed her in her ticklish spot just above her waist. She shrieked and nearly dropped the pizza as she danced back. "Tickling is no fair."

His grin widened. "Neither is forcing down cold pizza." He pointed to the sofa. "Go to your corner and I'll stay in mine." He lifted one of his pizza slices. "Ooh, nice, stringy, *warm* cheese."

It was the first time they'd joked with each other like the old days. Still smiling, Paradise reclaimed her spot beside Jenna and found Blake's mother watching them with a bemused smile. She didn't say anything, but she didn't have to—her joy in their clowning around was clear to see.

"Blake, I'm going to go see Frank, but the two of you need to help me come up with a good reason to ask to see him. I don't want him to think I'm going to sell out."

Blake swallowed his bite of pizza. "Don't you have a class reunion coming up? I thought I saw a postcard about it."

Jenna gasped. "You're right. All I have to do is pull him to one side. I hadn't planned to go, but the deadline for the RSVP isn't until next week, so it's not too late. I'll contact our class president and change my answer. We generally have ours in the winter because it's outside and we don't have to deal with the heat and humidity. I have to admit, I didn't want to go by myself. It's so soon after Hank's death that it will hurt to go alone. But I'll take one for the team."

"I could go as your plus one," Blake said. "It's not unusual to take a date."

"That's a great idea. Everyone knows I'm recently widowed, so they won't think anything about your escorting me."

"And I can take care of the boys." Paradise fixed a severe stare on Blake. "I'll need frequent text updates."

"I'll agree to that stipulation as long as you bake your favorite magic bars while we're gone. I haven't had those since you left, but I sometimes dream of them."

A laugh bubbled up in her chest, the kind of mirth she hadn't felt in so very many years. "Deal."

Jenna uncurled from her spot on the sofa. "I think I'll head to bed and leave you two to duke out the terms of the surrender."

Blake took her abandoned spot. He popped the last bite of

pizza in his mouth and wiped his fingers on the paper towel in his lap. "Just you and me, kid."

Paradise wiped her fingers on the paper towel and rose. "I think I'd better get to bed too."

"Coward," he said under his breath as she fled for the bedroom.

———

Final round of the night with the birds hushed and the park devoid of squealing children and boisterous teenagers. Blake loved strolling through the Thursday night darkness, listening to the sounds of predators interacting with their packs and exploring their spaces. The stars twinkled like diamonds on velvet in the inky sky. He should bring the telescope out for the boys again. The only thing missing in this moment was Paradise.

One minute she'd acted like she wanted to talk about *them*, and the next second she pulled back. Just like last night, but he couldn't blame her when he felt the same way. There would be time to face their feelings when they got to the bottom of who was plaguing the park. If he didn't discover the culprit, or culprits, behind the constant attacks, their donors would pull out and these animals would have to find new homes.

There had to be a common denominator, but he couldn't see it no matter how hard he examined the evidence.

He checked the entrance gates and found them secure. Time to head to bed, though it would be a wrestling match all night on the sofa. His pillow never wanted to stay under his head. He could sleep in his apartment with a gun by his pillow, but things had heated up so much, he wasn't sure how safe it would be to leave his family unprotected. He could install an alarm for the door, but truth be told, he liked being in the same space as Paradise. And he wanted to protect his family. An intruder would have an easy time slipping into the main house since it was on the ground floor.

He thought again about what Mary had said about Hank's death. The thoughts had churned in his brain since yesterday. Could the roots of all of this upheaval lie in what happened to his stepdad? It had never made sense. Hank had no reason to be in the hayloft. The Sanctuary bought hay and had it delivered, and teenage boys willing to work for minimum wage took care of tossing it down when they needed it. Hank had been a good guy—the best. He'd respected Blake's manhood and hadn't tried to treat him like a kid but as an equal. They'd become good friends, and his death wasn't fair. But was it murder?

Had he heard something in the hayloft? Hank left nothing to chance in the park and was constantly checking out the buildings and making sure things were running great. He could have been lured up there. Or maybe he'd never been there and the body was staged under the loft with the rail damaged and hay around to throw them off. It was such a puzzle to figure out on their own.

Mom missed Hank so much, and it hurt to see her bravely carrying on without him. And Blake couldn't let himself think about the boys missing their father or he couldn't function. A brother, even a present and loving one like he tried to be, could never replace a father. Hank had loved his boys so much and had taken them everywhere with him.

Blake shook his head and turned to go back when he heard a soft sound. Was that someone crying? The noise came from a copse of trees near the fence around the African safari, and he moved that way. The sobs grew louder, and he stopped as he tried to decide if he should make it his business. Sometimes people required a moment to themselves to deal with hard stuff. His intrusion could make things worse, not better.

It was clearly a woman crying though, and he couldn't walk away when he might be able to help. Keeping silent in case his presence was an intrusion, he sidled toward the trees and stepped into the cool wash of their leaves. He waited a moment for his eyes to adjust to the deeper shadows, then spotted Lacey on the grass with her knees hugged to her chest as she wept.

Not a good situation for him. Ever since she'd made her attraction clear, he'd tried to avoid her, and this moment of tears could have something to do with that.

She must have heard some slight sound he made because her head came up and the sobs stopped. "Who's there?"

Trapped. "It's just me. I'm sorry if I'm intruding."

She swiped at her face. "You're not intruding. Sometimes life gets overwhelming."

"I'm sorry. Anything I can do?"

"Not really." Her voice trembled. "I don't know if you knew it or not, but I'm raising my niece after my brother d-died two years ago."

It must have happened before Blake came back to help. "I hadn't heard you lost a brother. I'm sorry. That's hard." While he hadn't lost a blood brother, he still deeply mourned Kent's death and missed him every day. "How old is your niece?"

"Three. She's very stubborn." There was a smile in her voice. "I love her though. It's really hard—I know you understand that since you're helping out with your brothers. She was in the house wh-when I found Clay."

Blake took a few steps closer. "Man, how awful. How'd he die?"

"Overdose of sleeping pills. I think it was on purpose. He'd been despondent over some financial stuff. I tried to help, but working as a vet tech isn't the most lucrative job in the world." She laughed, but it was more bitter than anything else.

"You were working here?"

"Yeah." She got up from the grass and brushed off her shorts. "I like working here, so I'm not complaining, but I blame myself, you know? If I'd helped out more, maybe moved in with him, it might not have happened."

"What about his wife—your niece's mother?"

"She died in childbirth. Crazy, right, in this day and age? Blood clot. She would have loved Kinsey. All she ever wanted was to be a mama. Now there's Kinsey and all she has is me and my mom. Sometimes I feel like such a failure."

He started to reach out to pat her shoulder, then reconsidered. "She's lucky to have you. She's in daycare?"

"No, my mom watches her while I'm at work, so that's good. Her health isn't great though, and it's hard for her to keep up with a three-year-old. I worry she's going to say she can't do it one of these days. When I'm working nights is easy for her though— she just puts Kins to bed and goes on to sleep, then I pick her up in the morning."

Lacey tucked her hair behind her ears and took a step toward him. "I don't know how you do it. Helping your mom with two little boys, running this place on a shoestring, and now all the problems hitting here at once. You're pretty amazing."

"All we can do is take it a step at a time. Did you happen to see Evan's key?"

"I thought he told me he found it in his car, but maybe I was mistaken. I'll bet Isaac was terrified."

"Not really. You know kids. He thought it was a great adventure." Blake backed away. "I'd better get back to the house. I'm sorry you're having such a hard time."

"Thank you, but I'll live. It was a weak moment, but I'll be fine." She brushed past him and headed for the parking lot.

The encounter was a reminder to Blake that it was impossible to know another's heartaches. And her comment about Evan sent a tingle of alarm down his spine. Had the lost key been a lie?

CHAPTER 27

WHEN BLAKE PARKED IN Evan's drive on Saturday morning, Paradise sat motionless in his truck and stared at the brick home. The dormers had been painted black to match the shutters. The cut grass undulated in a green carpet toward the front door, but she couldn't make herself get out. The nightmare she'd had last night lingered in her fatigue and dry eyes, and she feared when the door opened, she'd see her mother's dead face like she had in her dream.

Blake touched her hand. "Paradise? We don't have to go in if you're not ready."

She licked her dry lips and shook her head. "I need to do this. Just give me a minute." She was still new at this prayer thing, but she sent up a silent request for courage. Inhaling, she reached for the door handle. "I'm ready."

Blake opened his door and climbed out. She waited until he came to her side of the truck before she took a step toward the house. Her legs were wooden pegs under her, and Blake took her arm.

"I've got you," he whispered. "Breathe. Nothing bad will happen. I think you'll like Honey."

His strong fingers holding her steady sent strength coursing into her legs, and she lifted her head and moved to the front door. It had been painted yellow and was a pleasing contrast to the black shutters. She pressed the doorbell and heard the sound of children playing inside. Moments later the door swung open, and the little girl she'd seen the day she arrived back in town peered out with curious blue eyes.

She smoothed the frilly pink princess gown she wore. "Hi, I'm Princess Polly. Are you here to see the king?"

Paradise bowed. "Yes, my lady. Is King Evan at home?"

"I think he's taking visitors. This way, please."

Paradise bit the inside of her lip to keep from laughing, and they followed the little girl. Polly led them to the living room where Evan, Nintendo Switch controller in hand, sat playing *Mario* with a little boy who appeared to be about five.

Evan turned and touched his daughter's head. "Thank you, Princess Polly. You want to finish the game with your brother?"

"No thank you, King Evan. My maid wishes to dress my hair in my bedroom." She curtsied to Paradise and Blake, then swished from the room.

Evan's grin widened. "Kids are so much fun." He touched the little boy's blond hair. "This is Kyle."

Kyle glanced over at the mention of his name. "Did you bring Isaac?"

"I should have, but I didn't bring him today. Next time."

"Okay." He turned back to his game. "I'll play for you, Daddy."

"Don't make me lose on purpose." He ruffled Kyle's hair.

Paradise took a moment to glance around the room painted a soothing taupe. The hardwood floors were stained a gorgeous light oak color, and the brown upholstered furniture was new.

The home had changed so much that it had retained no trace of memories for her.

"Want to wander around?" Evan asked. "Honey is getting groceries, but she'll be back any minute. Walk around and take it all in. Every surface has been touched in here. Not much left of the way it used to be."

Paradise nodded and walked through the small dining room to the kitchen with its white cabinets and white-and-gray-granite counters. The sweet scent of maple syrup lingered in the air. The floors were wood in here too. The bathrooms were fresh and new as well, and she peeked into Polly's open bedroom door into a fairy princess room of bubble-gum-pink walls and a matching comforter. A book absorbed Polly's attention, and she didn't seem to notice Paradise in the doorway.

The closet door stood open, and the hanging dresses, jeans, and tops were close to the same size hers had been when she lived here. Her lungs compressed, and she stared into the dark shadows of the closet. That corner was where her cousin had found her cowering and crying silently. She pressed her hand to her head. If only she could remember.

She backed away before she disturbed Polly and peeked into the other bedrooms. Nothing held a trace of her family, so she retraced her steps to find Evan and Blake in the living room.

Evan stopped midsentence in a discussion of a football play. "Done already?"

"Yes, thanks. Your home is lovely. You've done a wonderful job with the remodel."

"Thanks. Honey has great ideas, and I follow directions well." He rose and picked up a tub by the door she'd missed. "Here's the box I told you about." He shifted it to Blake.

"Heavy," Blake said.

"Papers and stuff weigh a lot. If you want to go through it now, you can use the dining room table."

"I think I'll take it home where I can take my time. Thanks for your hospitality, Evan."

"My pleasure." He hesitated, and his brown eyes searched her face. "I lived across the street."

"I remember." She kept condemnation from her voice. "You used to mow the yard. Did you ever notice Sheriff Davis coming to visit?"

Understanding settled in his expression. "It was always when your dad was gone."

So it *was* true. She nodded. "So I've heard. Did you hear anything that day? Screams, arguments, anything?"

Evan crossed his arms over his chest. "I saw the sheriff's car there, but that was all. I'm sorry, Paradise. It had to be hard to come here."

"It wasn't as hard as I expected. You made it easy." She turned toward Blake. "We'd better get back. I've got a grizzly to check out, and you'll have some safari tours. Thanks again, Evan."

"My pleasure." He walked them to the door.

Paradise followed Blake out of the house and to the truck. She said nothing until he'd stowed the tub and was behind the wheel. "At least I saw it all. There's nothing left of my family inside."

He reached over and took her hand. "Are you convinced it was the sheriff?"

"I think so. I'm closer to closure at least." She squeezed his fingers. "Let's go home."

Visitors wandered the high deck by the giraffes with leaves they'd purchased from the keeper. Angel, the park's oldest giraffe, meandered over to take a bite of a little boy's offering of vegetation. Blake grinned at the boy's obvious delight. This group was his last safari of the day, and they'd been fun and interested in his jokes and animal stories.

He rounded them up for the final excursion back to the gift shop and counted heads on the bus to make sure he hadn't left anyone. One short. Just great when he was already late. Mom had asked him to take the boys when he was done here so she could have an employee meeting about security changes with the keys.

He held up his hand at the front of the bus to ask for quiet. "Who's missing? Anyone know?"

An older man, bald on top and with his lower hair in a ponytail, held up his hand. "That girl with the green hair. I don't see her now, but she was sitting along the back."

Blake remembered her. She'd asked a lot of questions at the lemur encounter and had been interested in volunteering. What was her name—Nancy? No, it was Nicole. Nicole Grant. "Did anyone see where she wandered off to?"

A kid about ten pointed toward the far fence. "She went that way with some leaves. I thought maybe she was going to try to feed Angel one last time."

His mother waved her hand. "We need to return as soon as possible. I forgot some medicine for my son in the car, and it's already past time for him to take it."

Blake spotted the giraffe keeper, Zach Kelly, leaving with his cash box and stepped down outside the bus to beckon to him. "Zach, could you take this group back while I search for a lagging guest?"

Zach nodded and boarded the vehicle. The forty-year-old had been the source of a lot of advice after they took over. He'd worked here when the Steerforths owned it.

The African delta exhibit was the farthest enclosure from the gift shop, and they'd have to hoof it back, but sometimes that happened. He'd probably find Nicole sitting somewhere watching the giraffes and zebras. He waved to the guests and took off in the direction where she'd last been seen. He walked the length of the fence, clear to the back of the enclosure. Beyond that final fence was still preserve property, but they hadn't built anything on it yet. The dream was to put up some yurts and glamping tents, but funds had been too tight for that just yet.

She wouldn't have gone out onto bare land, would she? He turned and gazed out across the Africa area. He spotted water buffalo, giraffe, antelope, and zebra, but no green-haired girl. He did a complete circle and tried to catch a glimpse of anything out of the ordinary, but nothing stood out to him as problematic. The first sense of unease rippled down his back.

He pulled out his phone and texted Paradise. *You done for the day? I have a missing visitor I can't find.*

Where are you? I can come right now.

Back of the African enclosure, east side. I'm on foot. Grab my Gator. Keys are in it.

Be right there.

He pocketed his phone and tried to decide where to search first. They couldn't go into the enclosure on the Gator. Though the animals were friendly, sometimes they were a little too friendly and rubbed up against the vehicles out of curiosity. The water buffalo could tip over the Gator, and the zebras liked to kick and bite. He and Paradise could ride around the back of the enclosure, though, and check out the bare land behind it as well as drive to the other side and see if anything was awry there.

He checked the cameras he'd placed around the property. All seemed calm. Visitors, their arms full of stuffed animals from the gift shop, had begun to make their way to the parking lot. He closed the camera app when he heard the Gator's engine. The wheels plumed red dust behind them on the dirt trail, and his spirit took a buoyant jump at the sight of Paradise's curly mane of hair blowing in the wind.

She stopped the utility vehicle and smiled. "Need a lift, stranger?"

"My mother has always taught me never to accept rides from strangers, but she never warned me about a beautiful woman with twigs in her hair." He reached over and plucked a sprig of pine entangled in her light brown strands.

He tossed it to the ground, but he couldn't resist touching those soft curls again. "You've got the most amazing hair. One of these days I'm going to bury my face in it and not come up for air for days."

Pink rushed to her cheeks. "It's always a mess. Living with frizzy hair is one of the biggest trials of my life. And you're spouting off compliments when we're supposed to find a wandering guest."

"Good point." He grinned and went around to climb into the passenger seat. "This happens all the time, so I'm not really worried. I suspect she wandered back to the gift shop on her own. I see no evidence she's out here, but we at least need to do a cursory search."

He pointed to the back pasture. "Let's take a drive out there in case she got lost. If we don't find her in fifteen minutes, I'll check with the staff. Maybe they've seen her. We aren't babysitters, and we like guests to be able to wander at their leisure."

She nodded and drove that direction. When they rounded a copse of trees, he spotted Nicole's bright green hair. Her backpack lay on the ground, and she bent over ten feet from it with a small shovel.

She was so absorbed in her actions she didn't notice the Gator.

Blake motioned for Paradise to stop the vehicle, and he got out and approached Nicole. He paused at her backpack and noticed a collection of pieces of coal. A hole exposed more coal under the dirt in the area.

Her face turned their way, and a stricken expression settled over her features. She hastily put the shovel behind her back, but not before he realized what she was doing. Looking for natural gas or oil deposits. The area she had targeted consisted of dying vegetation as well as black coal deposits sticking up here and there through the dirt. Why had he never noticed there might be something valuable underground here? Why would she care if the land had oil or gas deposits?

CHAPTER 28

GAS OR OIL. BLAKE'S gaze swept the surrounding area, and he noted things he'd never consciously picked out in his walks around the property. How had he never noticed the terrain before? He turned his attention back to Nicole.

"Who sent you?" he demanded. It didn't take a rocket scientist to realize whoever had discovered this possible windfall might be behind what had been going on with The Sanctuary.

"No one. I'm a geological student, and the terrain caught my attention. I took pictures and wanted a coal sample to write an essay about it for my class. I didn't mean any harm."

Paradise hovered nearby to his right. "That makes no sense, Nicole. You came prepared with a shovel in your backpack."

The girl's chin tipped up, and she stared back with defiant green eyes. "I always carry a foldable camping shovel in case I notice something interesting."

Should he believe her? The words didn't ring true to Blake. "You took off without telling me where you were going, and I find you in an area that's clearly marked *Do Not Enter*. What do you think I should make of that?"

She shrugged. "I'm telling you the truth. It's a school project, nothing more."

"Where do you go to school?"

"TGU."

Tupelo Grove University was down the road. Maybe she was telling the truth, but something smelled off about it. "Hop aboard the Gator and we'll run you back to the parking lot."

Nicole grabbed her backpack and shouldered it before shuffling to the utility vehicle. Blake motioned for her to take the passenger seat while he hopped in the back for Paradise to drive them. His thoughts jumbled in a tangle of questions. If oil or natural gas was out there, did someone want to force them to sell before they discovered it? And what if they had it surveyed for their own purposes? The funds might help his mother immensely. But if they went that route, the expansion dream out here would be dead. It would have to be his mother's decision.

They reached the parking lot, and Paradise braked to let Nicole disembark. The girl glanced at Blake as if to see if he planned to detain her, but he shrugged and she scurried off to her car, a rusting green Subaru that matched her hair.

He took a quick snapshot of the license plate as she pulled away. He didn't know her last name, but he would. And Rod might find it interesting. He didn't see any reason to inform Creed Greene of the encounter. The detective wouldn't let facts interfere with his quest to pin everything on Blake, but the sergeant might be able to rein him in.

He settled in the passenger seat. "Let's take this back to the barn and head for the house. I need to tell Mom what we found."

"This could be good news, right?"

"I don't know yet." He told her his thoughts about how it might go. "If Mom doesn't want to give up her dream of yurts and glamping, we might still be dealing with someone trying to push us out so they can pick up the property for a bargain."

Her brow knitted. "It's so hard to know what's happening. Finances are still pretty dicey?"

He shrugged as she drove toward the barn. "I'm considering running some ads. Our visitor count is down compared to a month ago, so the negative publicity is having an adverse effect."

"What about social media? I'm pretty good at it. I know you shut it down because of the haters, but it's time to work on it again. I was thinking about it last night, and we could do funny memes of what the animals might be saying. Tourists would love that. Show the keepers interacting with the animals. What's the status of the zip line?"

"Nearly ready to go. Thrill seekers will love it, but I'm having an engineer take a final survey to make sure it can't dump a visitor in an unexpected place. With the way things have gone lately, I'll have to keep a close eye on things."

"Good call. If you don't mind, I'll take pictures and create some memes to use on our socials. We do still have the accounts, right?"

"Yeah, I just locked them down. I can get you the logins and passwords."

She pulled into the barn and turned off the vehicle in its corner spot. "Your mom is awesome. I want to help however I can."

He sneezed at the straw dust motes kicked up by the wheels. "You've been great. I'm glad you're here. In more ways than you know."

He longed to tell her how he really felt. To hold her and talk about the future. It was smart to stay focused on the gargantuan task facing them—especially since today had shown previously unknown obstacles—but now that she was back in his life, he wanted her to know he didn't take it for granted.

She turned off the vehicle and got out. He got out too and took her hand. "I'm late, so let's grab the boys from the employee meeting Mom has started by now. We could run into town and get pizza with them. Bring some back for Mom."

Her amber eyes smiled up at him with a promise he had no trouble deciphering. *Patience*, they said. It would be worth it in the end.

———

Light traffic dotted the streets of Pelican Harbor. Paradise had kept the boys entertained on the way to town by playing the license plate game, but they'd begun clamoring for pizza by the time Blake parked his truck in the parking lot. Pelican Pizza had been around since she was a teenager, and the aroma of garlic, cheese, and pepperoni made her mouth water when they entered. The iconic statue of a pelican guarded the entrance with a slice of pizza in its mouth, and the boys had to stop to touch it.

The hostess greeted Blake and led them to a back table near the arcade games. Levi and Isaac immediately asked to play, and Blake got up to get them passes. An hour pass for each was ten dollars, and it would satisfy the kids. They ordered pepperoni pizza and followed the boys from game to game until their food came.

Back at the table the boys dug into their slices, and Paradise nearly groaned when she bit into her first bite. "I'd forgotten how we used to love this place."

"We all still do," Blake mumbled around his full mouth.

Paradise never ate the pizza crusts, and she couldn't resist tossing a tiny piece at Blake like the old days. It hit him on the chin and left a tiny red smear. She wiped it off with her napkin and moved her crusts out of the way before he could retaliate.

The good feelings fell away when Creed Greene appeared next to him. "I'm surprised you're out celebrating after a tiger nearly took your brother."

Blake set his glass of sweet tea on the table. "Please don't talk about it in front of the boys."

Eyes wide, Isaac glanced up. "Where was Tigey trying to take me?"

The detective scowled and didn't answer. Maybe he'd allowed a little sense to enter his head.

Blake had said it wasn't worth talking to Greene, but Paradise wasn't so sure. His perpetual harassment had to end if he realized someone out there had an agenda and it wasn't Blake. "Detective Greene, we discovered something interesting today." She glanced at Blake. "Do you want to tell him?"

"I doubt it will do any good." Blake took a sip of his tea and shook his head. "We discovered someone digging in our back pasture a little while ago. From what I can gather, we might have natural gas or oil back there."

"Anything to try to throw suspicion off you, right, Lawson? I'm onto your games." He tipped his hat at Paradise. "Y'all enjoy your dinner. The food isn't nearly as good in prison." He sauntered out the door.

"Sorry," Paradise said. "I should have known he wouldn't listen. I thought maybe hearing more evidence would finally get through that thick head."

"I've given up."

"I haven't. Today's information is huge, Blake. How can we find out what's under the ground?"

"An official survey is probably pricey. I've never had one done, but I can only imagine how much it costs."

"What if we talk to some utility companies and see if they would sponsor the survey if you agree to let them put in the wells and pay for the gas or oil?"

"It might work." He straightened when his gaze landed on something over her shoulder. He rose and waved.

Paradise turned and saw Molly and her husband, Karson, waiting to be seated. She hadn't seen Molly since the family dinner, and her cousin's face lifted in a welcome that warmed Paradise. She'd wondered how things would be when they met again.

Blake arranged for more chairs to be brought over. "Glad you could join us."

Molly settled beside Paradise and hugged her. "What a treat to run into the four of you! Blake, your brothers are adorable."

Karson pulled out a chair by Blake, and the two launched into a conversation about football.

Isaac preened and scooted his chair closer to Molly. "I'm Isaac. I'm five."

"And a very cute five. I'm Paradise's cousin Molly. I heard you decided to visit one of the tigers the other night."

He nodded. "Tigey likes me."

Molly exchanged an alarmed glance with Paradise. "But let's not do it again, okay? Tigey might decide she wants you for lunch."

"She eats meat. I'm a boy." Isaac went back to eating his pizza.

Molly lowered her voice and leaned closer to Paradise. "Greene called Karson to ask about Blake this morning. He wanted to know if Blake owned a hunting knife. A big blade was used to kill the Mason woman. Like a hunting knife."

Karson's sporting goods store would be the likely place to check first. "I would guess lots of men in town have hunting knives."

"And Blake would have a military knife, right?"

"I don't know." But of course it was likely. He had been in the Marines. Wouldn't he have been issued a knife?

"The town is abuzz with speculation about the preserve. Is it true visitor counts have fallen off?"

Paradise didn't want to add to the speculation. "I don't have anything to do with visitors, but the parking lot has seemed full to me." She would do everything she could to turn around the negative perceptions floating around the area.

The preserve catered not only to out-of-state visitors but to locals as well. Some people had annual passes and came frequently. The ballooning issues would do serious damage to The Sanctuary's reputation if they didn't take steps to alter public opinion.

They finished their pizza over less controversial discussions and rounded up the boys to drive home. Paradise couldn't decide if Molly was concerned about The Sanctuary or trying to dig up dirt she could tell her friends. Her cousin seemed sincere, but Paradise had been burned too many times over the years to trust Molly's intentions. Paradise wanted to believe her family was on her side, but they'd never come to her aid in the past.

She helped get the boys settled in the back seat, looked over their heads, and locked gazes with Blake. These little guys, their mom, and Blake had quickly become more of a family to her than she'd ever experienced before.

CHAPTER 29

THE PRESENCE OF THE tub from her old home had been an itch between Paradise's shoulder blades since they'd picked it up this morning. Once Blake took the boys to their room for story time, she got the tub and carried it to the sofa, where she settled with it beside her. She eyed it and decided to wait to examine the contents until he joined her. Nervous energy—and not just the lingering odor of the pizza they'd brought home—cramped her stomach.

Fifteen minutes later, Blake entered the living room and dropped down on the other side of the tub. "I thought you'd want to do this right away."

He'd changed into athletic shorts and a tee for sleeping, and it was all she could do not to stare at his muscular legs. It wasn't just his physical strength and handsome face that drew her though—it was mostly that inner moral compass that radiated from him.

She touched the lid. "Where's your mom?"

"She and Isaac went to bed. They didn't even watch a little TV. She was exhausted."

"Levi is on the top bunk in my room?"

"They were both in Mom's bed, but he fell asleep halfway through the Justice League book I got him a couple of weeks ago, so I carried him to your bed before I came to find you. By the time you get in there, you'll have to move him to his side. Or sleep on the top bunk." He grinned her way.

Just the two of us. Warmth flowed through Paradise. Being with Blake centered her and tempered the pain she suspected she'd feel when she opened the tub lid.

He unclipped the ends of the lid and removed it. "You want to go through everything piece by piece? Let's make sure we check pockets and any possible hiding places. There has to be a reason your mom or dad tucked this away."

Inside she spied an old jewelry box, a packet of letters tied with pink ribbon, and a baby book. The clothing appeared to be infant clothing as well as some adult items. She lifted out the jewelry box. It would be the most likely place to hide something important.

Before she opened it, she examined it for the brand and any other information on the outside. She ran her fingers over the iconic LV monogram top in green canvas. The gleaming brass latches and lock added beautiful bling, and it had a leather handle at the front. "Blake, this had to have been expensive. My dad never would have been able to afford Louis Vuitton. Can you see what you can find about a value or original price?"

He nodded and took out his phone while she lifted the lid to reveal microsuede trays. A gorgeous set of sapphire earrings lay nestled in a compartment. A ring with a huge topaz stone rested in the next spot over. Paradise didn't remember her mother ever wearing such beautiful pieces. Where had she gotten them, and why had she felt the need to hide them here with the expensive jewelry box?

Blake leaned close to show her his screen. "Found it. The price right now is over six thousand dollars. I couldn't find its original price, but you know it had to be expensive. It's from the late 1980s or early 1990s."

"I was born in 1995, so Mom could have been seeing someone before she married Dad."

She turned her attention back to the contents of the jewelry box. One by one, she lifted out each of the trays to uncover more jewelry. A diamond tennis bracelet with matching earrings—and in the very bottom of a tray she found a diamond engagement ring in a velvet box.

Blake was close enough for her to catch the scent of his eucalyptus soap, and it soothed her agitation. He took her hand. "Whoever gave her this stuff was wealthy, Paradise. It couldn't have been Sheriff Davis, not unless he was on the take somehow."

"She might not have even known him then. I think this was someone she saw before she married Dad in 1992. Who gave my mom all this stuff?"

It was a rhetorical question, and she put the jewelry box aside with its contents and went through the other items. After she examined every pocket and fold of clothing, Blake checked them out too. Nothing had been hidden in the baby clothing or the maternity tops.

Something struck her. "Blake, the baby clothes are blue. I'm an only child. Could this belong to someone else?"

He picked up the baby book and flipped it open. His mouth sagged as he read the first page before he turned it around to show her. "Brace yourself, Paradise."

Andrew James Bartley.

"Bartley is Mom's maiden name."

"I remember."

She touched the line under it. "Born May 1, 1989. Just over five years before me." The implications hit her. "I have a half brother? Where is he?"

"That's the big question, isn't it? Did he die? Did she give him up for adoption? Maybe Lily would know."

Her lungs felt stuffed with cotton, and she couldn't pull in oxygen. All this time she'd thought she had no one. What if she had a brother out there? Everything could change. If he was alive, did he know about her? And if he did, why had he never contacted her?

"I—I can't take it all in." The last items remaining in the tub were the letters, and she reached for them. Her fingers fumbled with the ribbon, and Blake had to take the packet from her numb fingers and untie the knot.

"You want me to read one first?" When she nodded, he took the first envelope and extracted two handwritten pages.

She watched his expression as he scanned the letter, but he didn't show any sign of emotion.

"It's a female's handwriting, all in cursive. And she only signed a single initial." He turned the page around for her to see the large *A* scrawled at the bottom of the second page. "I think it's a letter from whoever adopted Andrew."

She had a brother. The knowledge tipped her world on its axis.

~

No matter how many times Blake searched for Andrew James Bartley, no leads popped up on his laptop screen. "I'm beginning to think his new parents changed his name."

They'd read all the letters, each one detailing milestones in the child's life—first step, first word, first time riding a tricycle, first day of kindergarten. But no hints as to who had adopted him. The few pictures showed the inside of buildings with no clue to location. There was no return address on the envelopes, and the post office stamp was Atlanta. It was a clue, but not one that helped much since the city was so large.

The clock on the wall sounded twelve times, and he yawned. Six would come way too soon, but he was too wired to sleep. And going to bed meant leaving Paradise, something he wasn't ready to do yet. He couldn't get enough of being with her. Ever since the tiger incident, she was different. More hopeful, warmer, and more willing to be with him.

He longed for the day the mystery was behind them and he could talk, really talk, with all their barriers down. The day was coming—he could sense it like skies clearing after a storm.

Her yawn followed his, and she leaned her head against his shoulder. "All we know is the letters were mailed from Atlanta."

"Yep." He could stay like this forever. Her faint plumeria scent settled in his lungs with a familiarity he never wanted to change, and the warmth of her pressed against his side was a comforting weight. It rattled his composure, and he had to struggle not to embrace her and tip her lips up for a kiss.

Soon, soon.

The reminder checked him, but it took determination to listen to his inner barometer.

"We should go to bed. I have a busy day tomorrow. I've got an otter with a likely heart problem I need to address after church, and I want to check on Rosy again. I think another fennec fox is picking on her. I might need to separate them."

"Your cousin comes to our church, and we could grab her after service before you go to work."

"That's a great idea. I thought I'd wake up early and put

something in the Crock-Pot for dinner. Your mom is worn out, and I want to start helping out with home chores."

He couldn't resist wrapping his arm around her and pulling her tight against his side. "Not many people would notice that. You're a good person, Paradise Alden." He rested his chin on her hair and pulled in another lungful of her plumeria scent. He'd never met anyone else who smelled like her—sweetness and light all wrapped up in a beautiful package.

One little kiss couldn't hurt, right?

Unable to resist, he touched her chin, and her face turned toward his without resistance. Her eyes radiated a calm promise that kicked his heart rate into high gear. He bent his head to capture her lips before she changed her mind. Her hand stole up to cup the back of his head, and he deepened the kiss. She gave a half sob, and he froze until she nestled closer.

When their lips parted, her hand moved to his cheek. "I wish I hadn't stayed mad at you so long. I should have come back as soon as I was of age."

"I should have gone to find you instead of escaping to the Marines."

"You joined up right away?"

He nodded. "It was a way of finding my dad. My uncle Ron recruited me, and Mom was ready to kill him. He was right though. It was time to be my own man, to find my own way. And I wanted Mom to find a life that wasn't all about raising me." He couldn't recover the lost years with Paradise, but they could go forward into a new future.

"Blake?" a small voice said.

He turned and saw Levi in his Spidey pajamas rubbing sleepy eyes. "Hey, buddy, you should be sleeping."

"I wanted you or Paradise and you weren't there." Levi's voice quivered. "I dreamed about Daddy."

"Oh, buddy." Blake rose and went to lift his little brother into his arms. "I know you miss your daddy. You'll see him someday in heaven. He's walking around with Jesus, taking in all the sights."

"But I want him *here*!" the little guy wailed, burying his face in Blake's neck.

A boulder formed in Blake's throat, and he wished he could take Levi's pain. He knew how it felt to lose his dad too, and even now, there were so many things he wanted to ask his father about. Mom had tried to be both mother and father to the boys, but it was impossible. Blake knew because she'd tried with him too. She was the best mom, but she wasn't his father. No one was.

He spotted Paradise wiping her eyes and knew she understood too. He wished the unrelenting pain of loss didn't have to be part of life, but it couldn't be changed. All the platitudes in the world didn't ease the hurt. It was something that had to be endured, not eradicated.

He squeezed his little brother tight and murmured comforting words in his ear. "You can snuggle with me here on the sofa," he said when Levi's sobs tapered off. "We'll lay there and think about fishing in the pond with the hippos."

Levi gave a small hiccup. "With Bertha?"

"Yep. She's back to burying herself in the water and spying on any fisherman who throws a fly her way. I'm sure she's lonely by now and wondering where you've been."

"Could we go tomorrow?"

"We have church, but we could go after work in the afternoon. Maybe Paradise will come with us, and we can teach her how to cast a fly. I'll bet she doesn't know."

"I don't have any idea how to do it. I think I need Levi to show me." Her voice held no trace of the tears he'd seen a few minutes ago as she rose and came toward them. She smoothed the little boy's rumpled hair. "I'm sure I can learn if you show me. Just like you told me what to call a group of hyenas."

He wiped his eyes. "A cackle." Levi lifted his head from Blake's neck. "It's pretty hard to throw a fly, but I won't mind if you miss it. I'll just show you again."

"Deal." She blew a kiss Blake's way and went down the hall.

CHAPTER 30

PARADISE TIPTOED INTO THE kitchen. Blake must be up somewhere in the house because the sofa was empty. She opened a window to let in the breeze before turning to her task of prepping for dinner. The boys loved Mexican, so she decided on her chicken fajita recipe. She found the slow cooker and plugged it in, then took chicken breasts from the freezer. She found peppers and jalapeños in the fridge and onions in the pantry, then grabbed the chopping board.

The sound of the park waking up wafted through the screen: the woodpeckers hammering, the lemurs cackling, the troop of monkeys screeching, and the water burbling from the artificial falls by the otter habitat. She inhaled the scent of early morning dew and the roses blooming in the backyard. This place held more and more allure to her, and it wasn't just because of Blake. It already felt like home.

She turned at a noise and spotted Jenna, dressed for church in a red dress that skimmed her hips and made her look twenty-five.

Her dark brown hair was up in a ponytail. "You're fixing dinner? I always knew I loved you."

"It's the least I can do for all the support your family has given me." Paradise eyed her. "You must have gotten a good rest. Your eyes are sparkling like you're ready to take on the new day."

Jenna stepped past her to take eggs and bacon out of the fridge. "Isaac stayed in one place all night, so I'm good. We have a busload of kids coming in at eleven and a group of seniors at noon. It's a good thing we have an early service. Should be a great day. At least some people haven't been put off by the rumors."

It was best to keep her mouth shut and not tell her boss about the rumors flying around Pelican Harbor. Paradise didn't want to dim Jenna's enthusiasm. "If it's okay with you, I'm going to do some social media posts. I'll get pictures." She told Jenna about her plans, and Jenna's smile widened.

"That's wonderful, Paradise! I haven't had time to do any of that. I'll text you the login information." She glanced toward the slow cooker. "What's for dinner?"

"I'm making chicken fajitas for wraps or quesadillas, whatever anyone wants to do with it."

"My mouth is already watering." Jenna put bacon on a cookie sheet and slid it into the oven, then cracked eggs into a bowl. She picked up a whisk. "You guys were up late."

Jenna had lived here a long time, and she had known Paradise's mom. Could she remember something from back then? "I found out something shocking last night, Jenna." Paradise put the lid on the Crock-Pot and turned to face her. "My mother had a son five years before I was born and gave him up for adoption. The evidence was in the old tub of belongings Evan gave me yesterday. Somewhere out there is an older brother I've never met."

Jenna's whisking paused, and she turned toward Paradise. "You never knew?"

Paradise studied Jenna's lack of surprise. "You knew?"

"Becky got pregnant her junior year. I was a sophomore, and we played volleyball together that year. She went off to stay with a cousin the summer between her junior and senior years. When she came back in August, she had no baby with her. I assumed she gave the baby up for adoption. I never heard if she had a boy or a girl."

"No idea where she went?"

The aroma of bacon began to rise from the oven. Jenna poured the whisked eggs into the skillet and grabbed a spatula. "She was closemouthed about it. I tried to ask questions but got shot down. I think your grandmother warned her not to say anything. Too bad she isn't around to ask."

Before Paradise was born, her maternal grandfather had died in a farming accident, and her grandmother died of cancer when Paradise was five. She had vague memories of a stern-faced woman with blonde hair who yelled at her a lot. Her mother had let her spend the night with her grandmother once, and Paradise had cried so much Mom picked her up at ten that night. There had been no grandmotherly snuggles or gifts that Paradise could remember.

"The letters from the adoptive parents were postmarked in Atlanta, but there's no guarantee that's where she had him. Blake suggested I ask my cousin Lily if she knows anything. I want to find him."

Blake spoke from behind her. "Hez might be able to help with that."

Paradise turned to see him. His hair glistened with moisture from his shower, and he wore khaki pants and a red shirt. "You're going to ask him?"

"I already called him, and he's going to see if he can find records."

Jenna checked the oven and pulled out a tray of perfectly browned bacon. "Is there a national database?"

Blake snagged a piece of bacon. "No, it's run by states. It would help if he had an idea where she went that summer. Hez will start the search in Atlanta."

"Another route would be a DNA test," Jenna said. "You hear stories about people finding relatives that way all the time. Maybe your brother had his done."

"I hadn't thought of that avenue. I think that's fast. I can order one right away. They're not that expensive. It's worth a shot."

"In the meantime we can check with Lily, and Hez can poke around. If Lily has an idea of where your mom went, he can target that state first."

The television flipped on in the living room and the sound of cartoons blared. "The boys are up. I'll call them for breakfast and make sure they're dressed for church," Blake said.

Paradise's thoughts spun with the possibility she might find her brother sooner rather than later.

———

Church was like a whole new world for Paradise. She hadn't stepped foot inside a church in years, and her soul drank up the words and music like a parched desert. Blake's shoulder pressed against hers on her left, and Jenna sat on the other side of him. Lily had come in after the worship music started, and her cousin had nodded in her direction.

After the ending worship song, Paradise shook hands as she edged her way toward Lily, while Jenna went to grab the boys from junior church. Blake caught Paradise's intent and helped create a passage through the throng so she could intercept her cousin before she escaped.

"Lily!" Paradise called as her cousin moved toward the exit.

Lily turned and reversed direction to come toward her. "I'm so glad to see you here, Paradise. I love that top on you. The orange brings out the red in your hair and makes me think of your mama."

"I really wanted to talk about Mom a minute. Do you have time?"

"Of course. There are several prayer rooms off the foyer. We can use one."

Paradise shot Blake an expression of entreaty, and he followed them to the room and closed the door behind him. He stood back and let her take the lead with the questions, but Paradise wasn't sure where to begin. If Jenna knew about the pregnancy, surely Lily did as well.

Lily's smile vanished. "Don't be scared, honey. I won't bite. What's wrong?"

"The owner of the house where Mom and Dad died found a hidden tub in the attic. Did you know Mom had a baby before I was born?"

Lily put her hand to her mouth. "That was in the tub?"

"You knew, right?"

Lily gave a jerky nod. "Of course, we all did. Grandma Penny was horrified. I thought she was going to kick your mom out onto the street, but she ended up sending her away. Your mom didn't want to give her baby up for adoption, but Grandma told her she'd have to find another place to live if she came back with a baby. They compromised with a private adoption where your mom got updates on the baby."

"Do you know where Grandma sent Mom?"

Lily shook her head. "Your mother was told not to tell anyone. I tried to worm it out of her—we were close after all—but she was terrified of Grandma. So was I, so I understood. All she admitted was she had a healthy baby boy. She met the parents and felt he was going to have a loving home. She never stopped mourning him though and lived for those letters and the occasional picture she got."

"Why hide that information in the attic?"

"She didn't want your father to know. He was from out of town, and by the time they married, she didn't think anyone would bring it up to him. Grandma had shut down any speculation, and once your mom left school, the episode faded away. There were new things to gossip about, so she felt safe."

Blake shifted by the door. "Do you know who the father was?"

Lily glanced his way. "I don't know his name, but I saw him pick her up in a shiny new Camaro after volleyball one night. He had to be ten years older than she was, maybe even fifteen or twenty. At first I thought it was a friend of Grandpa's, but she leaned over and kissed him before she shut the door. The interior lights showed it was no friendly peck on the cheek. This guy wasn't afraid to throw his money around a little. And like I said, he was much older."

Which would explain the expensive jewelry box and jewelry inside. Mom probably had to hide all of that from her mother before she ever became pregnant. Grandma Penny would have taken a gander at any of those pieces and known Mom wasn't dating a high school boy. No one in Pelican Harbor lavished so much money on their son that he could give gifts like that in high school. And Lily had seen an older man.

"Do you know where he lived?"

"No idea. I only saw him the one time, and your mom didn't

disappear every weekend, so I don't think his visits were common. Maybe every two or three weeks. Honestly, she was so secretive about him I thought he might be married. Why else keep it such a secret?"

"Because he was older?"

"But if he was wealthy, I don't think Grandma and Grandpa would have cared about that. You were so young when Grandma died you probably never knew she grew up poor and pushed Becky and my mom to marry well. I don't think your dad ever measured up in her eyes. Mine either, for that matter."

"Did my dad ever find out?"

"Not that I know of." Lily glanced at her watch. "I'd better get going unless you have another question?"

Paradise shook her head. "Thanks for your time. It helps me understand a little more."

But it brought her no closer to finding her brother. She and Blake walked out with Lily and found Jenna and the boys waiting in Jenna's van. The busy day stretched ahead, and Paradise hoped she'd be able to forget all about this for a while.

CHAPTER 31

BLAKE DROPPED HIS MOM and brothers at the house. Then he and Paradise headed to the drugstore to buy her a DNA test. They grabbed one and hurried back to the van for their busy afternoon.

Paradise buckled her seat belt and turned her phone around. "Look."

He saw the cute picture of Bertha yawning. The caption read: *I'm tired of waiting for you to visit.* "Cute."

Her frown indicated it was anything but cute to her. "No, read the first comment."

And we're tired of having a murderer next door. Your sins will find you out.

He exhaled. "Wow, a hate message already. See who left it."

"I already did and it's not a real profile. The person duplicated someone in New York and the profile only has five friends, so it's been done recently. It's almost like someone was watching to see if we started using the socials again."

"Can you delete it and block them?"

"Yep. I'll do that now." Her fingers moved across the screen.

"Whoever is behind this campaign to smear us may make another account, but I'll try to stay on top of it."

"I'll ask a few friends at church to make encouraging comments. And some of our loyal visitors may start commenting too. Thanks for doing this."

"You're welcome." She dug out the DNA test and flipped it over to read the back. She groaned. "Oh man, it takes six weeks for results. I'd hoped to hear something quickly."

"The time will fly. In the meantime we can continue investigating who might be targeting the park." A pothole loomed in the road ahead, and he swerved to try to miss it, but one tire thumped hard into the crater. Something rattled under the seat and continued to clatter on the smooth highway. "Could you see what that is?"

She leaned over and reached back under the seat. "Ouch." She withdrew her hand with one finger bleeding. "It's got a sharp edge whatever it is." She grabbed a napkin and blotted the drop of red from her finger. Then, using the napkin, she reached under again and gasped at the item in her hand.

Blake glanced down and automatically braked at the sight of an orange hunting knife in her hand. He swerved to the shoulder of the road and stopped the van. "Paradise, someone has planted the murder weapon in the van."

The knife slipped from her fingers and hit the carpet by her feet. "What do we do?"

"I don't know. If we give it to a deputy, it'll have your fingerprints and blood on it. With Greene's determination to pin the murder on me, it would be more ammunition for him." He reached for his phone. "I'd better see what Hez has to say about it."

Before he called the number, Paradise put her hand on his wrist. "No, don't. It's not fair to put him in the position of telling you to do something illegal. We need to figure this out ourselves. We could wipe the knife and report it."

"But then there'd be no evidence to glean from it."

She sighed and stared down at it gleaming in the light streaming through the window. "What if we have it examined for evidence ourselves? Well, with Hez's help."

"That's not a bad idea." He placed the call, and Hez answered almost immediately. "Big problem here, Hez." Without waiting for a hello from his cousin, Blake launched into the discovery of the knife.

"It's your mom's van?"

"Yeah, I only drive it when we all go to church together."

"Whoever planted it might have tipped off the police to check it out, so we'd better move fast. Savannah's best friend is a forensic tech here in Pelican Harbor. We're having lunch with her in a few minutes. Can you bring it to me in the parking lot by Billy's Seafood?"

"I'm only fifteen minutes away. We'll be right there." Blake ended the call and put the transmission in Drive. "Hez says we need to get this thing out of our possession. We're meeting him at Billy's Seafood."

───

Paradise kept her foot away from the side of the knife as if it were a tarantula waiting to jump. If it had been planted after the murder, the evidence was likely very contaminated from rolling around under the seat for nearly three weeks. She couldn't believe

Creed hadn't shown up with a search warrant. Or was someone waiting for the perfect moment to tell him about it?

"How's your finger?"

"Fine. It was only a scratch." She spotted Hez standing with a woman with shoulder-length auburn hair and green eyes. "That's Savannah?"

"It sure is. I haven't seen her in a while." Blake pulled into a parking space beside them and got out to envelop Savannah in a hug.

Paradise left the knife on the floor and went around the front of the van to greet Hez. Fine lines fanned from his blue eyes, and he was still very trim and fit. The sea breeze lifted his dark hair, and somewhere out on the water a boat horn blared. "You've been such a big help, Hez. I don't know what we'd do without you."

His voice, as deep as a cello, rumbled against her ear as he hugged her back. "Blake is my cousin as well as my best friend, so you're part of the family by extension." He released her. "This is Savannah."

Paradise knew their tragic story and immediately bonded with Hez's ex-wife. They were still dealing with their own problems. "It's great to finally meet you. I'm sorry we're butting into your lunch date."

"I'm not. I told Hez yesterday I wanted to meet you." Her smile faltered when she glanced toward the van. "I'm sorry there's more trouble looming for you both. Nora should be here any minute. I told her to meet us in the lot by the pier and to bring an evidence bag. That's not something Hez carries around with him, though he should."

"With you two around, I'd better invest in a box of them," Hez said. "There's Nora now."

A white Nissan pulled into the lot and parked on the other side of the van. A brunette with glasses got out and came around the van to join them. "You started the party without me."

Hez introduced everyone. "Someone planted a knife in the van, Nora. Paradise found it under the seat, and it cut her so it's going to be contaminated with her DNA. Just telling you that up front. We suspect it's the Danielle Mason murder weapon."

Nora's brown eyes darted to Blake. "You should call the detective handling the case."

"Greene has already told me he's pinning this on me. He'd haul me in and toss me in jail. Someone planted that knife. I've never seen it before, and we found it accidentally."

Nora chewed on her lip before she gave a reluctant nod. "I'd likely be the one who runs the evidence on it anyway. I can tell Sergeant McShea how it came into my custody."

"Please run the evidence first, just to make sure Greene doesn't yank it away from you and plant fake evidence on it."

"You really don't trust him, do you?"

Blake's brows rose. "Do you?"

When Nora didn't answer, Paradise took that as a yes. "I left it in the van and didn't touch it with my bare hand again."

"I'll need to do a complete sweep of the vehicle as well." She glanced at Savannah. "I won't be able to join you for lunch. This will take some time."

The woman didn't seem disappointed, more determined and focused, so Paradise thought she didn't mind the intrusion into her day too much. Nora went to her car and popped the trunk to extract a case of equipment that she carried to the van. She got out a pair of nitrile gloves and an evidence bag, then picked up the knife gingerly and dropped it into the bag.

It was the best view they'd had of the hunting knife, and Para-

dise had never seen one like it. The bright orange blade would
stand out, and it would be a deadly weapon.

"That's some knife," Blake said. "It's not military issue."

Nora studied it through the plastic. "It's a Benchmade Raghorn."

Blake started to step toward her, then stopped and put his
hands in the pockets of his jeans. "Not familiar with the brand,
but then, I'm not a hunter."

"I'm not either, but Greene will find out more about it." Nora
laid it aside and pulled out her phone. "I'll call for help to process
the vehicle. Go ahead and have lunch."

"You and Paradise want to have lunch with us?" Hez asked.
"You're going to be stuck here awhile anyway. Savannah and Paradise can get acquainted a little better."

Blake glanced at Paradise, and she nodded. Hez might know
more about her brother, though she assumed if he'd discovered
anything, he would have dropped that news already.

Paradise watched Nora begin gathering hairs and fibers at the
driver's door. This could be the moment that turned the investigation around. It might clear Blake and point to the real killer.

Or it could be another boulder on his back that would sink
him, and they'd all go down with him.

CHAPTER 32

THERE WAS NO AROMA like the blend of grilled oysters and seafood gumbo, and Paradise realized she'd skipped breakfast after doing her PT. Their table at Billy's Seafood had a view of the marina with its boats bobbing in the waves, and the place was full.

Hez slipped his arm across the back of Savannah's chair. "I'm glad we've got a minute. I had an unexpected call last night—the box containing the evidence collected after the Alden murders turned up. I ran up to Bay Minette and picked it up. It turned up some interesting information."

Paradise tensed beside Blake, and he put his hand on her knee. "Steady," he whispered.

Paradise had thought she was ready to hear it, but Hez's somber expression caused acid to churn its way from her belly to the back of her mouth. "What did you find?"

"The Nike shoe belonged to Sheriff Davis. My informant believes that's why the evidence box was buried in the basement. There are witness statements that his truck was parked down the street and a neighbor saw him running from the house before law enforcement arrived."

Finally, an answer to the question she'd wrestled with for twenty years, yet somehow it left her feeling cold and bereft. Shouldn't a resolution carry a sense of peace? "So that's it then. It's over."

"I can bring this evidence to McShea so the truth is out."

"Then what would happen?"

"People would know the truth."

"Truth." Bea's sorrowful face in her memory segued to her beam of pride about her grandchildren. She'd kept quiet to protect her family. Did Paradise want to explode the peace they'd found by saying this was the truth? "I'm not sure truth is what I wanted. I think it was justice, and Davis is already dead and gone. Digging up these bones would hurt his wife and children who did nothing."

Hez nodded. "It would be a bomb exploding in their lives, but it might be worth it for the case to be wrapped up with no more questions."

"It wouldn't be worth it to Bea and her kids who have gone on to build their lives. She's so proud of her grandchildren. The truth would trash the memories they have of Gerald, and it wouldn't change anything for me. My parents are still gone. I think I'd rather focus on finding my brother, no matter how long it takes."

Blake's approving smile warmed her and maybe even crept a bit into that cold space where the memories of the night of her parents' murder had begun to stir. "Hey, Savannah, can you get into the TGU enrollment records?" He laid out the story of the student digging on the property.

"My sister can. I'm happy to get it for you. Or you can meet me at TGU tomorrow if that works better in case you have more questions."

"I'd like to meet you there, if that's okay. I might have more questions. Is eight too early? That would give me time to get back for the park opening."

"That's fine." Savannah gave him directions for where to meet.

The server brought their food, and they chatted over lunch. Paradise liked Savannah more and more. Maybe she'd found a new friend in the area.

By the time they finished their meal, Savannah had a text from Nora. "Your van's ready for you to take."

Blake's phone sounded with a message too, and he glanced at it. "Mom says the boys are dying to go fishing, so I guess our afternoon is planned out for us."

Paradise was ready for a day of mindless fun with the boys so she could evaluate how she felt about this turn of events. The resolution of one question had come, but finding her brother might prove to be even more difficult.

Tupelo Grove University was showing its age and lack of funding. Blake noted the overgrown landscaping and weedy walkways. The massive tupelo trees in the quad needed limbs removed. He parked in the lot on Oak Lane. Only a few students were out and about.

He and Paradise got out of his truck, and he pointed out a gator sunning itself by the pond in the greenbelt. "There's Boo Radley."

She gasped and a delighted chuckle emerged. "He's still here? He's grown a lot."

"He's an icon around the school, and I think the students feed him even though they're not supposed to." He examined her face.

"You got a little sun yesterday out fishing. I'm going to cook up our fish for dinner tonight."

He pointed out the administrative building to Paradise and steered her that direction with a light touch on her elbow. They entered the wide hall with its soaring ceilings and followed the signs to the CFO's office. A young woman in her early twenties greeted them. "May I help you?"

"We're supposed to meet Savannah Webster here to chat with her sister. I'm her cousin, Blake Lawson." While she and Hez weren't remarried yet, it wouldn't be long.

The secretary nodded. "I'll let them know you're here." Her sneakers squeaked on the marble floor as she went to the tall door to Jess's office and vanished inside.

Seconds later, the door opened and Savannah exited with a welcoming smile. "Blake, you made it. Come on in. Ms. Legare has a few minutes before her first meeting of the day, and I was about to clue her in to the issue."

Jess's secretary exited behind Savannah and stood out of the way for them to enter the office. Blake knew Jess and Savannah's family ties ran deep at TGU. Jess rose from behind the desk. She wore a green sleeveless dress that contrasted with her blonde hair and deepened the flecks of green in her hazel eyes. Piles of paperwork covered her big desk and a window overlooked a green space with park benches under towering live oak trees.

Blake shook her hand. "This is the park's vet, Paradise Alden."

Jess indicated for them to have a seat in the chairs facing her desk. Savannah perched on the corner of the desk since there were only two seats.

"Welcome to TGU," Jess said. Her curiosity about their visit hung in the air.

"I'll try not to delay you, but I wondered if you could help us.

I'm sure you know about the constant barrage of attacks at The Sanctuary."

"Oh yes. I'm sorry you're having to deal with it."

"We had a new wrinkle over the weekend." He told her about Nicole Grant and her claim she was working on a school project. "Her story *could* be true, but it seemed a little too convenient."

Jess frowned. "And if it was for a school project, she should have contacted you or your mother and asked permission. We certainly wouldn't condone her taking coal or digging on your property without authorization."

"Have you heard whether there might be a project like that in your geology department?"

"Hang on, let me see what classes she's taking. I can direct you to her professor." She jiggled the mouse on her desk and leaned toward her computer screen. After a few moments of study, Jess leaned back in her chair. "We don't have a student named Nicole Grant. We have no Grants at all and no Nicoles. I checked in case she gave a false name."

"I had a feeling her story was bogus."

Savannah hopped off the edge of the desk and came around and hugged him. "You've been so good to Hez, and I'm grateful."

"He's like a brother instead of a cousin. I'm glad to see things are going so well for both of you." He released her.

She turned to Paradise and hugged her too. "I'm sure we'll be seeing more of each other, Paradise. I'll walk the two of you out." Savannah waggled her fingers at her sister. "Thanks, Jess."

He and Paradise added their fervent thanks as well, and moments later the two of them stepped out into the sun as Savannah headed back to her office.

"I like her so much," Paradise said.

"She's great. I'll tell you more about their story sometime.

They've traveled some rough roads together and made it to the other side." He walked with her back past the greenbelt toward his truck. "I'll shoot Hez that plate number and see what he can discover about Nicole Grant."

He opened the truck door for Paradise, and she slid in. He shut the door and noticed a man watching them. He climbed under the wheel of his truck. "See that guy across the pond? Do you recognize him? The tree shadows are hiding his face, so it's more his shape that's familiar."

Paradise stared through the windshield at the figure who continued to watch them. "Let's go find out." She hopped out of the truck and started that way.

Blake followed and stepped in front of her. "Let me go first. He could have a weapon."

"I don't think he's dangerous. He's not running and doesn't seem to mind that we've seen him."

The man stepped out of the shadows, and Blake recognized him instantly. "It's Clark Reynolds." Had he followed them to continue his vendetta against Blake?

CHAPTER 33

NO THREAT LURKED IN Clark's brown eyes, and his smile was stiff but not threatening. It was like watching an angry turtle attempting to smile but failing. He stood with his hands thrust in the pockets of his jeans. Dogs barked off to Paradise's right, and she caught a glimpse of his two German shepherds trying to escape his truck's interior, but the windows were only open six inches.

"Hey, Clark." Paradise kept her tone even and friendly.

"You didn't expect to see me on a college campus, huh? I graduated high school by the skin of my teeth, but I'm no dummy."

"I know you're not," Blake said. "Kent always bragged about how you could fix anything with your welder but a broken heart and the crack of dawn."

A genuine smile tugged Clark's lips higher. "I forgot he used to say that."

"How'd you find us here?"

"I was coming to The Sanctuary and saw you turn out and head this way. I followed." He yanked his hands from his pockets and stared at Paradise. "Why'd you do it?"

"I've been in a tough spot where I didn't know where to turn myself, and God told me to do it." Would he receive the truth? Even if it made him mad, it had to be said.

"God, huh? God hasn't bothered with me in a long time."

"God is never the one who moves," Blake said.

Paradise shot him a glance of thanks. "Blake knows more than me. I'm new at this God thing myself, and all I know is I felt a nudge telling me to help you out, so I did. I hear this new walk is one step at a time."

Clark's gaze went from her to Blake and back again. "This wasn't a trick to get me to 'forgive'"—he made air quotes with his fingers—"the guy who killed my brother?"

"I didn't even think about that."

"Weird." He turned toward his truck and yelled at the dogs to be quiet, and they quit barking. "I'll pay you back."

"I don't want to be paid back. It was a gift."

"I don't take charity."

"You ever get a gift from someone before?"

"Only from family, and you aren't family."

"Maybe not, but it was still a gift. Help out someone else if you like."

"How's the old truck running?" Blake asked.

"Like a spring chicken hunting for bugs. It hasn't purred like that in forever. I went to town and got welding supplies and happened to acquire a new customer. She wants her Victorian iron fencing repaired. It's a big job that needs to be done on-site, and I couldn't have taken it without wheels. No way to bring my equipment there without the pickup." He shuffled his feet. "So thank you. I appreciate it more than you know."

But Paradise did know, and her fingers went to the ache in her shoulder. "You're welcome." She'd come here as a last resort to find her life again. Jenna and Blake had been there for her, and she finally saw a way through the maze of pain her life had been.

Clark gave a final nod before plodding toward his truck. His shoulders were squared now as if having his truck lifted the weight from his shoulders. Paradise watched him get in the truck and drive off. He waggled his fingers through the open window one last time.

Blake draped his arm around her. "When you wanted to do that, I thought you were crazy. You did a good thing, Paradise. He seems like a different guy. I don't know that he's able to move past Kent's death yet, but he's one step closer."

She nestled against his side and lifted her face to the morning sunshine. "To be honest, I thought it was crazy too. I hope it makes a difference in his life. So now what do we do?"

"We wait for Hez to find Nicole's address, and then we'll follow up with that. And I think I should find someone to come and see what we've got underground. I need to talk to Mom about it, but I haven't had a chance yet. I mean, she knows about Nicole and that there might be oil or natural gas on the property, but I need to find out what she wants to do if there's a valuable deposit under there. I hate seeing her work so hard."

"She loves the place though."

"She does, and it's been her dream for a long time. But it was Hank's dream first, and maybe she'll decide she wants something different for her life without him. We haven't talked about things of the heart like that." He pressed his lips against her hair. "Maybe she'll open up to you. Girl talk, you know. I'm her son and sometimes I think she doesn't want to worry me."

"I can see if she opens up. I really love your mom. She's a special person."

"More than you know. She didn't even date when I was a kid. It wasn't until I was grown and off on my own that she was willing to find out what she wanted for herself from life. I worry she's doing the same thing now with the boys, and I hate to think about her sacrificing everything for her family."

"I doubt she considers it a sacrifice. Jenna has always been about family."

"She's a great mom, but she's so much more than just that. Smart with business and with people. I want her to have a full life."

"You're more like her than you want to admit. You threw over a job you loved to come help her raise the boys. Did you consider it a sacrifice?"

His low chuckle rumbled in his chest under her cheek. "Got me. No, of course not. Nothing is a sacrifice when you love someone."

It was a truth she was only beginning to realize herself.

———

Paradise could smell fennec fox in her hair after work, so she took a quick shower, pulled back her mane, and went to help Jenna with supper. There shouldn't be much to do since she'd put the ham and beans in the slow cooker this morning. She found Jenna pulling cornbread out of the oven, and the sweet aroma mingled with the salty tang of ham.

"Wow, that smells great." She spotted green in it. "Green chiles in it?"

Jenna nodded and grabbed a knife to cut it. "Blake loves it that way. I'll have to give you the recipe."

Paradise bit her lip to keep from smiling at Jenna's blatant

assumption that Paradise might want to cook for Blake sometime. It wasn't a wrong way to think. "I'd like that." She lifted the
steamy lid of the cooker and checked the bean soup. "It's done
whenever we want to eat it."

"I already chopped lettuce too. You want to wash the cherry
tomatoes?"

Paradise took the bowl of tomatoes to the sink and turned
on the water. "We spoke to TGU today. Jess told us Nicole isn't
registered at the university."

Knife aloft, Jenna turned and gaped. "It was all a lie?" She
went back to her task of prepping the cornbread.

"Not a word of truth. Hez is tracking down the license plate
number, so we're not at a dead end yet. What do you think about
that whole gas or oil thing? Have you thought about what finding it on your property might mean?"

"I haven't had time to think about it. It shouldn't really change
anything other than I wouldn't be able to do the glamping out
there. There's another spot I could use, or I could forget the whole
idea. The campground could be very lucrative though."

"What if the land was so valuable you could sell it all and
never work again?"

The question hung between them, and as the seconds dragged
out, Paradise wasn't sure Jenna was going to answer. Had she
never considered how her life could change if she wasn't running
this very busy animal refuge?

Jenna used a spatula to put pieces of cornbread on the serving
plate. "Selling out isn't an option. It would mean giving up Hank's
dream. As long as I have this place, he's still close. I see him everywhere on the preserve. Playing with the baby goats, feeding the
animals, splashing in the pool with the tigers. He's everywhere,
Paradise. I can't walk away from that." Her voice quivered.

"I'm sorry, Jenna. Your pain is still too fresh. Blake and I would love it if you didn't have to work so hard. Between The Sanctuary, homeschooling the boys, church, and housework, you never have a minute to yourself. You don't sleep well either. You can't keep burning the candle at both ends and not have a health crash eventually."

"I'm fine. I like to keep busy. I don't know what I'd do with myself if I didn't have The Sanctuary." She glowered at Paradise. "Did Blake put you up to this? Without the preserve to run, he could go back to the Marines. He loved his job so much, and I hated for him to give it up."

"He'd never leave the boys. You should know how much he loves them."

"I do know, but I also know he loves you. He always has, Paradise. He never really got over you. People think young love doesn't last, but I know better."

The direct and pointed statements struck Paradise squarely in the heart. "H-he's never said that."

"He won't yet. Not until he's sure of how you feel and probably not until he's out from under suspicion for the murder. If we're having a heart-to-heart, just how *do* you feel about him? I'd hate to see his heart broken again."

"I don't plan to do that, Jenna. Life doesn't offer second chances very often. We haven't talked about the future yet because we have to focus on whoever is out to destroy The Sanctuary. But I have no plans to leave."

She couldn't tell Blake's mother that she loved him. Not when she hadn't yet spoken the words to Blake. And the time wasn't right.

Relief washed over Jenna's face. "I'm glad to hear it. I'll stay out of your business. Just know I never want me and the boys to stand in your way."

"That would never be an issue. I love you and the boys. You are a great mom, and all three of your boys are pretty wonderful. Blake worries about the sacrifices you've made for him, and he wants to see you happy again."

Oops, she shouldn't have said that. Now Jenna would know for sure Blake had asked Paradise to talk to his mom.

"I'm as happy as it's possible to be with Hank gone. The Sanctuary keeps me busy and content. I wish money wasn't so tight, but God has provided week by week. This brouhaha will pass. The truth will come out. It always does eventually."

Paradise finished washing the tomatoes and laid them on a paper towel to dry. Did truth always come out? In her experience the bad guys continued their secret work unhindered and justice never came. But she was new at this whole trusting God thing. The old saying "The wheels of justice turn slowly but grind exceedingly fine" came to mind. God had exacted justice on Gerald Davis by now, but the thought only made her shudder.

CHAPTER 34

BLAKE HAD INVITED PARADISE on a walk through the refuge once the boys were asleep. He loved the park at night with the predators' eyes gleaming as they passed and the other park animals sleeping. February was two days away, and the chill felt good after the warmth of the kitchen. Paradise shivered, so he draped his arm around her.

She moved a little closer. "I should have brought a jacket."

Her hair was still a bit damp from her shower, so he wasn't surprised she was cold. "I've got a jacket in the barn. We can stop and grab it." He quickened their pace toward the building looming ahead in the dim glow of an overhead light.

She kept pace with him, and they stepped into the barn, which smelled of hay and straw. He grabbed his lined denim jacket hanging on a nail and draped it over her. Her face tilted up toward him, and he couldn't resist the temptation to brush his lips across hers. Her arms came up around his neck, and he pulled her into a tighter embrace, deepening the kiss. Her lips were soft and welcoming, and he relished her response.

He pulled back and thumbed her lower lip. "How did I ever live without you?"

Her mouth curved up under his thumb. "I thought we weren't going to talk about us yet."

"I never said that."

"It was in your eyes."

"Oh, so now you're a mind reader?" He tugged the jacket back onto her shoulders. "I guess it doesn't take much of a mind reader to know how I feel about you."

She stilled, and her expression tensed as if she wasn't sure she was ready to hear it. And maybe she was right and this wasn't the time.

His phone sounded in his pocket. "Saved by the bell?" he whispered. He glanced at the screen and swiped open the call from Hez. "Hey, bro, you find something?" He kept possession of Paradise's hand and walked with her out under the stars.

"Yeah, it came up under a stolen plate. Some guy in Birmingham reported it stolen a month ago. I also searched for Nicole Grant online, but none of them in the area matched her age and description. No hits."

"So it appears she was part of the bigger picture of the attacks on The Sanctuary."

"I'd say so."

"Well, thanks for checking, Hez. I appreciate it. Put it on your bill."

"Oh, I did, and it will require a full day of fishing at the pond out there."

"You got it." Smiling, Blake ended the call and told Paradise about the dead end.

"What about a reverse image search?" Paradise asked.

He steered her toward the vet facility since she wanted to check on Rosy, who was back in the infirmary with another sprain. "What do you mean?"

"I snagged a picture of her on my phone as I got there to pick you up. I could upload it and have the search engine try to find Nicole's picture. If she's got her photo out there somewhere, we might find out who she really is."

"That's brilliant! Let's give it a try."

"Let me check Rosy first." They reached the building, and she pulled out her key and unlocked the door.

A breeze touched his face, and he frowned. "You feel that? Did someone leave a window open?"

"I checked the windows and doors before I left tonight, and everything was locked up. Let me see if Rosy is okay." She rushed to the room down the hall where sick animals were housed in crates.

Blake followed her. If someone was in here, he didn't want her surprised by an intruder. Rosy was the only animal in the kennel room, and Paradise already had her crate open. The little fox lay curled in a far corner. "Is she okay?"

Paradise did a quick exam. "Seems to be." She latched the door back in place. "Let's check out the other rooms. The window in here is locked."

"Let's check the office." Blake hurried down the hall to the office door that stood open. "Was this locked when you left?"

"I locked it myself." She reached past him and flipped on the light.

The breeze intensified, and he spotted a side window open. The screen that should have been in it lay damaged on the floor. "Someone knocked it in." He turned in a half circle around the room and spotted the safe standing open. "We've been robbed. What was in here?"

"Just a little money for miscellaneous supplies we buy in town. Some research Lacey was working on. Some of the more dangerous anesthetics we use. That's all I can think of."

"See what's missing, and I'll check with Lacey too."

Paradise nodded and went to kneel by the safe. She pulled everything out and began to go through it. "None of the drugs are missing, which seems strange. I would have guessed the burglar was searching for drugs. I'll check the drug cabinet."

He followed her to the locked metal cabinet where she consulted a page that listed the contents. "It's still locked." She unlocked the cabinet and ticked off quantities of drugs. "Nothing missing here either."

"So what was the intruder searching for, and did they find it?" He launched the camera app on his phone and called up the playback for the lens outside the vet building. Frame after frame was black. "Someone erased the video feed or managed to turn the camera off." He showed her the screen. "There's nothing on it."

"There was the break-in at the house too. The guy is searching for something, but what?"

He put the screen back in place, then closed and locked the window. "I think I'll put up a couple of secret cameras. I need to get to the bottom of this. But first, let's try that reverse search."

———

Paradise opened her laptop. Blake sat close beside her with his arm on the top of the sofa behind her. It would be difficult to concentrate on the reverse search when she wanted to lean against him and talk about the future he'd been ready to discuss before

Hez called. Maybe it had been a blessing in disguise though. They should stay focused on the problem at hand.

She found a reverse photo search and uploaded the picture from her phone. They watched the progress circle and several photos appeared. "There she is. We have to pay to unlock the app and view the details, but wow, that was fast."

He whipped out a credit card and handed it to her to type in the number. Minutes later they had her real name: Nicole Iverson. He leaned closer. "She's thirty and is a private investigator."

"What on earth? Who would have hired her—and why?"

"Whoever is trying to drive us off. And I have a strong feeling it's all about the oil or gas deposits under the land. I need to find out what's there and what it's worth. It could be the key to everything."

A murder, an arson, shots fired at them, break-ins, possible deposits underground—how did it all tie together? They'd missed something, but she struggled to think what it was. Something tickled the back of Paradise's mind. "What about Hank's death? We have left it out of everything we've examined. Who had reason to want Hank dead? Someone who thought your mom would be an easy mark to get her to sell? Or could it be some personal reason?"

"I don't know of any enemies Hank had."

Paradise shifted and tried to keep her excitement in check. "So let's find out. Let's start at the beginning, before things went wrong. Let's examine the history of how he and your mom bought this place. How long were they married?"

"They were married a year before Levi was born. And Hank died six months ago, so seven and a half years before his death."

She launched a page in the word-processing program and notated Blake's answers. "He was always interested in exotic animals, and working for him a few days a week is what got me interested in veterinary work. When I left here, I knew I wanted to be a vet. What happened to his first wife? I can't remember her name."

"Susannah. She had a brain aneurysm and died during childbirth. The baby died too. I think you'd been gone about two years when that happened."

Paradise put her hand to her mouth. "That's terrible."

His blue eyes went somber. "She ran the office, and he hired Mom after Susannah died. She'd worked for him for about three years when he asked her to go to dinner." A smile slipped out. "I was home on leave, and she was like a schoolgirl trying to figure out what to wear. She wasn't sure she should accept—she was ten years older. But by then she knew she cared about him. Before that, he'd hinted around that he'd like to date her, but she managed to fend him off. He finally caught her with her defenses down."

Paradise's heart ached for the pain in his face. She took his hand and laced her fingers with his. "You loved seeing your mom settled and content."

He nodded. "I'd never seen her so happy. They dated two years just to make sure, but I knew the first time I saw them together that it was meant to be. She married him and moved into his big farmhouse that abutted this place. The next thing I knew, she was pregnant with Levi, and they were both so thrilled. Hank was a great dad. He loved those boys with everything in him." Blake's voice thickened.

"And when he died you flew home to help your mom and the boys." She leaned her face against his, and his breath mingled with hers.

Talking about this kind of loss scared her. What if she opened her heart fully and lost Blake again? She didn't know if she could take it. She released his hand and ran her hands across the rough stubble on his face.

His fingers grazed her chin and lifted her gaze to his. "Don't be so scared. We can't borrow trouble, like my grandma always used to say. One day at a time is the only way to live life. Mom doesn't regret a moment of that life with Hank even though it ended with such heartache. She wouldn't have the boys or the memories."

His head came down, and she welcomed his kiss. The tenderness in his lips reverberated all the way to her toes. He was right. What did anyone achieve by being afraid to live? Loneliness was hard no matter how it happened.

"I'm glad you're here. We all want you with us. Me most of all, but Mom and the boys need you too."

"I feel the same way." She leaned her forehead against his. "So let's dig into Hank's life before he died. Maybe there's something." She drew back. "I talked to your mom before dinner too. She has no interest in replacing Hank anytime soon. She sees him everywhere here, and she doesn't want to sell this place. Maybe not ever. She finds purpose here. Your mom has a giving soul, not just to her family but to the animals in need too. She would never want this park closed and housing put in its place. She asked if you put me up to it so you could go back to the Marines."

He gave a snort of laughter. "Oh man, that would be a trip. I'm not leaving my girl now that she's back in my life."

With his arms wrapped around her, she wasn't going anywhere either.

CHAPTER 35

BLAKE HAD TAKEN FULL buses on the safari tours today, and his smile felt broken. Paradise's new social media blitz must be having some positive effect. He loved the job, but the weight of the refuge having a target on its back pressed down on him and made it hard to be himself with the visitors. After a shower, he went in search of his mother and found her with Paradise on the back deck cooking chicken on the grill.

The late-January day was a warm seventy, perfect for an outdoor supper. The boys dug happily in the sandbox in the middle of the backyard—far enough away for them not to hear the questions he intended to ask.

He gently elbowed his mom out of the way. "I'll take over that duty. Go sip some iced tea with Paradise." The aroma of grilling chicken made his mouth water, and he lifted the lid and flipped over the pieces before brushing on barbecue sauce. Veggies steamed in foil packets on the top shelf. "What else are we having?"

"Paradise made potato salad and I made white chocolate–

macadamia cookies with the boys for dessert. I think there are still some left after the boys 'helped' me."

His mom's chuckle was relaxed and happy, which eased his worry. Blake shot a glance at Paradise, who nodded for him to go for it. "Um, Mom, Paradise and I were talking last night about everything hitting the refuge at once. She pointed out that we haven't taken a hard look at Hank's death."

She trailed a finger over the lip of her glass of sweet tea. "You mean you still think Hank's death might have been the first attack?"

"It's possible," Paradise said. "We thought we should talk about the months leading up to his fall from the hayloft. Had he mentioned any incidents that puzzled him? Had there been any threats against him?"

His mom's forehead creased. "No threats that I'm aware of. He did seem strained the month before he died. Kind of skittish, peering out windows—that kind of thing. I asked him why he seemed tense, and he brushed it off as employee problems at the clinic in town."

"He maintained his vet business after acquiring the refuge?" Paradise asked.

Jenna shook her head. "Hank signed the vet business over to Owen Shaw for quarterly payments on its worth. Owen was gone for three weeks on an anniversary trip, and Hank agreed to fill in for him. I thought his stress was from trying to keep everything going."

"Did anyone talk to Owen about Hank's death?"

"Not in relation to it possibly being murder. He got back the day before Hank died."

Blake flipped the chicken again. "Did you ask him about the employee issue?"

"He dismissed it when I tried, and things were hectic here with starting to homeschool Levi. I should have pushed it more." Mom's voice wobbled.

Paradise reached over from her chair and took his mom's hand. "It wasn't your fault, Jenna. Don't ever think that. And maybe it's not connected, but it seems very strange for such a weird accident to happen and then for all this stuff to start."

Mom sighed and stood to tell Isaac not to throw the sand out of the box. She settled back in the chair. "It's been six months though. If it was connected, why the delay?"

"Maybe to let things die down," Blake said. "I think I'll talk to Owen. He likely has heard of our troubles, at least some of them. It's possible he knows something."

He removed the food from the grill and turned it off. "Food's ready," he called to the boys. "Go wash up." While they ran into the house to wash their hands, he carried the food to the table under the pergola. Tableware and bright blue plates had already been set around the glass-top table along with the cookies in a covered plastic container to keep the bugs out.

The boys came running out of the house in high spirits, and Levi wrapped his arms around Blake's waist. "Blake, can we go fishing after dinner?"

Blake lifted him in his arms. "It will be dark, buddy, and we just went two days ago." He pointed to the sun already sinking in the west over the tupelo trees. "But it's a clear night. We can bring the telescope out and search the skies. We can see Jupiter."

"And its four moons!" Levi hugged his neck and Blake put him down.

"You're right. You're getting good at astronomy."

"Mom's been teaching me. Did you know Daddy wanted to be an astronomer when he was a teenager? I think I should be one."

"I didn't know that." Blake glanced at his mom, whose eyes had misted over at the mention of Hank.

The boys wolfed down their dinner so they could have cookies, and Paradise helped Jenna clear the table while Blake set up the telescope. He'd forgotten it had been Hank's. Somehow it had always seemed to be here, and he thought maybe Jenna had gotten it for the boys. As he adjusted the lens, he stopped and stared at it. This was a high-end piece of equipment and it took pictures. Hank had been using it with the boys the night before his death. Could he have snapped any suspicious photos of the area around the yard? It was unlikely, but after Blake was done here with the boys, he wanted to check it out.

—————

Paradise and Jenna watched Blake with the boys at the telescope. The clear night would provide great viewing. With no breeze it was a comfortable temperature as well, and the peaceful setting with the buildings and enclosures around them made for a perfect evening. Paradise was envisioning a walk with Blake again tonight. Maybe this time they wouldn't be interrupted by the knowledge of another break-in.

"He's so good with his brothers," she said.

"He was a kid magnet even when he was ten. I've always thought he would make a great father, and he jumped right in when Hank died. There aren't many men who would give up their career and rush to help out."

"He's pretty wonderful." She cleared her throat to give her a moment to push away the images of Blake with his own children. With *their* children. "What do you think of our theory that Hank was the first casualty of this war against the refuge?"

"I've never thought it was an accident, but I tried not to dwell on it. The thought made me a little crazy. And honestly, I couldn't think why anyone would want to harm him. You remember what he was like—always kind to people and animals alike. He often took care of animals for free when the owners didn't have the money. After his first wife died, the trauma made him even more considerate of others. Why would anyone deliberately toss him out of the hayloft?"

"Why would anyone send a dead body to the park? Or shoot at us at the grizzly enclosure, or try to tempt a tiger to hurt someone? All the attacks have seemed random and unrelated, but there has to be a reason for all of it."

"To get me to sell."

Paradise gave Jenna a one-sided hug and released her. "Hold tight, Jenna. We will figure it out." Blake gestured for them to join him. "I think we're being summoned." Jenna on her heels, Paradise got up and walked across the deck to where Blake and the boys clustered around the telescope. "See something exciting?"

Isaac took her hand. "You have to see Jupiter's moons, Paradise! Look." He dragged her to the telescope, and she peered in. It took a moment to adjust to what she was seeing. A bright star with four pinpricks of light, one on the top left and three trailing off the bottom right, came into focus. "Wow, you're right."

"Can we show her Polaris?" Levi asked. "It's my favorite."

"Sure." Blake moved the telescope to accommodate his brother. "Have a peek."

She peered into the eyepiece again. "It's so bright through the telescope."

"That's the North Star. It's like the Bible of the sky. It helps sailors navigate," Isaac said. "Just like the Bible helps us navigate life."

The total trust in his voice struck her, and she took another peek at the bright star. Until now she hadn't been navigating her life by any sort of standard, yet these boys had been taught so much about faith already. She had a lot to learn.

"Boys, bath time," Jenna said.

"Oh man," Levi complained. "Can I see Polaris one more time first?"

"You have two minutes," his mother said.

Paradise stepped out of the way for him to take another peek. She studied it with bare eyes. "The Big Dipper points right at it."

"It makes it easy to find," Isaac said. "I want to see too."

Levi stepped out of the way for his brother, and when both boys were finished viewing, they turned to run to the house with their mother. Their happy voices faded as they went inside, and the chirping of crickets took their place.

"Could you shine the flashlight on your phone this way?" Blake asked. "I've been waiting to search the SD card in the telescope."

"Sure." She turned on the app and focused the beam on the telescope. "It takes pictures?"

"Yeah, and I wondered if Hank could have caught anything suspicious on it. He sometimes used the telescope to snap pictures of the animals out in their enclosures and the buildings in the distance. It's a long shot, but I have to check. I didn't want the boys here when I did it in case there was something problematic to see."

She watched him fiddle with the compartment and pop out a micro SD card. "I'll grab my laptop and card-reader adapter." She rushed inside and retrieved the equipment, then hurried back where she found Blake waiting at the table.

He took the laptop and slipped the card into the adapter, then opened the files. "There are twenty-one pictures."

The screen changed to pictures of the night sky, and he flipped through sixteen of them. The seventeenth photo was of tigers prowling the enclosure, and Paradise's pulse blipped. Blake studied it before moving to the next one, hyenas staring at the fence.

He studied it. "Nothing out of place there. I think he was taking pictures for social media."

The screen changed to the barn where he'd died, and she leaned forward to study it with him. "Is that someone in the shadows?" She pointed out a dark blob on the west side of the barn.

"It might be." Blake enlarged the picture. "I think it is. The person is short. See what appears to be the head and its relationship to the light switch on the barn wall?"

"Maybe it's a woman?" They had ten female employees. "Check the next photos. There should be two more."

He advanced to the next picture, which showed the same scene as the prior one. "The figure is still there."

In the last photo the figure was illuminated by the overhead light. "That's Lacey," Paradise said.

"She often wanders around at night."

Was that all it was? Paradise had her doubts.

CHAPTER 36

WHEN WAS THE LAST time Blake had been to the old vet building in Nova Cambridge? Before his mom and Hank bought the preserve three years ago, he had stopped in to bring them both lunch one day when he'd been on leave. Mom had been pregnant with Levi, so it was over seven years ago.

He opened the door for Paradise and they stepped into the waiting room. The after-hours cleaning had left it smelling fresh with only the faint odor of dog. "Owen said he'd be in the back and to come on in."

They walked through the office to the door leading to the back kennel area where the vet held overnight patients. Owen was a short, stocky man in his midforties with thick red hair and freckles.

When the door closed, he slid a food bowl into a dog crate before turning an open, friendly expression their direction. "Blake." He shook hands and Blake introduced Owen.

The two dogs in crates began to bark, and Owen gestured toward the door. "Let's go into my office and let these two settle."

They followed him into a crackerbox office barely large enough to hold a metal desk and two chairs. He perched on the corner of his desk and gestured for them to be seated in the chairs. "How can I help you?"

Blake launched into all that had happened in the past few weeks. "But it all started with Hank's death. I wondered if you heard anyone complain about him after you got back from your trip."

"Complaints?" Owen shook his head. "Everyone knew and loved Hank. There was nothing to clean up after I got back other than having to find a new vet tech. Lacey decided she couldn't handle two jobs and had to quit one. She picked this one to torpedo instead of The Sanctuary. She said Hank really needed her help."

Lacey. Was there any connection? It didn't seem likely. Lacey was all of five-two and 110 pounds soaking wet. She wouldn't be able to toss a big guy like Hank over the haymow. And someone had stabbed Danielle Mason to death and gotten her into the horse trailer. Lacey didn't have the strength.

"Would you mind if we went through your files?" Paradise asked. "There might be something that would jump out at us."

Owen gestured to the front office. "They're all in there. Help yourself and lock up when you leave. I need to get home for supper and a play at school. My daughter has the lead role, and she'll have my hide if I miss it."

Blake stood when Owen did. "Thanks, Owen. It shouldn't take long, and we'll lock up."

They filed out of the tiny office, and Owen exited through the back while they went to the front office. Paradise yanked on the top drawer and took a handful of files. "You start with these, and I'll grab another batch."

Blake sat in front of the stack of files and began to go through them. Dry reports of cuts, kidney problems, sterilization procedures. Nothing stood out.

Cross-legged, Paradise sat on the floor. "Here's something."

She handed him a file. "It's an employment file. I'm not sure Owen even knows this. It reads that Lacey was fired for cause. Hank caught her in a clinch in the back with Karson Asters."

"Whoa. That's not good." He studied the statement. "Paradise, this was the day before Hank died. Could Karson have wanted to keep the liaison under wraps? Maybe he went to see Hank and they argued in the barn and he killed him."

"You don't really know if he fell from the hayloft, right? He was found dead at the bottom of it with a broken neck."

"Right." Blake's thoughts spun. "Karson is a quiet, congenial guy. It's hard to imagine he'd be that violent."

"It's the best lead we've gotten though. I think we should talk to him. It won't do any good to ask Greene to do it. He'll blow us off again."

Blake glanced at his phone. "It's five thirty. Karson's outfitter store closes in half an hour. Let's try to catch him. When we're done, I'll take you to dinner. How's Jesse's Restaurant sound? You'll have to behave there though. No throwing pizza crusts. I told Mom not to wait on us because we'd be late, so we don't have to be home early. Mom even said not to try to be home for bedtime. I won't know how to act if I stay out past nine."

Her laugh always lit up her eyes and warmed her cheeks with color. He loved to hear the joy in it too. "I take it you're down with dinner alone?"

"Are you saying I have to behave? I mean, I'm not sure I can promise that."

His grin widened, and he carried the stack of files back to the filing cabinet. "Would you settle for some spilled coffee instead of flying pizza crusts?"

"As long as you replace it. Coffee is a precious commodity." Her smile flashed, and she put her files away too.

He caught her hand and walked with her to the front door, where he pulled it shut and tested to make sure it was locked. Karson's Sporting Goods was across the street, and the parking spots were all open. Maybe they'd catch Karson alone. They waited for a sports car to zip down the road and then jogged to the door of the business. Through the plate-glass windows he spotted Karson at the register. There were no customers Blake could see.

The door jingled as they entered, and Karson smiled when he saw them. "Blake, Paradise, what a nice surprise. What are you searching for tonight?" He was a big guy, muscular with sun-streaked blond hair. He wore a purple polo shirt with the store logo on the front.

Blake released Paradise's hand and approached Karson. "Just a little information. You've likely heard of the attacks at The Sanctuary." He waited for Karson to nod. "We realized we hadn't considered Hank's death as a possible link."

Karson paled under his tan. "I thought Hank died in an accident."

"Mom and I never believed that. It was very unlikely he was in the haymow. So we started poking into the weeks before his death. Were you angry when he fired Lacey after he caught the two of you making out in the vet office?"

Karson grabbed the edge of the counter and gaped. "No. I mean, it wasn't my business." He shot a panicked glance at Paradise. "Molly doesn't know about this. Please, for the sake of our family, don't say anything. I haven't seen Lacey since that day."

"Did you go see Hank? Maybe try to talk him into letting Lacey keep her job?"

"No, we never spoke of it again. Actually, I never talked to him after that confrontation. He died the next day." He blinked and inhaled. "I mean, that sounds bad, doesn't it? I didn't mean it that way. I went home to Molly and my kids that night and never strayed again. You have to believe me."

Blake wasn't sure what to think, but he'd gotten all the information Karson was going to give out willingly.

———

Jesse's Restaurant was busy as usual. Blake had opted for the newer location on the bay out on Fort Morgan Road, and it was Paradise's first visit there. Their legendary blue-crab-and-crawfish gumbo was the first thing she ordered for her appetizer.

She had been on plenty of dates over the years, but she couldn't remember a time when she had more butterflies taking up residence in her stomach. Maybe the first time the man across the table from her tonight had asked her out as a gangly teenage boy had come close. But the Blake of today had erupted into the full potential she'd glimpsed in him all those years ago. And he was too handsome for words with his shock of dark hair and eyes as blue as the water in the bay outside the window.

Blake set down his glass of iced tea. "You're staring at me. Did I do something wrong?"

She shook her head. "Sorry. Just thinking about what Karson said." *Liar, liar.* If she tried telling him the truth, what would he say? His humility wouldn't let him accept any of the thoughts teeming in her brain right now. "Did you believe him?"

"I don't know. He's strong enough to have killed Hank, and his panic at his affair getting back to Molly was very real. Would that kind of raw fear be enough for him to kill to keep it quiet? Maybe so. But I'm not sure he has murder in him."

His phone dinged with a message. "He couldn't be sure no one else knew either. But we don't have a better suspect right now."

He glanced at his phone. "The predator zip line is ready for testing. Mom will be excited. We got the report from the engineer, and that thing is strong enough to hold an elephant. I need to tinker with the lighting a bit, but I'll do that in the next couple of days and we'll be ready to fly." He grinned. "Pun intended."

"Visitors are going to love it."

"We hope so. It's been in the works a long time. We had to jump through all kinds of hoops to make sure it's safe." He reached across the table and took her hand. "But enough about that. Have I told you lately how beautiful you are?"

Her cheeks heated and she found it impossible to think with his thumb rubbing lazy circles in her palm. "Not lately, no. You're a handsome guy, Blake. And smart and kind. Why are you still single?"

The light eked out of his eyes, but he kept possession of her hand. "I traveled with the Marines a lot, and there was a certain amber-eyed girl whose memory stepped between me and any other woman I dated. Three or four dates and I was usually sent off somewhere again. Anyone I dated soon vanished from my thoughts, and I realized I didn't care enough to try managing a long-distance romance."

"I don't think that's all the story."

"Maybe it's not *all* the story, but it's the most important part."

His thumb continued to drive her crazy, but she didn't want it to stop. "And the rest of it?"

"I had this sixth sense that Mom might need me. I can't explain it, but it was enough to halt any interest in laying down roots anywhere else. This place called to me: the tupelo trees and the Spanish moss, the gators and the pelicans. They all tugged at my heart no matter where I went."

"That makes a lot more sense than your carrying a torch for

me." Though every cell in her body wanted to believe that was the root of why he was still here for her.

His thumb stilled, and his fingers tightened around her hand. "Don't discount that, Paradise. I know it's hard to accept. We were kids, but what we had was real. It wasn't some stupid teenage crush. I've always seen you and known you inside. And you have always seen me. You know it's true."

She gave a jerky nod. "I felt it too, but I tried to tell myself it was stupid and childish." His thumb stilled, then resumed its lazy circles. "Is there going to be a future for us?"

He opened his mouth, but the server came with their appetizers. Just as well. If she let herself think about the future, she wouldn't be able to keep her brainpower focused on who killed the Mason woman. And Hank.

CHAPTER 37

PARADISE ADJUSTED BLAKE'S TIE. "You clean up pretty well."

The soft expression on her face melted his heart. "Wish you were going with us."

"What? And give up sticky fingers all over my face after making caramel corn and playing Candy Land? My evening will be much more fun than yours. You'll have to listen to old people reliving their glory days of the eighties. If you see any of the ladies with bodacious big hair, I want pictures."

His mom's heels clicked on the hardwood flooring in the hall-way. "I heard that. I'll have you know in my heyday at seventeen, my hair could have made the best mop you've ever used on the floor."

"That's just sad, Mom. Your heyday was at age seventeen?"

"Your dad fell for it. How do you think I got pregnant so young?"

She'd never hidden the mistakes she made as a teenager, and her honesty had helped him avoid a lot of missteps. He wished he remembered his dad, but all he had were pictures and a few old-time movies of his impossibly young father chasing Blake as a one-year-old around the yard. He hadn't run off when he discovered Mom was pregnant but had immediately married her and loved her until his tragic death at nineteen.

Blake winked at Paradise and stepped back to extend his arm to his mother. "Your carriage awaits, my lady. Or maybe it's a dirty van."

She wrinkled her nose. "I hope you cleaned out the pizza boxes."

"I'll have you know, once Nora was done with it, that van has never been so clean. Well, except for fingerprint dust." He'd spent an hour cleaning the cleanup. His truck was even cleaner, but he didn't want his mom to have to hoist herself in a snug skirt and heels into his pickup.

They were still smiling fifteen minutes later when they entered the gymnasium at the high school. It had been decked out in gold and white. A giant dance ball spun near the ceiling, and Blake spotted several photo-op areas set up with memorabilia from high school as well as one with giant balloons attached to the wall. Whitney Houston crooned "I Will Always Love You" from the speakers, and several couples swayed to the music along one side of the gym.

His mother elbowed him. "Wipe that incredulous smirk off your face. At your thirtieth class reunion you'll embarrass your kids too."

He grinned. "I have to say you're prettier than anyone here, Mom. That red dress will wow them." Before she could respond, he spotted Frank Ellis walking their way. "Get ready, here he comes," he whispered.

His mother's smile widened as though he'd said the funniest thing, and she threw back her head in a laugh that rang out through the room. He'd never heard her laugh like that—was that her high school persona she'd just slipped into?

Frank, looking smart in khaki slacks and a navy blazer, headed for them like an ant zeroing in on cherry pie. "Jenna Mitchell, I was hoping you'd be here." His thick blond hair fell onto his forehead, and he pushed it off to take in her appearance. "As beautiful as ever."

She turned wide eyes his way. "Frank! How are you?"

Her delight appeared genuine, and she hugged Frank's stocky frame. Blake noticed how reluctant the man seemed to drop his arms after the hug. Where was his wife?

His mom tucked her hand into the crook of Frank's elbow and steered him toward the refreshment table. "I'm sorry to hear about your divorce, Frank. You doing okay?"

Frank shrugged. "A little poorer and wiser is all. She was having an affair with the tennis pro. That sounds like something you'd hear on *The Real Housewives*, not at our country club. I gave her the house because I didn't want my girls to suffer for her behavior. It's life, I guess. I wanted the old Steerforth place, you know, but the divorce hit at the wrong time and I lost it. I'm glad you got it though. I'm sure it's a great distraction now as you're grieving."

That explained a lot. Blake hovered near his mom in case she got into trouble, but she seemed a pro at handling this guy. He'd never seen this side of her.

Frank grabbed drinks for them and handed one to Blake as well. "You're a good son, Blake. The whole countryside knows you came running to help your mom and brothers. Jenna deserves it too. She's the finest woman I've ever met." His eyes glistened and went a little red. "It was my loss in high school, but she took one look at your dad when he moved to town, and it was all over between us."

Blake noticed his mom's cheeks go pink and her expression soften. Did she still have a tender spot for Frank? Until tonight

Blake hadn't been around the developer much. He'd only heard stories, but Frank was different from what he expected from the scuttlebutt. He seemed to have a soft, kind center—at least where Mom was concerned.

"We've had some trouble, Frank. You're the kind of businessman who hears everything. Do you know why someone might be trying to force us to sell?"

He frowned. "I've tried to squelch rumors when I've heard them. I thought it was simple bad luck that the activists targeted you. You think it was a deliberate attempt to shut you down?"

Mom sipped her sweet tea. "There's been a target on our backs for months, starting with Hank's death. We don't think it was an accident."

Frank's scowl deepened. "That's terrible, Jenna. If there's anything I can do to stop it, I will. And to put your mind at ease, my failure to buy the property ended up being for my own good. My daughter is engaged to the son of a big farmer on the other side of town. Ryan's dad was wanting to quit the business and retire. Ryan is going to go into business with me, and I'll have more work developing that land than I know what to do with. God works in mysterious ways, doesn't he?"

Blake's mother nodded, and Blake watched them wander off, still chatting. While he could be mistaken, Blake didn't think Frank had anything to do with what was going on. His gaze stayed fixed on his mother, who seemed to be having a wonderful time with Ellis. Blake wasn't sure how he felt about that.

———

After the boys' baths, Paradise was as wet as they were, and she slipped on athletic shorts and a tee after she cleaned up the floor in the bathroom. Even her hair was damp and stood out around her head in a frizzy halo. She smoothed a little argan oil on it and went to tell the kids a story.

While Blake was allowed to read a story, she always had to make one up. Levi in particular liked her to make up stories about things they'd seen or done that day, and she always had to include Twilight Sparkle in the story. When he flushed and grinned every time he talked about the little pony, she thought it was the sweetest thing she'd ever seen.

Tonight's story was about how superhero Levi and his sidekick Isaac had to rescue Twilight Sparkle from an evil dragon who'd penned her up in the jaguar habitat, and big brother Blake had to rescue all of them in the end.

They were asleep in her bed by the time she heard a noise at the door and turned to see Blake leaning against the jamb with a tender expression on his face. She tiptoed out and shut off the light, then pulled the door closed behind her.

The amusement on his face glinted in his blue eyes. "That big brother Blake sounded like he could leap buildings in a single bound."

"Which is why he'll find magic bars awaiting him in the kitchen. He needs to keep up his superhero strength." In the hallway she leaned against his chest, and his arms welcomed her. "And he's devilishly handsome as well."

He pressed a kiss against her hair. "And he's pretty confused by the evening."

She let him lead her to the empty living room. "Where's your mom?"

"Frank is bringing her home. They went for ice cream."

Paradise's mouth gaped and she snapped it closed. "You let her go alone with Frank Ellis?"

"Let her? I didn't have a choice. Those two took up together like they'd never been apart. Mom turned all giddy. I'd never seen anything like it." He dropped onto the sofa and pulled her down beside him. "But to be honest, I liked the guy. I didn't think I would, but he's actually nice. He had eyes for no one but Mom. And get this—the reason he couldn't buy this place was because of a nasty divorce." He told her the details he'd learned.

"Could the rumors be wrong?"

"They were wrong about us. I never believe rumors."

She settled into the cradle of his arm. "Have you been listening to the news? We've got a big storm coming in that's likely to spawn tornadoes. Massive amounts of rain too and flooding likely. Hitting late tomorrow or on Friday."

"I hadn't heard. I'll make sure we've got plenty of bottled water and kerosene for the heater. And plenty of food for the animals. If flooding starts, you and Mom can take the boys to TGU. They usually have a center set up in their gym with cots, food, and water."

Unease flickered down her back at the thought of him staying here alone. "What about you?"

"Someone will need to feed the animals. Evan usually stays to help me. We've never had the house flood, but it's come close a few times, and I had to use sandbags."

They were used to storms and floods in the South, but preparation was key, especially for the park. He would feel responsible for everyone—including the animals.

He nuzzled her hair. "I got a call from Roger Dillard. He found what he thought might be the crime scene of Danielle Mason's murder in a corral on the west side of his property. He's going to call the sheriff's department, but he wanted to give me a heads-up. I asked if I could look at it in the morning before he makes that call. He said he's fed up with the way Greene is handling the case and wanted to make sure I'm not railroaded into jail."

"It's kind of him, Blake, but you're not a crime-scene expert. What can you do? Should we maybe take Nora? I suppose it's too soon to hear anything from her about the knife."

"It's not a bad idea. She's separate from the sheriff's department—they borrow her at times, but Jane is her boss. Savannah and Hez are friends with Jane. I'll ask Hez what he thinks." He pulled out his phone and made the call.

Paradise listened with half an ear to his side of the conversation as Blake thanked his cousin and ended the call. "Hez wants me to have Dillard report the site to Pelican Harbor PD. Then Jane can send Nora. Hez will give Nora and Jane a heads-up. We can meet them out there in the morning. I'll call Roger now."

It was the best they could hope for. She sipped the cold remains of her herbal tea while he notified Roger.

He ended the call and set his phone aside. "That's settled. Maybe it will be a break in the case." He twirled one of her fat curls around his finger. "I love your hair."

"Are you trying to distract me from the case?"

He pressed his lips against her hair and spoke into the thick strands. "Maybe."

"Maybe it's working."

He captured her lips when she turned her head and pulled her into a tighter embrace. When he kissed her like this, she could almost forget the problems looming.

A car door sounded, and he pulled away. "So you made me magic bars?"

"The boys might have left you a few."

He grinned down at her as his mother entered the house. Paradise tried to hide her surprise at Jenna's windblown appearance. The updo she had when she left here was now a down-do that straggled onto her shoulders.

"Uh, Mom, have you looked in the mirror?"

"I must be a mess." Jenna combed at her hair with her fingers. "Frank put the top down on his convertible." She kicked off her heels before settling into a chair opposite them. "I'd forgotten how much fun Frank always was. He hasn't changed a bit." She must have noticed their astonishment because pink rushed to her cheeks. "It was just a fun night. It's been a long time since I've laughed like that."

"I have to admit I've never heard you laugh like a hyena before," Blake said in a deadpan voice.

Paradise put her hand over her mouth and giggled. "Blake, stop. Your mom would never sound like a hyena."

"You didn't hear her tonight. I thought she dropped thirty years off her age the second we got inside that school."

Jenna's gaze darted from him to Paradise before she laughed. Her belly laugh rang out in a way Paradise had never heard before, and she giggled again. Then Blake's bellowing laughter joined them. After so much tension it felt good to be able to let it go.

CHAPTER 38

DAWN BARELY REDDENED THE sky when Blake stood with Paradise and Nora at the corral fence line on the Dillard Ranch, and he caught a whiff of impending rain on the wind. He nodded at the brilliant color spreading in the east. "Red sky at morning, sailors take warning."

Roger, a big man with grizzled hair and sloped shoulders inside a red-and-black-plaid flannel shirt, put his foot on the lowest rung of the fence. "Got a bad one coming in. Glad I found this spot before the rain washes it away. It's already been almost a month since the poor lady died, but this drought maybe saved your butt, Blake." He jabbed his finger at Nora. "If your friend here can find anything."

Nora gestured to the padlock. "Could you show us the spot, Mr. Dillard?"

Roger took out a key and opened the padlock. "It's on the back side of the hayfield. I only noticed it because I was out here to see how much hay needed to be taken to the barn before the storm hits, and I saw some stacks of bales had been moved. I poked around and saw the brown stains. Looked like blood to me, but

I didn't want to disturb too much so I didn't move them back into place."

Nora was the first one through the gate. "Smart move, Mr. Dillard."

Blake and Paradise followed her across the dry grass toward the stacks of hay bales on the back side of the corral. Horses grazed on the other side of the fence in the last corral. It was a low-lying area, and Blake imagined it flooded. There would have been no evidence left.

They reached the piles of large bales and Roger pointed out the stain. "I nearly missed it."

"I would have," Blake said.

Nora squatted at the stain and opened her backpack. She laid out a sheet five feet away. "It's going to take a while, guys. Blake, would you put on booties and nitrile gloves to lift off the hay bale covering most of this? Lay it off to one side because I'll need to examine it as well. I want to see how much blood we're talking about before I go any further. If it's the possible crime scene, I'll need to call in help from my team."

He donned the booties and gloves she handed him before grabbing the twine binding the hay bale. Moving slowly and carefully, he lifted it and deposited it a few feet away on the sheet she'd spread out. His gut clenched at the sight of the massive amount of brown staining the dry grass and weeds. This had to be it.

Nora pulled out her phone. "I'll need help. All of you stay back, and in fact, feel free to leave the site to me and my team. Once I'm done I'll let the sheriff's department know we were called to the site. Mr. Dillard, there may be pushback from Greene that you called Chief Dixon instead of him."

The big rancher turned and ambled back toward the gate. "I

can handle Creed Greene," he said over his shoulder. "He's a gator looking to bite, but I've dealt with his kind before."

Blake didn't want to leave, but they were in the way, and he wanted to talk with Roger, who was away when the murder happened. He suspected the old guy had some insight into the events. He and Paradise walked a few paces behind the rancher, who went to grab the halters of two horses in the next paddock over.

"Roger may know more than he's told anyone," he whispered to Paradise.

She nodded. "He let the activists camp on his land. Let's find out why. Was it because he's a nice guy, or did he know someone in the group?"

Blake took her hand and they quickened their pace until they were jogging after Roger, who led the horses, one halter in each hand, toward the big barn. Once they were a couple of feet behind, Blake slowed to a more leisurely stride and held back as Roger opened the barn door and got the horses settled in stalls.

"I should be readying the park too," he told Paradise.

"What do you have to do there?"

"Get all the animals in their shelters and set out sandbags in areas I suspect might flood, especially around the house and the food barn. Make sure we have enough food to last for at least a week, just in case it's bad. Make sure I have enough fuel for the generator to at least run the well pump." He examined the sky with no sign of clouds yet. "Though we might have a little longer than initially thought. It might hold off until tomorrow."

She walked into the barn beside him and inhaled. "I know it's crazy, but I love the smell inside a barn—the hay and the straw on the dirt floor mixed with the scent of the horses and their leather. There's nothing like it. It reminds me of being a kid. I learned to ride starting at five, and my mom would bring me to the stables here where I took lessons with his daughter Abby. It feels like home somehow."

He slipped his arm around her, and they watched the old rancher feed a sugar cube to each of the horses. "Those were the good old days, but I think the future is going to be just as good. We're going to get through this—together. And why do you need a horse now when you've got a whole park full of exotic animals?"

She leaned her head against his chest. "I like how you think."

Roger glanced up and nodded when he spotted them. He plodded toward them in his old brown work shoes. "You need me, kids?"

"The activist group camped out on your back pasture. Did they move in and you didn't want to kick them off, or did they have permission?"

The older man pursed his lips. "My granddaughter asked if they could stay there, and I can't tell her no. Abby's daughter, Quinn, who's ten. She was doing a school project on zoos and wanted to hear what they had to say. They filled her head with all kinds of nonsense. I suspect she let them into the back paddock where we found the crime scene. Not sure why, and she isn't talking." He gestured toward the house. "She's inside if you want to talk to her."

Blake did indeed.

———

Though Paradise knew Quinn was ten, she looked about fourteen. Her curly red hair fell nearly to her waist, and she was already outgrowing her gangly awkwardness. She sat cross-legged on the living room floor with nail polishes and nail stickers spread out in front of her.

"Quinn, these are some friends of mine," Roger said. "They'd like to talk to you for a minute."

A slight frown marred the perfection of the girl's face, and she didn't glance up. "Just a second, Grandpa. I'm almost done with my polish." She layered another coat of bright blue on her pinky nail before glancing up at Paradise and Blake.

Paradise settled on the hardwood floor in front of her. "I went to school with your mom. My name is Paradise." Out of the corner of her eye, she saw the men walk toward the kitchen and heard Roger say something about coffee.

Quinn's turquoise eyes widened. "That's a bussin' name. Did your parents name you that, or did you find it yourself?"

"My parents called me that. I was born in Hawaii when my dad was in the military. I don't remember it though because we moved here when I was a baby." Paradise did some calculations in her head. "You're in fifth grade? Middle school?"

"Uh-huh." The girl blew on her nails.

Maybe bluntness would receive a reaction. "Why did you let the activists into your grandpa's back pasture?"

Quinn continued to blow on her nails for a long moment. "Grandpa never cares what I do."

"Why did they want in there?"

"They wanted to make a video."

That was unexpected. "Why there?"

"It was a video about how wrong it is to use horses. It was pretty cringe. I love our horses and they love me. That's when I realized that group was ick."

At least they hadn't misled the girl for long. She might be

young, but she was more astute than she seemed. "Did you hear them say anything about the animal park?"

"The Sanctuary? Sure, they wanted to shut it down and turn all the animals loose." Her red curls fell across her face, and she pawed them away with the back of her hand so she wouldn't smear her wet nails. "They got into a fight that day about who got to pretend to be dead."

"Pretend to be dead? How was that supposed to work?"

"One of them was going to have fake blood smeared all over her and have this big orange knife sticking out of her chest. They were going to use the horses. They were salty about old Moses going to the park."

"So they planned all along to have one of them get in the trailer with Moses and pretend to be dead?" And an orange knife was used. That was a very interesting detail considering the knife planted in the van was orange. Was it originally in the possession of the activist group?

Quinn nodded. "And then it was *real*. I don't know what happened."

"Did you ever see anyone else with them—someone local?"

Quinn frowned as she thought. "Well, the vet was there."

"Dr. Shaw? Out to check on the horse?"

"I don't think so. He was talking with them and never examined Moses. We all knew the old guy had a strangulated bowel and couldn't live. He was in pain too."

"Did you hear what Dr. Shaw talked to them about?"

"He seemed to be agreeing with them that the park should be shut down."

"Did he say why?"

"No, but the rest of them seemed to think he had inside information about how the animals were mistreated or something. You're the vet out there, aren't you?"

Paradise nodded. "The animals have great lives there. They're well-loved with lots of enrichment times and fun things for them to do. They seem very happy."

"I always thought so when I went to visit."

"Did you tell the detective any of this?"

Quinn peeled a nail decal of flowers off the sheet of stickers and attached it to the index nail on her left hand. "No one ever asked me. I'm just a kid, you know. But I see things. I stay with Grandpa after school until Mom gets off at six, and I know everything about the ranch."

"Did you see what they did with the knife?"

"The vet took it."

The information sucked the moisture from Paradise's mouth. Could Owen be involved in this? She couldn't see why he would want to shut down the park. He and Hank had been friends, longtime friends. And he had no skin in the game at the park, so none of it made sense.

Maybe Blake or Jenna would have some idea how this all made sense.

Blake returned with Roger and coffee. "I just got a text from Nora. It appears the knife we found is the murder weapon."

Paradise rose. "Quinn was very helpful. She saw that knife, and Owen Shaw took it with him."

CHAPTER 39

OWEN SHAW COULDN'T BE involved. Blake turned the information over and over in his head as he drove to Nova Cambridge, but no matter how he thought about it, he couldn't see what motive Owen would have. Blake parked the truck at the curb. "Let's go talk to Owen and see if he can clear any of this up. I can't stay long—I need to make preparations at the park for the storm."

"There's probably a good explanation."

"I hope so." Blake reached the door and stopped at the sign on the window. "Closed for lunch."

He glanced at the sky. The greenish-black clouds had begun to gather low on the horizon, and the air held the taste of a storm— humid and breezy. "I don't have time to wait. I want to grab some cases of water while we're here and some extra sandbags. I have some in the barn, but maybe not enough. They're passing them out at the town hall."

"You grab the sandbags while I pop into the grocery store and buy some cases of water."

He nodded, and she went across the street to the market while he drove the truck to the town hall. Half an hour later, he pulled the truck into the grocery's lot and shot her a text to let her know he was out there.

Almost ready. Could use some help.

He got out and started for the front of the market when he spotted Owen coming out of the drugstore. He paused long enough to shoot Paradise a message that he would be a few minutes, but when he looked back up, Owen was gone. And the office was still closed.

He continued into the market and grabbed three cases of water from Paradise while she wheeled a cart full of canned goods toward the truck. "Not taking any chances, are you?"

She shook her head. "I got some canned cat food too, just in case we were low. And plenty of stuff for the boys. I hope we don't have to leave. The thought of holing up at the park with the animals and the boys sounds fun. We'll make fudge and caramel corn while we play games and watch cartoons. It would be a perfect couple of days."

He eyed the glowering sky again. "I don't know. I have a bad feeling about this storm. The radar is intense. They're saying we could get hit with dozens of tornadoes. I'd guess we might lose power, and our generator will only be enough to keep the well water going and the freezer."

She studied the sky too. "I don't mind wind and rain since we're in a drought, but tornadoes wouldn't be good. You have a basement?"

"A storm cellar just out the back door. I should make sure it's cleared of spiders and snakes."

She shuddered. "I'd appreciate that."

"I saw Owen just before I came in. That's what delayed me. But he disappeared and I didn't see where he went. It's going to have to wait for a better time."

"Do you want to hang around and see if he opened up the office again?"

"Better not. There's a lot to do." He loaded the water and groceries in the back, and they climbed in for the short drive home.

The lot was nearly deserted when they arrived back at the park. Only a few vans and cars dotted the usually clogged parking lot.

"What can I do to help?" Paradise asked when he drove through the lot to the house.

"Pray."

"I've been doing that." She hesitated. "I never realized having the resource of prayer was such a big deal. It's somehow comforting to know events are outside my control and that's okay. It makes me realize I never had the control I thought I had."

He leaned over and cupped her face in his palms. "Some Christians go their whole lives and never articulate that." He brushed her lips with his before releasing her. "Let's unload this stuff and I'll start piling up sandbags."

"Can I help with that?"

"Sure. The boys will want to help too. It takes both of them to drag one sandbag, but they'll love it anyway. They should be finishing their schoolwork in Mom's office if you want to grab them."

"I'll be right there. Where are you putting the sandbags?"

"There's a low spot by the lions and a bigger one by the hyenas. Let's try to bulwark that as much as possible. I'm going to get them into their shelter before the storm hits too. There are high shelves and spots for them to hang out if the water manages to come in. I'm praying there's no flooding though. That's the worst-case scenario."

She got out and grabbed several bags of groceries to take with her, while he carried the flats of water into the garage. He wasn't worried—not yet. But he had a strange feeling tonight would not be the cozy scenario Paradise had in mind. He hoped and prayed he was wrong. A fun evening of treats and games with the boys would be welcome after the stress of the past few weeks, but their safety was his job. And not just their safety, but the welfare of the whole park depended on him.

Preparing for the storm seemed like a huge job right now. If the park had to be evacuated, how would he protect the animals? A few years ago several storms and flooding had forced a local zoo to evacuate the animals, but Blake had no idea how he could do that. He didn't have enough trucks or even a place to take them where they'd all be safe.

All he could do was depend on God to protect them—and that was the best thing anyway.

Nearly bent over and faces red, the boys each carried one end of a sandbag toward the line of defense Paradise had pointed out to them. Her muscles were already sore from hefting countless bags herself, but the barricade in this area was nearly done. No rain had fallen yet, but the forecast had grown more and more ominous throughout the afternoon. The taste of rain was in the air, and greenish-black clouds billowed on the western horizon.

She helped the boys place the final bag. "Good job, guys! You worked hard. When we're done, who wants to help me make fudge?"

Isaac's hand shot up and Levi's did a moment later. "Can I stir in the butter?" Isaac asked. "It's my favorite part."

"You sure can, and Levi can help spread it in the pan." She stretched out the kinks in her back and glanced around for Blake.

The last glimpse she'd had of him was a distant view of him checking fences and opening gates to bring the animals out of the weather. Even the safari animals like the antelopes and zebras had lean-tos to shelter in. She turned and scanned the area near the back of the house and saw the storm shelter doors were open. Moments later he emerged with a broom. It might be safe for her down there if they had to seek shelter. She eyed the mounting clouds again. It might be necessary in the night.

"I think we're done here, boys. Let's get cleaned up and head for the kitchen."

"Yay!" Isaac scampered ahead of her and Levi, who took her hand and walked with her.

"I'm glad you're here, Paradise. Don't ever go away, okay?" he said.

She squeezed his fingers gently. "I'm glad to be here too, big guy. Being with you and your family has been the best thing that's ever happened to me."

She made no promises about never leaving. While she was hopeful about the future with Blake, she'd learned early in her life that circumstances might flip on a dime and upheaval could follow. It would make her happy if she never left this little corner of the world again and could watch Levi and his brother grow to manhood, but that was out of her hands.

They headed straight for the bathroom and washed up. She changed her clothes and had the boys do the same so none of them tracked sand through the house. In the kitchen she got out a heavy pan and the ingredients for fudge. She set Isaac to buttering the square glass dish while Levi helped her measure out sugar, cocoa, and milk. The sweet chocolaty aroma began to fill the kitchen.

A door slammed and Blake entered the kitchen. Cobwebs draped across his hair, and his grimy face told her what a mess the storm cellar must have been.

He held up blackened palms and acted as though he was going to touch her. She squealed and danced back with the wooden spatula in her hand. "Oh no, don't you dare touch me with spidery hands. Are there spiders in your hair?" With sick fascination she watched for anything crawling on his dark hair.

"I don't think so. I tried brushing anything living off me, but I'm going to take a shower."

"I think that's a very good idea."

"I stocked the place with water, clean cots, and blankets just in case. And a few snacks as well. I put everything in spider-proof tubs and plastic bags so we're all set for the storm season. I didn't remember you were so scared of spiders. You face down all kinds of large creatures but run from spiders."

She shuddered. "I can't explain it, but I hate them. Thanks for making sure I can go down there."

Isaac put a wet hand on her arm. "Me and Levi will protect you, Paradise. We're good at squashing bugs."

Blake nodded solemnly. "They are indeed. I taught them myself."

His phone sounded, and he gingerly pulled it out. "This thing will need a bath too." He frowned at the text message. "It's Hez. He says Greene wants to interrogate me again, but that he's putting it off until after the storm."

He typed in a response. "I asked him if there was any news from Nora's evidence collection."

Paradise stirred the bubbling fudge. "Greene is a menace. I don't know how you're going to get off his radar."

"I don't think it's possible." Another message sounded and he read it, then glanced at the boys. "Hez says the evidence matched."

So the blood on the knife was a match to Danielle Mason. "Did you tell Hez what Quinn said about Owen?"

"I did. He didn't know what to make of it. I still want to talk to him, but it will have to wait until the storm mess is over." He pocketed his phone. "I'll shower and come help with dinner. What does everyone want to eat tonight?"

"Tacos!" the boys said.

Blake ruffled Isaac's hair. "My specialty. I'll need some help."

"We always help," Levi said. "You don't even need to say it."

"Point taken, big guy."

Paradise watched him leave, then checked the fudge. "It's at softball stage. Get the butter ready, Isaac. Levi, grab the spatula and get ready to spread. It's a finely tuned dance to make sure it's not too hard and not too soft."

And wasn't that like life? There were hard places and soft ones, but the trick was remembering it didn't ruin the delight.

CHAPTER 40

BLAKE AWAKENED TO HOWLING wind and pounding rain trying to batter its way into the house. Isaac cried out, and he heard Paradise comfort him. Levi would be scared too. Blake tried to flip on a light, but the power was out, so he found his way through the dark house and down the hall to where Paradise slept with his little brothers. Both boys had crashed in there last night—Levi on the top bunk and Isaac with Paradise.

Blake struggled to see in the dark. "I should have brought my phone so I could use the flashlight. Everyone okay?"

"We're fine," Paradise said. "My phone is across the room on top of the dresser if you want to feel around for it."

Levi whimpered. "I want you, Blake."

"I'm coming." The storm outside obliterated every bit of light, and he felt his way through the dark until he bumped into the bunk bed. "Here I am, guys. Nothing to be afraid of."

"I can't see you, Blake," Levi said. "Can you get me? I'm in the top bunk."

Blake ran his hand up the bedpost and touched Levi's leg. He found his brother's arms and pulled him out of the bunk. "I've got you."

"I'm with Paradise," Isaac said to his right.

He heard his mother's bare feet hurrying down the hallway to check on the children. A faint glow entered the room with her phone flashlight illuminated. "Everyone okay in here? We knew the storm was coming, remember?"

Lightning flickered outside and the glare pushed its way past the blinds. Levi's arms tightened around his neck. "I'm scared," he whispered in Blake's ear.

"We're safe and snug in the house."

The lights flickered outside and then came on. The welcome glow showed enough for him to see the white moon of Paradise's face with Isaac clutched to her chest. His mother strode to the wall switch and flipped on the light. Her hair was mussed, but she was calm.

Mom held out her arms. "It's only three, guys. Anyone want to sleep with me?"

"I do," both boys chorused.

Levi reached for her, and she tucked him into one arm while her other grabbed for Blake's littlest brother.

"You've been abandoned," Blake told Paradise. "Aren't you scared?"

She rose from the bed and came to stand in the circle of his arms. "Do you remember when we were teenagers and we used to sit on your porch in the old neighborhood and watch the storms roll in off the Gulf? Sometimes we'd go to the beach and shelter in a pavilion and watch the waves from a tropical storm."

"I remember. That one time we nearly got caught in a storm surge. You always were a daredevil when it came to storms." He rested his chin on her head and inhaled the plumeria scent in her hair. "You sleepy? I can let you get to bed."

"Not in the least. We could watch a movie until we get sleepy."

He opened his mouth to tell her he was game to watch a chick flick, but her phone began to wail with an alert. "Sounds like a tornado warning. Let me check the radar on your phone."

She handed it to him, and he checked the weather map. The storm was bearing down on them.

"We've got to get to the shelter *now*. It's coming this way."

They ran for his mother's room, and the boys weren't asleep yet. Blake scooped up Levi and handed him to Paradise. "We're going for a campout, guys. Mom, you carry Isaac, and I'll run on ahead and open the door. It's tough to lift, especially in a wind. Hurry."

He didn't have to spell it out for his mother. They'd weathered plenty of storms over the years, and she didn't wait to slide her feet into shoes. He dashed ahead, pausing only to grab the boys' iPads, then splashed through mud and the ongoing deluge toward the storm shelter. Lightning slashed the black sky and thunder ricocheted off the trees and buildings. The pungent scent of ozone hung in the air. The heavy metal door pushed against the wind, but he finally managed to throw it back.

He descended the steps and dropped the tablets onto an old wooden crate he'd brought in to use as a table, then turned on the battery-powered lantern he'd left charged and ready to use. The warm glow pushed back the complete darkness in the small space, and it seemed cozy to him with the camp chairs set up. He'd had a sixth sense they would need them tonight and had arranged them in a circle on an old rug.

Holding the lantern aloft, he went back up the steps and saw the rest of the family hurrying toward him. The boys, eyes wide and frightened, clung to the women. Isaac had his head thrown back and was staring at the low clouds. Blake spared a glance up too but didn't see a funnel cloud. Not yet anyway. He prayed the park would be spared any direct hit. The animals were probably frantic out there, but there was nothing he could do.

He grabbed Isaac from his mom and passed him back to her once she reached the bottom step. Paradise and Levi went down next, and he glanced at the sky one more time before he descended, pulling the door shut behind him. He locked the door with the inside security bar, and the dank scent of the underground space rushed at him. At least he'd ensured the spiders were gone, for now anyway.

Levi held up a dish of fudge. "We grabbed this on the way past. Paradise said we could have a party down here. Did you bring down some games?"

"We've got Go Fish, Candy Land, and Uno. And I grabbed your iPads." He snatched a piece of fudge from Levi and popped it in his mouth. "Who's ready to party?"

The boys jumped up and down, and Blake exchanged a long glance with Paradise. They'd do their best to keep the boys from worrying, but the adults in the room had their own share of fears. He reached over to the old boom box he'd brought in and turned on the *Moana* soundtrack.

Paradise squatted beside it and cranked it up until music filled the small space and drowned out the creaks and groans above their heads. As long as the door didn't fly off, they should be safe, but that was a mighty big *if*.

———

Carrying Levi, Paradise blinked in the drab light as they exited the storm shelter into the torrential rains that continued to fall.

She ran for the back door with the little boy, and the rest of the family was right behind her. At one point the door had billowed in and out, and she'd been sure it would go flying off, but it had held tight.

She paused on the back deck under the overhang and spared a glance around the property. Tree limbs and leaves lay battered and heaped around the yard. The house's roof hadn't gone flying off, and she spotted only a board or two swinging from the big barn. The tornado hadn't carried off anything she could see.

Blake set Isaac down and opened the door. "Go on in, guys. Mom will make you some breakfast. Paradise and I need to check the animals and make sure everything is okay." He pointed to Paradise's muddy feet. "You might want some boots though, Simba."

She laughed. "So we're back to that, are we?"

"You were quite the lioness last night protecting the boys. I don't think you slept at all."

"Neither did you," she countered.

"It's my job."

"No, you just love well." He always had, but she'd been too angry and blind to see it. Blake wasn't someone who spoke flowery words of love—he was a man of action who showed his love for those close to him with every decision he made.

She went to the hose spigot four feet away and rinsed off her feet, then darted to the door. Jenna had left a stack of towels by the door, and Paradise grabbed one. She toweled off her hair and face so she could see, then dried her feet and ran to her room to grab socks. She yanked them on and went to dig her boots out of the stack of shoes and boots in the laundry room. With her boots on, she rushed for the door and paused long enough to grab yellow rain slickers for her and Blake. If they could keep even some of the pounding rain off, they might stay warmer.

She hurried outside to an empty deck and saw him moving in the doorway of the barn. She exited the yard through the gate and ran to catch up with him. "Here, put this on."

He took the rain slicker and pulled it over his head. "I think trying to stay dry is a lost cause. The barn seems okay. Let's check the animals."

They slogged through the mud and rain to pen after pen. The mud on the soles of her boots made her legs heavy, but they made it through the park and found all the animals and structures safe.

"The twister must not have touched down here," Blake said. "But I don't like the depth of the water rising in the back field. The last time it was like that, the level went high very quickly and surrounded the house. We were trapped inside. I think you and Mom should take the boys to a shelter in town. The rain isn't supposed to stop anytime soon."

Paradise wrinkled her nose. Ugh, a shelter filled with other people. "Maybe we could rent a motel and make it fun for the boys? I'd like to stay with you though."

"I don't think you'll find a room. Hez said some friends had to go clear to Montgomery. It's probably just a night or two. Besides, the boys will have a blast with the other children at the shelter." He touched her cheek. "I would worry every second if I didn't know you were safe. I'll be fine."

"Will you promise to text me every hour or so and let me know everything is all right?"

He gripped her shoulders and kissed her. It was a quick caress, and she sensed his stress in the rigid line of his spine and the press of his fingers.

She stepped back. "Okay, I'll go tell your mother and we'll pack up some things." She'd rather stay here with him, but Jenna might need help corralling the boys. Plus, having another calming presence would soothe Jenna's worries about what was going on out here.

Paradise felt Blake's gaze on her back as she ran for the house in the deluge. She didn't remember ever being in this kind of rain before, and unease shuddered down her spine at the pool of water on the other side of the driveway. The parking lot was full of water too, and she wasn't sure they'd be able to get out with the van. The standing water might flood the engine.

She reached the house and stepped under the overhang before she removed her slicker. She shook the moisture from it and from her hair, then stepped inside and grabbed another towel. She left her muddy boots outside and padded in socked feet to find Jenna, who was with the boys in their bedroom.

Paradise beckoned to her from the doorway, and Jenna rose from the floor where they'd been playing with their dinosaurs.

Jenna grimaced. "It's bad, isn't it? I've never seen it rain like this."

"It's already flooding. Blake thinks we should go to the shelter. I suggested a motel, but he said we'd probably have to go to Montgomery to find one."

"The shelter won't be so bad. We'll know people, and we're all in the same boat. I'll pack some clothes for me and the boys, and you can grab your things."

"I think we should take Blake's truck."

"But what if he needs to escape? He'd be stranded here."

"I'll come back and get him. I don't think the van will make it out."

"Okay, as long as we have a plan. I know you won't let anything happen to my boy." Jenna turned toward the boys. "How'd you like to have some kids to play with tonight? We're going to go to the university and stay in the gym."

The boys gaped for a moment, then jumped to their feet and began gathering toys. "Only four things," Jenna warned. "We don't want anything left behind."

Before she started packing, Paradise shot a text to Blake explaining the vehicle dilemma, and he approved the plan. At least she'd have good wheels if she needed to come back here. She had a very bad feeling about all of it.

CHAPTER 41

IT WAS BEGINNING TO feel like the biblical account of Noah's flood. Blake eyed the low-hanging clouds pouring down the greatest amount of rain he'd ever seen. Wind lashed the rain across his face, and there wasn't a dry spot anywhere on his body. Even his feet were soaked from splashing through the cold rain. His teeth chattered as he rode the Gator, food pails loaded in the back, from area to area to feed the animals.

At eight in the evening, only the hyenas still waited to be fed. The Gator's headlamps barely punched through enough of the darkness to drive out toward the far fence around the hyena encampment. The field was badly flooded with water only a few inches from rushing into his cab. The front passenger tire slammed into a hole, and the vehicle tilted heavily to the right.

Blake spun the wheel and tried to recover, but the slimy mud and water had made the area incredibly treacherous. The Gator ricocheted off a metal fence pole, and the next thing Blake knew, he was suspended upside down in the Gator's seat belt. The top of his hair dragged in the floodwaters below him.

His head spun, and his arm hurt when he tried to unbuckle the belt. He fumbled with the clasp and finally managed to loosen it. The fall to the water and ground below jarred him, and his teeth slammed together. He sucked in water and came up choking and spitting.

For a moment he didn't know which way was up or down. He shook his head to clear it and grabbed a piece of the vehicle to help him stand up out of the foot-deep water.

His phone had been on the passenger seat beside him, and he searched for it, but it was lost in the floodwaters and mud. He retrieved a flashlight from the vehicle and turned it on. There was nothing he could do about the Gator, so he slogged through the water, now nearly to his knees, toward the far exit. Some sixth sense made him turn, and the dim glow of eyes bounced off the flashlight he aimed at them.

The hyenas are in here with me.

The inner fence separating them from the outer enclosure must have washed away in the flood. They circled toward him, and he cut a glance to the right. Open field, so no help there. On the left was a large tree, and he just might make it.

He spoke in a friendly voice. "Hey, Clara. Want some food?" Backing away, he reached down into the water and found the pail of food. He continued to walk as he tossed pieces of meat as far away as he could. At first the hyenas ran toward the food, but the pieces of meat landed in the water and they turned their attention back to Blake.

He tried tossing pieces of meat so they landed on the partially submerged Gator, but the wind derailed his aim and most still landed in the muck. The hyenas ran that way and managed to gobble up a bite or two, but with so many misses, they turned back to approach him again.

He was nearly to the tree though. A few more feet and he'd try to clamber up. It had several low-lying branches, but the trick would be gaining the safety of the higher branches before one of the hyenas could latch onto his leg and drag him down.

In spite of the cold, sweat broke out on his forehead. He had so much to live for and didn't want to end up dying out here in this flooded field. Heaven awaited him, but his mom and brothers would never recover from losing him, and he didn't want to leave Paradise either. For their sakes, he had to live.

He touched the rough bark of the oak tree, then tucked the flashlight into the waist of his pants. He tossed the empty pail away, and one of the hyenas went to nose around it, but she quickly left it. Out of the corner of his eye, he saw Clara start to make her final charge. He grabbed hold of the closest limb and swung his legs up out of the water and tried to get purchase on the tree trunk with his wet shoes. One foot slipped back toward the dominant hyena's laughing jaws, and he kicked out to push her back.

She yelped and came at him again, but she slipped in the water. The slight hesitation was enough for him to clamber onto the limb six feet above her head. She could leap that far, so he knew he should climb higher. Holding the tree trunk, he managed to stand on the wet limb and reach up to the next one. He yanked on it and decided it would be sturdy enough to hold his weight.

His hands kept slipping off the wet bark, and it was useless to try to wipe the moisture away on his saturated clothing. Clara was on her hind legs snapping at the limb a few inches below him. Through the wet leaves he spotted a platform above the tree branches.

The platform for the zip line! It would give him a better spot to settle and wait for help. He'd be at the mercy of the storm, but at least he'd have a more secure perch. If the hyenas lost interest, he could climb down and escape.

He was already getting tired clinging to the tree limb, so it was now or never. He let go of the tree trunk, and balancing on the limb, he leaped up and caught the edge of the platform with both hands. He got his legs swinging and managed to hook one over the limb supporting the platform. Moments later he was well away from the hyenas' hungry jaws and sitting on the platform.

Please, God, send help.

Paradise checked the time again. Nine fifteen. Only fifteen minutes had passed since she'd last checked it. Blake hadn't answered any of the three messages she'd sent him in the past hour, and the notifications showed he hadn't seen them. What did that mean? That he was busy or that he was in trouble?

Could the storm have knocked out the cell coverage?

The gymnasium throbbed with life. People of all ages had claimed cots, and groups of teens had teamed up to play hoops on one end, while younger children squatted over games more suitable for their ages. She spotted Mr. and Mrs. Adams from across the room and had felt faint for a few minutes until she reminded herself that they had no power over her. But she made sure to stay well away from them. She found Jenna watching the boys play dinosaurs with three other boys about the same age.

"Did you hear from Blake?" Paradise asked.

Jenna shook her head. "He hasn't seen my messages either."

"Nor mine. I'm going out there." Saying the words cemented her decision. "I'll keep you posted on what I find, but I can't stay here not knowing if he's all right."

Moisture glimmered in Jenna's blue eyes. "Thank you. I'll pray for safety for both of you."

Paradise accepted Jenna's fervent hug and held her for a long moment. "I'm sure he's fine."

"I see the worry in your eyes. I feel it too. Go find him."

Jenna released her, and Paradise grabbed her yellow rain slicker and yanked on her muddy boots again. What could be happening out there? In her heart she was sure something was wrong. If Blake could text them, he would have. He knew they would be worried, and he never liked to cause his mother or Paradise concern.

She pulled up the hood on her rain jacket and ran through the deluge toward the truck. Conditions had worsened considerably since they'd gotten to TGU. The water was up to her calves, and she was thankful for Blake's four-wheel drive. The van would've been stuck here.

She climbed behind the wheel and drove slowly past the partially submerged smaller cars and out onto the road. There would be low spots between here and the park, and she could only pray the truck would make it through them.

The first bit of trouble was at the bottom of a hill. A barricade warned of high water, and a squad car, lights flashing, sat blocking the road. She ran her window down and leaned her head out into the rain. "I have to get through to The Sanctuary. I'll risk it."

An unfamiliar male officer studied her expression and nodded. "I advise against it, but it's on you, miss."

"I'll take the chance, thank you."

He moved his vehicle out of the way, and she inched down

the hill and through the water that sloshed against the door of the truck. It seemed forever before she glimpsed the sign for The Sanctuary through the driving rain. She turned onto the gravel road, which was mostly mud with little purchase for the wheels. She lowered her speed even more and managed to stay on the road.

The entrance should be just ahead, but the dark, rainy night stole any sense of direction, and she was at the gate before she spotted a truck idling at the entrance on the right shoulder. She braked beside it. What was Clark Reynolds doing here?

She ran the passenger window down, and Clark cranked down his. "Are you okay, Clark?" The wind blew drenching rain into her face, and she wiped it out of her eyes and tried to use her hand to shield herself from more water.

Clark peered out of his window. "I came to help out, Miss Paradise. You helped me when I was in a tight spot, and I figure one good deed deserves another. I wasn't sure you all made it out, and I was sitting here trying to decide what to do."

"Blake isn't answering his phone, and I'm worried. He stayed behind to care for the animals, but he has no way to get out since we had to take his truck. I'm so glad you're here. I didn't know what to do or if I could find him on my own."

"Are the kids out? And Blake's mom?"

"Yes, they're at the TGU shelter. We all got out but Blake, who didn't feel right about leaving the animals."

"I'll follow you to the house, and we'll figure out how to find him."

"Thank you, Clark. God sent you." She knew it in her soul. He'd seen this problem before she'd ever met Clark and decided to help him.

"I don't know about that, but I'm here to help."

He cranked his window back up, and she drove slowly toward the cluster of buildings. A light caught her attention, and she braked on the way to the parking lot. Was that a beacon out there? And if so, who had turned it on?

It was so dark she couldn't see well, and the light flashed again and again. *SOS* in Morse code. Then she spotted the figure moving around in a tree flickering the light. Wait, were hyenas around the tree? It had to be Blake trying to signal with a flashlight.

———

When Blake heard the first shot ring out, he thought it was thunder, but a bullet plowed into the platform, digging a rut through the wet wood. It sounded like a .223 round. With the second shot he caught movement from atop the barn on the outside of the enclosure. He peered through the dark rain but couldn't make out the person's identity. Either they were a terrible shot or they didn't want to hit him. Were they trying to knock him off the platform and into the jaws of the hyenas milling around below?

His murder would appear to be a tragic accident. He shifted position on the platform so the metal support pole sheltered more of his body. The shooter would need to change positions to hit him. Had waving the flashlight signaled his position? A little earlier he'd decided to try an SOS signal in case Paradise had gone to the house. It was too far from here to see well, but he'd thought he caught a flash of light along the drive and had tried to signal. Whether anyone had seen it was the question.

A bullet struck the metal pole, and he flinched. The rain continued to pound his head and saturate every inch of his body. He couldn't stop shivering. He peered down through the leaves below and saw the hyenas had taken note of the shooter's presence and moved toward the far fence. There was no way out, though, with them blocking the gate. If he dropped to the ground, they'd be on him in moments.

If only he'd been able to retrieve his phone. The longing didn't fix a thing, and he would have to figure this out by himself. He could go down into the shelter of the leaves and branches for a while, but he feared he wouldn't be able to hang on with his hands numb from the cold. And his perch down there would be thinner and slicker. It would be a precarious position.

Wait.

The inner prompting to stay on the platform was too strong to resist, and he clasped his wet arms around his shivering torso and tried to ignore the desire to *do something*. He hadn't been able to text Paradise or his mom, so they were undoubtedly worried. He thought it likely Paradise would try to find him, but the roads might be flooded and impassable.

His watch glowed the time. Nearly midnight. All he could do was pray and wait.

CHAPTER 42

PARADISE FOLLOWED CLARK BACK toward the parking lot and prayed Blake had seen her flick the lights on and off on his truck, but the angle and the rain made her doubt he'd seen it. She'd intended to give him hope that help was on the way.

But how? She couldn't crash the truck through the gate to get to him without releasing the hyenas into the wild. Rounding them up before they harmed someone might not be possible. Blake wouldn't want her to try that. There had to be another way.

She parked behind Clark and got out into the storm. He rushed to her side. "Someone's shooting a rifle!"

She turned and tried to see through the darkness. "Where?"

"On top of the barn." He reached into his truck and pulled out his rifle. "He's shooting toward Blake but missing. I think he's trying to knock him into the hyenas. I'll try to knock him off the barn, or at least distract him."

Thunder rumbled overhead and she looked around for another vehicle. "How'd he get in here?"

"Hard to say. Someone else dropped him off? Maybe a neighbor and he walked?"

Clark started toward the barn and she followed. "Hey, I thought of something," Paradise said. "Blake has night-vision binoculars in his apartment above the garage. There's a line of sight to the barn from the window up there too. I'll go fetch them. It will just take a minute."

"You go ahead. I gotta stop him from knocking Blake down."

She nodded and ran for the house. The side door to the garage was unlocked, and she threw it open and raced for the steps at the back. The sandbags hadn't kept the flooding from the garage, and she splashed through six-inch-deep water. The house might be as bad.

She pounded up the steps and used her phone to find the flashlight Blake kept by the door at the apartment. Its beam pushed back the dark, and the cone of light swept the room and landed on the binoculars where she'd last seen them by the back window. She snatched them up and pressed them to her eyes to peer out the window toward the barn.

The greenish images were sharp and she spotted the figure on the barn. She adjusted the view and gasped when the man turned. Owen Shaw held a rifle in his hand and aimed it toward the tree.

When she lowered the binoculars to go back out and help Clark, another movement by the barn door caught her attention. She brought the binoculars back to her face and focused them. Lacey's face jumped into view. Behind her through the open barn door was a pickup. They'd hidden the vehicle.

Paradise took the binoculars and flashlight with her and went back outside to find Clark. When she reached him in the shelter of the overhang of a shed, he was aiming the rifle at the barn roof.

"It's Owen, the vet from town. And his girlfriend is waiting in the barn with a truck for it to all be over." She brought the binoculars up to her eyes and found Owen again. He didn't seem to know anyone had spotted him and was aiming the rifle again.

"They're both about to get a big surprise." The rifle gave a small kick against Clark's shoulder.

Through the binoculars Paradise saw Owen turn and slip. He caught his balance and brought the rifle around toward where they stood. "He's seen us."

"Don't matter." Clark aimed the rifle again and fired.

The bullet plowed into the roof by Owen's feet, and he teetered again. This time he fell onto his backside and slid down. His arms and legs flailed as he tried to catch his descent, but the roof was too slick from the rain. He plunged off the edge of the barn and landed in the water near Lacey, who ran to him. Owen didn't move. She lifted his head out of the water and held it.

Paradise swept the focus of the binoculars to the tree where Blake hunkered beside the pole. His head hung low and he shivered violently. She lowered the binoculars. "Let's get over there and make sure they're no longer a problem. We've got to get Blake out of there as quickly as possible. I don't know how much longer he can hang on."

Clark nodded and led the way toward where Lacey squatted beside Owen. The vet tech huddled in her yellow slicker, but her jeans and shoes stood in six inches of water.

Lacey's shoulders were slumped. "You killed him."

Paradise knelt and touched his neck. His pulse was strong. "He's not dead, just unconscious. Clark, I'll grab rope if you can drag him into the barn. We'll tie them both up until the police arrive."

There would be time to ask questions after Blake was rescued. She found the rope and Clark helped her tie up Blake's attackers. Paradise turned toward the doorway and made sure Blake was still clinging to the platform.

"How we gonna get him?" Clark asked. "We can't get in the gate without lettin' out the hyenas."

The platform. Paradise gasped. "I know how we can get him out. Come with me. I'll need help."

———

The rain began to lessen as Paradise led Clark up the wooden steps to the high platform of the new zip line. She pointed out Blake's platform anchored to a big live oak in the middle of the hyena enclosure. "That's the first stop. The next one is over the tigers, and the next is at the wolf enclosure. The final stop is across the lion enclosure."

She focused the flashlight on Blake's figure, and he turned his head. His dejected posture straightened, and he struggled to stand on the platform. At least he knew help had arrived and they were working on getting him out of there.

Clark opened the small shed next to the launching pad. "Lucky for Blake the platform was built. The hyenas aren't in a hurry to leave the area." He eyed the harnesses and setup. "We have a problem. There won't be anyone to catch you guys once you leave the first platform. There are three more to navigate, and you could miss the platform. If you do, you may not have enough velocity to reach the next one and will be left dangling between stands."

Oh no. Paradise let go of the harness in her hand. She'd been about to climb into it. "What do I need to do?"

"Have you ever been on a zip line? You know how to operate this thing, Miss Paradise?"

"I get enough thrills with the wild animals. I just hang on, right? And make sure I can stop on the platform?"

"Yep." He wove the line of the harness next to hers through her harness. "Gotta keep it near you so it doesn't slide away. The harness has to be in your reach, so hang on to it here." He showed her the line to hold. "I'm going to attach a line to slow you down at Blake's stand, but it isn't long enough to go all the way. Once you proceed to the others, you're on your own."

"We have to try."

The rain picked up again and started its incessant drumming on the wood and the shed. "Gotta hurry. Even if the rain stopped now, the flooding is just startin', I think."

Her pulse leaped into overdrive, but she had to do this. Help wasn't coming. They *were* the rescue team. "Ready."

He led her to the edge of the platform and attached the line to slow her down at the right time. "Here ya go."

His shove into the middle of her back took her breath away. Then she was soaring over the flood below. The wind and rain buffeted her face and every inch of her body. She wanted to scream, "Too fast, too fast!" but fear kept her mouth shut. Blake's face grew closer, and she kept her gaze locked with his. She was almost above the platform. A few more feet would be perfect.

Then she was traveling faster again. Clark must be having a tough time hanging on to the wet cable. She let go of her hold on the doohickey on the cable and grabbed the cable itself with gloved hands to slow it down. Her rate of travel slowed slightly.

"Catch me!" She screamed the words out into the wind and rain and prayed Blake heard her. "We took out the shooter."

Blake's white face was turned up toward her, and he caught her in the middle of the platform. He was as cold as granite, and his teeth chattered. She clung to him. "Are you all right?"

"I will be once we're both out of here."

"There won't be anyone to catch us on the other platforms. I'm not experienced enough to know how to land. Do you know how?"

"I've done it a few times. I'll wing it."

She helped him into the second harness. "Ready?"

"Past ready." He put his arms around her waist from behind and pushed them off.

The rain pummeled both of them as they zipped to the next platform. She prepared to plant her feet and stop them from falling off the other end as best as she could. Two white tigers noticed them and splashed through the water to follow along. One leaped and gave a playful swipe of its great paw, but it was far below them. The other one watched while standing still.

Then they were over the wolf enclosure, but it was empty of animals. The platform loomed ahead, and she braced for impact. She'd seen pictures of how it was done and prepared to run along a few steps and stop the forward motion. She bent her knees a little and they were there. Her feet slipped on the slick surface, and she grabbed the hold above her head to keep from falling.

Blake felt like a deadweight behind her, and his bulk propelled her along the platform. "Blake!" Her shout roused him from his stupor, and he planted his feet. Together they managed to stop at the edge of the platform.

She unlatched the harness and turned around. He tottered on his feet. How was she going to get him down the steps to safety? She hugged him to her. "You're okay, you're okay."

His closed eyes fluttered and managed to open. "I always knew waking up to Paradise would be a good thing," he muttered.

CHAPTER 43

BLAKE WAS FINALLY WARM as dawn pinked the sky outside the window in Savannah's living room. She had invited them all to stay with her for the next few days while the floodwaters went down. Her house was full to bursting with all of them. The boys had a blast "camping out" with their sleeping bags in the spare room with their mother. The boys hadn't made an appearance yet this morning, but it was only six fifteen, and his mother sat in a chair with her hands wrapped around a coffee mug.

Blake sipped his hot cup of coffee. *Bliss.* Even more like heaven was the wonderful woman curled up beside him on the sofa, who'd braved storm and flood along with tigers and hyenas to rescue him.

Clark snored in the chair across from them. The road to his house had flooded out, and he had nowhere to go, so he'd parked his truck outside and had slept in it for a few hours before coming in for coffee—and promptly falling back asleep.

There were more people in the kitchen—Jane Dixon, Savannah, and Hez banged around fixing breakfast while talking over the events. Last night Jane, Rod, and Nora had gone over the interrogations with Hez and figured out what had happened. Blake had been too exhausted to care then, but he cared now, though not enough to disturb the sleeping beauty beside him. All the whys and wherefores could wait while his gaze traced the sweet curve of her lips and jaw.

They had challenges yet to face. He couldn't picture leaving his mom and the boys on their own just yet, but one obstacle was out of the way. Still, last night had proven Paradise was the sticking kind. He could have died last night—she could have too. Yet here they were, safe and sound. And warm. Warmth was something he'd never take for granted again.

Jane entered with Hez trailing her. "Breakfast is almost ready, but I wanted to hear again what happened. You were in severe hypothermia last night and weren't making much sense."

They'd tried to make him stay at the hospital, but the rooms were all full so they'd opted to bring him here. "I'm a lot more clearheaded now."

Paradise stirred and sat up. "Is it morning?"

"Sure is." He pulled her against him. "But you can go back to sleep."

She shook her head. "I want to hear what Jane found out."

Jane dropped into a chair. "It's a long story. Owen's in financial trouble. He invested his savings in some stocks that tanked, and he started gambling over in Mississippi to try to hit it big. He was siphoning off funds to pay his gambling debts instead of making his business payments. When he went on vacation, Hank poked through the books and found the discrepancies. He confronted Owen about it and told him he was going to report it. Owen begged for a chance to put the money back, and Hank gave him three months."

Blake's mother put her mug on the table beside her. "Owen has skipped most of the payments since Hank died. I haven't bugged him about the business payments because I've been concentrating on making things work at The Sanctuary."

"You should have told me," Blake said. "I could have talked to him."

"You had enough to worry about without that. Finish what you've learned, Jane."

Jane took a sip of her coffee. "Hank sent him a message and said he was going to file charges, so Owen went to see him to plead for more time. He found Hank in the barn, and they argued. Hank refused to give him more time, and Owen shoved him. Hank stumbled and hit the railing in the haymow at the right spot and toppled over.

"Though he hadn't intended to kill Hank, Owen thought he was home free and no one knew about his embezzlement or his involvement in Hank's death. But his money woes were far from over, and a loan shark started hassling him to pay the money he lost gambling. He lived a lavish lifestyle, but no one knew what he was doing to fund it. When Lacey was working for him, they began a relationship, and she saw his money as a way of getting out of her own financial problems. She's raising a niece and is struggling."

"She told me about that," Blake said.

"Lacey had a friend who worked for one of the gas companies in the area. He told her there were some valuable gas deposits on the property here. She told Owen about it, and he convinced the loan shark that he could force Jenna to sell and would cut him in on the profit from the gas deposits. He gave him six months to get it done, and time was running out."

Blake absorbed the news. "What about Danielle Mason's death? Was it related?"

"The Mason woman was Owen's cousin, and he enlisted her help with the blockade and media attacks. She wanted a bigger cut of the pie when it came, and they argued about the terms. Danielle slapped Lacey and called her a tramp and said she wasn't good enough for Owen. Danielle was holding the knife, and the two women fought over it. Lacey got control of it, and Danielle was 'accidentally' stabbed." Jane made quotation marks with her fingers. "Not sure how you accidentally stab someone to death."

"So they continued on with the sabotage without her?" Paradise asked.

"Lacey did. She had access to everything, and she sabotaged the enclosures to harass the family even more. She arranged for activists to shoot at the bear enclosure. They were running out of time." Jane hesitated. "One more thing—they claim to know nothing about the break-ins. There were three, right?"

Blake nodded. Could they be lying? "Why try to shoot me tonight?"

Jane lifted a brow. "'Hell hath no fury like a woman scorned.' Lacey was furious with you, and she convinced Owen that without your help here, Jenna would *have* to sell."

"She wasn't wrong," his mother said.

Blake pulled Paradise closer to his side. This all could have gone wrong in so many ways.

"What happens to the veterinary business?"

"Hez is going to go over the agreement, but it's been in default, so he thinks ownership will revert to your mother. It's unlikely Owen's wife will be able to come up with that much money. Your mom will have to find another purchaser or simply sell the building and move on." Jane turned back toward the kitchen. "There's fresh coffee and pancakes in here."

"Be right there." It was a lot to take in. An idea began to coalesce in his mind. He tightened his arm around Paradise. "What if you took the veterinary business?"

———

Paradise was barely aware of moving to the kitchen to choke down a pancake and chase it with coffee strong enough to dissolve her spoon. Blake's suggestion was outrageous—wasn't it? She didn't know anything about running a business. While medical needs for the animals here didn't really require full-time work, she liked filling in. It kept the day interesting.

Did she really want to upset her happy place here by taking on that kind of challenge and responsibility? Her work had been with exotic animals, and while she was trained on the household variety of pets, her heart was with the wild kind. But in spite of all that, the thought of being in control of her own home and business tugged at her. When she was in foster care, she had no control over anything—not even where she'd sleep at night. This would be *hers*.

After breakfast she slipped away to the front porch to evaluate the yard. What was left of it. The wind had torn petals from the azaleas and roses, and rain had flooded the low areas. It would recover though.

She settled in a rocker and the door opened behind her. She didn't need to turn around to know Blake had followed her.

"Mind if I join you?" He dropped into the other chair without waiting for a response. "My suggestion floored you, didn't it? I saw the color drain out of your face."

"It's a lot to think about. I don't know how to run a business."

"You could do it." He blew out a breath. "Hez just dropped a bombshell. He doesn't think Sheriff Davis killed your parents."

She gasped. "What has he found?"

"A DNA profile was part of the original investigation, and the sheriff submitted his DNA to rule him out. The report wasn't in the printed file, and Hez tracked it down through his contact in Pelican Harbor. He wasn't a match according to the report."

"Then who killed them?"

"The investigation stalled, and the killer was never found. I hated to tell you because at least you had closure. Now you're back to square one."

Her stomach cramped, and she folded her arms across her midsection. She was so tired. Investigation was exhausting, and she wasn't sure where to look next. Maybe she should forget it and concentrate on finding her brother. But could she live with knowing justice hadn't arrived for her parents after all?

Blake's suggestion about taking over the vet business had hit hard too. Was he trying to get rid of her after everything they'd been through? Her feelings of inadequacy were going to take longer than she'd thought to heal. One suggestion and she was questioning how he felt.

Her gaze lingered on him. What a good man. While she wanted to be his wife with every fiber of her being, he didn't need the distraction right now. All of this news would cause a media storm, and not all of it would be good. This could torpedo The Sanctuary, and Blake had to focus on ensuring the long-term stability of the business so his brothers could take it over eventually. It shouldn't take long—maybe a year to turn things around. And in the meantime she could become part of the fabric of the town, the warp and weft of building a life here.

She cupped his face in her hands. "I'm going to do it. I'll work alongside you here, and I'll take over the animal care in town. I'll be in town and I might get to know my family a little better. And I can focus on finding my brother and whoever murdered my parents."

His immediate smile came as if he couldn't believe it. "We'll get through these next few months, and it will be worth it."

"I have a few stipulations."

"Name them."

"Can we do pizza with the boys every Friday night?"

A tender expression lightened his face. "Anytime you want."

"How about s'mores by the campfire on the weekends? And fishing with Bertha on Saturdays?"

"You could ask for that North Star up there and I'd try to give it to you."

He'd shown her the true North Star by the way he lived and loved. "You already did." She wrapped her arms around him and kissed him.

They had twists and turns to navigate, but one thing she knew—at Blake's side was where she belonged, no matter how long it took to figure things out.

A NOTE FROM THE AUTHOR

DEAR READER,

I first visited Out of Africa Wildlife Park for my grandson Silas's birthday, and I immediately envisioned a series with a similar setting. The park is huge with so much more room to roam than a zoo, and we were smitten with Cypress, a sweet grizzly at the park. She showed off with a leg show during our visit aboard the safari bus, and her story of rescue cemented the idea.

I decided to have my Sanctuary in the Gulf Shores, Alabama, area near Pelican Harbor and Tupelo Grove to give readers a little glimpse of the characters from those series as a bonus. Plus I personally love the area! I hope you enjoyed the visit.

I loved the name Paradise when I first thought of it. Can't you imagine the teasing she experienced through the years? But it made her stronger, and I do love a strong heroine. I was blessed to have a predator keeper, Addam Krauch, advise me on things behind the scenes, and we chatted about the danger of working with the big cats. He has a few scars himself, and I was intrigued by the way keepers deal with the danger day in and day out. They take security seriously and do a great job with the animals.

I love hearing from readers, so drop me an email and let me know what you thought of *Ambush*. I hope you love it as much as I loved writing it.

Love,

Colleen

https://colleencoble.com

colleen@colleencoble.com

PS: Oh, and before I go, if you enjoyed meeting Gwen Marcey, you can get to know her better in the Gwen Marcey novels by Carrie Stuart Parks. You'll love them!

ACKNOWLEDGMENTS

Special thanks to Addam Krauch, predator keeper at Out of Africa Wildlife Park. The first time I met Addam was after the Tiger Splash at the park when we took my grandsons up to feed the tigers. I mentioned I was a writer and asked if he would be willing to help me with details. Any errors are mine, not his. Addam, you've been tremendously helpful—thank you very much for your kind and thoughtful answers to the many questions I peppered you with!

Thank you, Team HarperCollins Christian Publishing, for all you have done for me through more than two decades! Thank you, dear editor and publisher, Amanda Bostic, for sticking with me through thick and thin and setting my suspense free to fly! And I'm thankful for my marketing and publicity team. You are the best out there, and no one has better covers than me. ☺

Big thanks to my freelance editor, Julee Schwarzburg. She has such fabulous expertise with suspense and story. She smooths out all my rough spots and makes me look better than I am. I'm truly blessed by your partnership on all my books.

My agent, Karen Solem, and I have been together for twenty-five years now. She has helped shape my career in many ways, and that includes kicking an idea to the curb when necessary. She's an animal lover and was quick to jump on the idea of a series set in an animal refuge. Thank you for your constant support, dear Karen!

My critique partner and dear friend of twenty-five years, Denise Hunter, is the best sounding board ever. Together we've created so many works of fiction. She reads every line of my work, and I read every line of hers. I'm so blessed by your partnership, Denise!

I'm so grateful for my husband, Dave, who carts me around from city to city, washes towels, and chases down dinner without complaint. But my Dave's even temper and good nature haven't budged in spite of the trials of the past year.

My family is everything to me, and my three grandchildren make life wonderful. We try to split our time between Indiana and Arizona to be with them, but I'm constantly missing someone.

And I'm grateful for you, dear readers! Your letters and emails make this journey worthwhile! God knew I needed you in order to be whole.

And all of this was God's doing. He knew the plans he had for me from the beginning, and I'm thankful for every day he gives me.

DISCUSSION QUESTIONS

1. Paradise was angry with Blake for interfering in her foster-care situation when she was a teenager. Was she right to feel that way? Why or why not?

2. Blake gave up a lot to help his mom and brothers. Tell about a time when you sacrificed something important in your life for someone you loved or when someone sacrificed something dear for you.

3. Do you think Jenna should have stopped Blake from upending his life to help her? Why or why not?

4. Paradise was traumatized by the injury she suffered while trying to help a jaguar. How do you deal with fear in your own life?

5. There's something special about your first love. Why do you think that is?

6. Paradise blamed God for her traumatic childhood. Have you ever struggled with feeling disappointed with God? Tell about that time.

7. Paradise's cousins weren't there for her when she needed them. Family issues can be hard to navigate. How do you patch what's broken in your family?

8. Blake is a "fixer." Are you one of those? If you are, why do you think you want to fix things for other people?

From the Publisher

GREAT BOOKS

ARE EVEN BETTER WHEN THEY'RE SHARED!

Help other readers find this one:

- Post a review at your favorite online bookseller

- Post a picture on a social media account and share why you enjoyed it

- Send a note to a friend who would also love it—or better yet, give them a copy

Thanks for reading!

LOOKING FOR MORE GREAT READS? LOOK NO FURTHER!

THOMAS NELSON
Since 1798

Visit us online to learn more:
tnzfiction.com

Or scan the below code and sign up to receive email updates on new releases, giveaways, book deals, and more:

@tnzfiction

THE SANCTUARY NOVELS

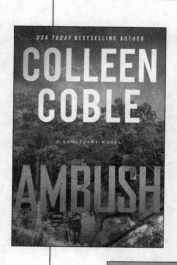

PROWL

Coming November 2025

DESCENT

Coming July 2026

Available in print, e-book, and audio

THOMAS NELSON
Since 1798

ABOUT THE AUTHOR

Photo by EAH Creative

COLLEEN COBLE is the *USA TODAY* bestselling author of more than seventy-five books and is best known for her coastal romantic suspense novels.

Connect with her online at colleencoble.com
Instagram: @colleencoble
Facebook: colleencoblebooks
X: @colleencoble